The Hopeless Life of Charlie Summers

The Hopeless Life of Charlie Summers

PAUL TORDAY

Weidenfeld & Nicolson

LONDON

First published in Great Britain in 2010
by Weidenfeld & Nicolson
An imprint of the Orion Publishing Group
Orion House, 5 Upper St Martin's Lane,
London WC2H 9EA

1 3 5 7 9 10 8 6 4 2

A CIP catalogue record for this book is available
from the British Library

ISBN 978 0 297 85526 2 (cased)
978 0 297 85839 3 (trade paperback)

Typeset at Spartan Press Ltd,
Lymington, Hants

Printed and bound in Great Britain by
Clays Ltd, St Ives plc

The Orion Publishing Group's policy is to use papers that
are natural, renewable and recyclable products and made
from wood grown in sustainable forests. The logging and
manufacturing processes are expected to conform to the
environmental regulations of the country of origin.

www.orionbooks.co.uk

My thanks to Tommy Fellowes for much hospitality and for introducing me to the landscapes of the Var, which inspired the beginning of this book; and to Algernon Percy for his advice and help about the world of fund management – the mistakes are all mine.

Prologue

The money came out of nowhere. In the first years of the first decade of the new century, money flowed around the world as it had never done before. The newspapers called it a 'tsunami of cash', with an enthusiasm that exceeded their accuracy. But that described how it felt to those of us in the money business at the time. Investment banks, hedge funds, prime brokers, mortgage lenders, retail banks: all of them threw money at everything and everyone. Did you want to buy a house? Then the industry would lend you the price of the house, plus another few tens of thousands on top to fit new carpets and hang new curtains and pay the stamp duty, and with luck there would be enough left over for a good long holiday once the deal was done. All you had to do was sign on the dotted line. You didn't really have to prove you had an income; all you had to do was sign your name.

Did you want to buy a car? The lease finance company barely needed your address in order to lend you the purchase price of almost any model you wanted: why buy a Ford; why not buy a Porsche? Did you want to buy the girl you love a diamond ring, but found that your credit card was at its limit? The solution, in these days of prosperity, was simple: get another credit card, at zero per cent interest for two years.

Around the world a metasphere of invisible, intangible money flowed through the Internet, coursed through the arteries of the electronic banking and trading systems that had sprung up in the last few decades of the previous century.

No one knew where the money really was: it was everywhere, and it was nowhere. It was a wonderful time to be in the business. We called our industry 'Financial Services' because that had a nice ring to it: as if we were a group of grey, respectable bankers cautiously managing your money and avoiding risk. But, while there were still a few of those around, most of them had been sidelined, or forced into early retirement owing to their lack of panache and imagination.

The people who had the money nowadays knew how to enjoy life, and how to spend their bonuses. Shortly after I started working in the City, after several years in the army and a brief spell in the private security industry, the first ten-million-pound flat was sold. Ten million pounds! For a flat! The mind boggled; but it was not long before you could spend twenty million pounds on a flat, thirty million, eighty million. It proved, if proof were needed, that the normal laws of economics – that boring, dusty subject as it used to be taught in universities – had been banished. The boom-and-bust cycle had been broken. It was official. One leading central banker cautioned the market against 'irrational exuberance'. But why was it irrational to be exuberant when you were making lots of money? The price of nearly everything almost always went up. If you didn't present it that way, it was probably your fault for being a bit slow, a bit nit-picking about detail, a bit painfully, boringly honest.

I was in the City myself for a few years: not a player, as some of them called themselves, but a minor character, a walk-on part. I had taken the most basic Financial Services Authority exams, which enabled me to offer advice to investors and still be legal. It didn't really matter: I was not one of the elite who had their own trading desks; or one of the mathematicians who occupied the top floor of our premises in Bloomsbury, devising investment strategies expressed in strings of algorithms, a language that few could understand; nor was I charged, like Bilbo, with the high priest's job of making this new religion comprehensible, irrefutable and irresistible. My business card said 'Director – Client Relations' but the job was humbler than that: I was what was known disrespectfully in the trade as a 'greeter'. I knew people, you see. I knew lots of people: from school, from army days; friends, and friends of friends. Some of them had money to invest, and I would lunch with them at White's, or entertain them in our hospitality tent at Cheltenham, or at Ascot, or at Wimbledon. I would take them for a couple of days' shooting in Devon or Yorkshire. I went every other week to assist at roadshows where high-net-worth individuals whose names had been gleaned from lists, no doubt bought from a bank or credit card company, were lured to the conference rooms of expensive provincial hotels with promises of free champagne, canapés and financial insights.

Everybody knew me as Eck, even though my proper name is Hector Chetwode-Talbot. I was Eck, good old Eck, not the sharpest tool in the box, but an officer in a decent regiment once upon a time, and thoroughly trustworthy. If Eck thinks it's a good thing to be in, then it must be a no-brainer. I would set up a meeting between the punter and Bilbo, and perhaps one of the traders from upstairs to add a whiff of cordite from the markets, and the rest was up to them. It wasn't only people I knew socially: there were acquaintances who worked as pension fund managers, or as corporate treasurers, who wanted some hedge fund action. I was at one end of the conveyor belt, buying large gin and tonics, shaking hands and making jokes; at the other end was the moneymaking machine.

The name of our particular machine was Mountwilliam Partners: one of dozens of similar firms that had set themselves up in the last few years in or near to the West End of London, and in the equivalent districts of New York, Paris and half a dozen other capital cities. We knew how to make your money work better than you did. You're getting a seven per cent compound growth already? Don't be pathetic! We offered ten, fifteen, twenty-five per cent compound. It would be negligent of you, we argued persuasively, to ignore these opportunities at the expense of your children, or your clients, and especially at the expense of yourself. Mountwilliam Partners was what was called a 'multi-strategy' hedge fund: we analysed other people's trading strategies and imitated the ones we liked. Our motto was: we can pick and choose, duck and dive, cut and run, just as the market dictates. For this you paid us a two per cent management fee, and a twenty per cent gross performance fee: two per cent per annum of a few hundred million pounds under management is a good income shared among twenty or thirty people, even after paying the rent. That was before the capital gain, the twenty per cent, which was reserved for the equity partners such as Bilbo. My calculator overheated every time I tried to work out what Bilbo might take home at the end of the year. The numbers were so big, they meant nothing to me.

I didn't care; I was incredibly well paid for what I did.

After I left the army, I had a brief spell working for a private security consultancy. I left that outfit too, after a nasty moment in Colombia. By then I was at my wits' end as to what to do with the rest of my life. That was when Bilbo rang, and what he told me over the phone and afterwards at lunch was enough to persuade me that the doors of Aladdin's cave had opened just a fraction; just enough for me to glimpse the sparkle of what lay inside.

Within two years of moving to London, joining Bilbo and then passing my exams, my salary was a multiple of what I had been contemplating before, and my bonus, if everything went to plan, would be a multiple of my salary. Everything always did go to plan: it was the best of times.

What Bilbo had discovered, along with everyone else in those wonderful years, was debt. It wasn't always called debt. It wasn't always recognised as debt. Sometimes it sat on one side of the balance sheet; sometimes on the other. The pension funds paid hedge funds to look after some of their money; the hedge funds borrowed money from prime brokers on margin, or deposited funds with banks, or spent the money on buying up senior and subordinated debt. It was hard to say who owed what to whom. Then money became too boring, too finite. After all, this market wasn't about tangible things like pound coins and dollar bills: it was about the pricing of risk. Our view of the right price for a risk was always going to be different to anyone else's: we bought something – a share, a bond – from people who perceived higher risk in it than we did; we sold to other people who perceived lower risk in it than we did – or sometimes didn't understand that there was any risk at all.

We bought subordinated debt from banks that wanted to get it off their balance sheets, and from bankers prepared to accept sixty cents in the dollar, because that way their bonus was less likely to be cut than if they had to write off the debt. We bought the debt because we believed we could move it on to other banks, or private equity traders at eighty cents in the dollar – or even wait, in the hope it might one day be redeemed at par value. Then all those debts suddenly became an asset: alchemy! We called them collateralised loan obligations, or collateralised debt obligations, but mostly we just used acronyms such as 'CLOs' or 'CDOs': it sounded more punchy, and we bought them and sold them as if they were US Treasury or British government gilts, with no distinction as to risk. We bought them and sold them as if they were sheep at the mart. We swapped futures contracts; we swapped interest rates; we swapped swaptions. We didn't need to buy shares: we borrowed them from stock lenders and traded on margin. We believed the market always went up in the long run, and usually bought long, or else bought contracts for difference so that we never actually needed to own the shares, just pocketed the difference in price between buy and sell. We didn't just use our own money. We leveraged twenty pounds for every one we deposited on margin with the prime broker. Bilbo once told me, in one of his confiding moods: 'To stay ahead in this industry, you need to leverage your balance sheet. We need to maximise our firepower.'

It didn't matter if the pound in the balance sheet was eighty pence of sub-prime loans and twenty pence of real money, whatever that was these days. We marked to market, like everyone else. Our balance sheet assets were what we said they were. Who should know better than us?

Farther down the chain, the rest of the world borrowed too: they bought houses with debt, they bought cars with debt, and none of it mattered because everything always went up. If you questioned the risk on a house purchase, the broker arranging your mortgage would say, 'They're not making land any more. You can't go wrong with bricks and mortar.'

The levels of debt rose, invisibly, and exponentially. Our counterparty exposure in Mountwilliam Partners (only we didn't recognise it as debt) was the same size as the external debt of Guatemala: yet we were only a small player in the hedge fund industry. The bigger funds were into sums of money so large that they could scarcely be computed: what *is* a trillion dollars? I don't know.

For a while it seemed as if the music would never stop. I didn't think about the bigger picture. Bilbo, I think, did know that the music would stop one day, but that is not what he said to the punters, or even to us. However much we made, it was not enough; however much we used our leverage, someone out there was bigger and better than we were, and had to be beaten.

You had to be big, because then the market did what you did. You became like the Pied Piper of Hamelin. You played the tunes, and the rats followed. Just when the music was at its loudest, I bought myself an Audi TT soft top. It was midnight blue, with a black leather interior, and stuffed with every sort of gadget the manufacturer could think of. When I say I bought the car, I didn't buy it with real money. I used some of my bonus to finance a deposit and borrowed the rest from the bank; the balance was hire-purchase finance. The salesman kept me for what seemed an age, filling out forms that neither he nor I cared much about, setting out my repayment schedules. Then came the champagne moment of sitting in the new car for the first time, smelling the new leather, and polish. I turned the key in the ignition for the first time, and heard the throaty rumble of the engine, growling like a beast not entirely tamed. It was the greatest moment of self-indulgence of my life so far: but, why not? My next bonus might be so huge I could pay off the HP debt;

or maybe trade in this car and buy a real beast, a Ferrari or a Maserati.

I drove the car to the South of France to play golf with Henry Newark. That was how I met Charlie Summers, and this is as much his story as mine. Some of it I heard later from Henry, some of it from others; mostly from Charlie himself, as he sat for hours in an armchair at Aunt Dorothy's, clutching a tumbler of whisky. But that was later on. Charlie wanted to get on the money wagon too, and his optimism was, for a while, no less than mine; no less than Bilbo's. All you needed was an idea, charm and some determination, and then the money would roll in.

Meanwhile, the invisible, locationless money ebbed and flowed around the world, a great tide of wealth. Each high tide was higher than the last; each low tide less marked. No one knew quite where it all was, or which debts were going to be repaid, and which not. Yet, here and there, one or two people were beginning to ask: where's the money?

For a while these people were dismissed: as lunatics, nutcases, Jeremiahs; people with their own murky agendas. Then there were more of them, and their mutterings could not be ignored. Loan defaulting began, at first in America, then elsewhere. In secure meeting rooms politicians and bankers began to discuss the unthinkable. Scenarios were painted for them by economists who spoke as if they had been asleep, like Rip van Winkle, since the Great Depression and had only now woken up, and were looking about them in dismay.

Then, somewhere, someone asked a new question. It was: 'Can I have my money back?'

We didn't know it then, but the money that had come out of nowhere was about to return to exactly the same place.

One

People change. I have changed since my army days, even since my days in the City. The other evening I heard a Mozart oratorio being sung in York Minster, an event organised by the charity I now work for. As I listened to the pure notes of the tenor singing *Ave Dominus*, the tears welled up in my eyes and ran down my cheeks. I prayed that no one would notice. Until a few years ago, the only musical pieces I reacted to, with perhaps a slight prickling at the back of the eyes, were the 'Eton Boating Song' and 'The British Grenadiers'. Now I can scarcely remember the words of either work, especially the latter, which once meant so much to me:

Rum tumtumtumtumtum; rumtum, tumtumtum
Of Hector and Lysander, and such great names as these
But of all the world's great heroes, there's none that can
  compare
With a tow, row, row, row, row row something *British*
  Grenadiers

Because people change, one becomes aware that it is difficult, if not impossible, to estimate the true worth of another human being. In the army we learned to sum up people very quickly: good soldier; crooked as a nine-pound note; one prawn short of a sandwich. As a simple system of categorising human types, it served quite well. But it was not adequate to recognise human potentiality: the possibility that, when one shone one's torch into the coal cellar, a refracted gleam might indicate the presence of a diamond among the sooty lumps of more basic forms of carbon.

Such reflections did not pass through my mind when I first met Charlie Summers. I was, in those days, still very much a man of business; and hoping one day to become a man of leisure, a state of being which I thought I might be able to afford quite soon, if things kept going smoothly for a year or two longer. I did not then reflect much on my life or on others' lives: I judged people at a glance. In Charlie's case, when I saw a rather grubby-looking man in his forties, wearing a navy blue blazer with the shine of age upon it and anointed with dandruff about the shoulders, I was inclined to place him as a typical middle-aged drifter; neither use nor ornament, as my mother used to say. The rest of his outfit was in the same vein: well-worn chinos that had once been white; scuffed suede shoes; brass buttons on the blazer, and a striped tie, hinting at military circumstances without committing to any specific regiment.

I had driven down to the South of France with Henry Newark, and our plan was to play golf and drink wine for a week. Henry was a very old friend, but he was also a potential punter in Mountwilliam Partners, and I felt sure we would find a moment to talk about money and investment in among the golf and the eating and drinking. That morning we were taking some time off from these rigorous obligations, sitting in the square of a small French town, in the hills above the Corniche. We had moved from cups of coffee to a glass of a sour white liquid, which was the only thing available in the form of an aperitif. It was as yet only eleven o'clock. The *Daily Mail* had been read, and Henry was now working away at the Sudoku puzzle. I was looking at the business pages, and saw that the Footsie 100 Share Index had reached another record high. House prices were up another ten per cent year on year. Everyone everywhere was making money: even me, in a small way. I put aside these reflections with my newspaper and settled back in my chair to watch the theatre that seems to be an integral part of daily life in small Provençal towns: a sinister-looking man, shuffling down a side street carrying a baguette, clearly intent on murder; a shop girl flirting with a customer who was by no means obviously her husband or her boyfriend.

At intervals, enormous trucks would climb the steep and winding roads from the plains below – vehicles large enough to be considered a problem to overtake on a motorway, let alone on the small roads that intersected the hillsides. As they arrived in the town square, their progress was impeded by a stone fountain, which might – or might not – have been intended for use as a roundabout. There they might be confronted by a people carrier full of Swedish tourists, whose driver, in the panic following a near-head-on collision with the oncoming truck, seemed unable to locate reverse gear. In the ensuing impasse the most optimistic outcome one could imagine was the demolition of the side of a house as the truck manoeuvred its way around the fountain, crushing to death the occupants of the people carrier as it did so. At the high point of this drama three madmen on Harley Davidsons flew between the opposing vehicles and roared off down the hillside. Then, all at once, the crisis was resolved, without anyone quite seeing how it happened: the people carrier had gone, and the truck was parked by the local supermarket, its driver handing over the tray of yogurt that he had come all this way to deliver.

'Excuse me, have either of you gents got a light?' said a voice near by. I looked up. It was the middle-aged drifter I had spotted earlier. He was bending over our table, a small unlit cigar in one hand – the kind that are made from sweepings from the cigarette factory floor – and an ingratiating smile upon his face. Henry, without looking up, indicated a lighter lying on the table next to his packet of Gitanes – a luxury he allowed himself when his wife Sarah was not with him – and the newcomer took it, clicked it open and lit his cigar. Then he stood for a moment expectantly, as if waiting: for an invitation to sit down; comments about the weather to be exchanged; or the offer, perhaps, of a glass of wine. None of these things happened. Henry continued with his Sudoku and I stared off into the middle distance. The new arrival was being treated, surely not for the first time, with the cruel indifference, bordering upon outright hostility, with which the English sometimes treat each other when abroad.

He left. Henry looked up then and said, 'He's your double, Eck.'

'I don't see it,' I said, rather offended.

'Apart from the fact he's older, he could be your brother.'

The thing was, Henry had a point. The man, who had retreated to a table at a neighbouring café, was the same height and build as me, though carrying a few more pounds and with rather more hair on top than I have now. His hair was the same reddish colour as mine, he had blue eyes and the same highly coloured, square-shaped face.

Henry Newark is one of my oldest friends. He is a landowner from Gloucestershire whom I first met when we were at school together. He is very rich, and rather pompous, but a kinder-hearted man I have never met. We have known each other a long time and are comfortable in one another's company. We are both equally bad at golf, which helps. These golfing excursions have always been more to do with Henry's need to get away, from time to time, from his rather tough wife, Sarah. I am happy to help out, and nearly always free if someone like Henry rings up and proposes an expedition of this sort. At the time, it was almost part of my job.

We said no more about the drifter, although from time to time I was conscious of a movement on the periphery of my vision, as if the stranger were circling us, waiting for a moment of weakness when he could pounce and get us to buy him a drink.

Half an hour later we toddled off to the villa we had rented from one of Henry's friends. There we helped ourselves to a light lunch that the French housekeeper, Valerie, had laid out for us. In the afternoon we played golf. In the evenings we usually dined out: preferring to take our main meal in a restaurant rather than risk exploring the limits of Valerie's goodwill or ability. Tonight, however, we were to eat in, because my cousin Harriet was coming to stay the night.

The problem of what to do about Harriet had been exercising me for some time. Sometimes it seemed as if I had been thinking about little else for most of my life, although this could not have been the case. It was only about three years ago that I went to her engagement party: a guest, as it happens, of her fiancé Bob Matthews rather than at Harriet's invitation. Harriet and I were cousins once removed, and not especially close. Bob Matthews, on the other hand, though not in my regiment, was a friend of some years' standing. When he was killed in action in Iraq – in circumstances that have remained unclear to this day – I was more affected by the news of his death than many others that had taken place – it seemed with increasing frequency – in that meat-grinder of a war. I was fond of Bob.

Harriet was devastated by the death. Such a word is used so freely now as to have lost most of its meaning. In her case it was exactly the right word to describe her state of being. She was like a country that had been laid waste: villages burned to the ground, fields of wheat trampled by marauding horsemen, orchards slashed and burned.

I saw her at Bob's memorial service in Hampshire. She was so pale that it was as if she, not Bob, ought to have been given funeral rites. She was very thin by then, much thinner than I remembered her at her engagement party. She spoke little; she thanked me for coming, as she thanked everyone who attended the service on that oppressive, drizzly day in August a year or two back. I'm not sure how much of it she took in. She still had that stunned look on her face, even though many weeks had passed since Bob's death was officially announced on the MoD website. I later heard that she gave up a high-powered job in London as a partner in a firm of land agents and went to live in France. There she stayed and eventually found work, as a fixer and project manager for well-off English people wanting to buy or develop property in the South of France.

The problem was this: on the few occasions when Harriet and I had met, at family gatherings or at parties and even – I must admit to myself – at her own engagement party, Harriet had made my heart her own every time she glanced at me. That she thought of me as anything other than a rather dull and distant relation, there was not the slightest evidence. No grounds existed, could even be imagined, for hoping that she had ever felt anything for me.

I wrote a letter of condolence to her, and eventually received an answer, which was formal enough. I wrote again once or twice and she made some effort to describe, in her reply, her new life and to explain why she had decided not to come back to England. To me it sounded like running away from life. She was like a bird with a broken wing which had crawled into a hedgerow until life ebbed away. Nevertheless, we became occasional correspondents, and after a while I noticed a change in the tone of Harriet's letters. They were less dutiful; she was not responding simply out of a sense of obligation or good manners. Perhaps, in a minor way, I had become a link to her old life, a sign that she had not altogether relinquished her past, her family, her existence over the last thirty-two years.

When Henry and I made our golfing plans, I looked at the map and saw that the place where Harriet lived was not impossibly distant from the villa we had rented. I wrote and proposed that she join us for lunch or dinner, and to my surprise, she agreed a date.

She arrived about seven. I had been standing on the terrace, looking at the view without seeing it, wondering when she would ring to cancel. That she would not come, I felt certain. The whole thing had been a mistake. If she did come, what would I say to her? What did we really have in common, except Bob? That was the last subject to chat about over a drink. Henry was inside, supervising Valerie's preparation of our dinner, and no doubt getting in the way. Then I heard a car door slam.

I went around the side of the villa and found Harriet standing by a small blue car, extracting an overnight bag from the back seat. I took the bag from her and received a kiss on the cheek.

'Harriet, it's good to see you,' I said.

'You're looking well, Eck. You've caught the sun.'

She smiled. She was exactly as I remembered her, and yet the memory and the real person were quite different, in ways too subtle to explain. She was still too thin; tall, not quite my height, which is six foot, but certainly five foot nine. She had cut her hair shorter. It was a golden blonde, and used to reach down to her shoulders. Now it was cropped at the base of her neck. Her face was as pale as I remembered it at Bob's funeral, as if she had never recovered her colour, as if it had drained from her face that August day two years previously, and had never returned. The smile was the only thing that was different since the last time I saw her.

'Come and meet Henry,' I said. We went inside and Henry was introduced, a bottle of wine was opened, and the three of us sat on the terrace and watched the evening sun going down over low, wooded hills on the other side of the valley. I could see that Henry was rather impressed by Harriet's looks.

'We used to see each other at children's dances a long time ago,' he told her.

'I'm afraid I don't remember,' said Harriet. 'I used to hate parties at that age. I was terribly shy.'

'I remember your father, the general,' said Henry. 'Is he still alive?'

'No – he died a year ago. He was in his seventies.'

'He must have married late, then,' said Henry.

'I was an afterthought,' explained Harriet. There was a silence. I tried to think of something amusing to say, but failed. Harriet looked at me and said, 'Eck, it was so nice of you to keep writing to me. I'm afraid I'm not much of a correspondent.'

'I'm not a fan of email when I'm not in the office,' I replied. I felt I was blushing, for some reason.

'It's so nice to get letters,' said Harriet.

'I love emails,' said Henry. 'I've been going to classes at the local college. I know all about computers now. You get such amusing jokes sent to you once you know how to get on to the Internet.'

'You never actually said what you are doing now, Eck,' said Harriet.

'He doesn't do anything except chat up clients for his new firm, and play golf or go on corporate days shooting,' said Henry, 'although considering the amount of time he must have to practise, he's still very bad at golf.'

'I do have a job, as a matter of fact,' I said. 'I work in London, for an investment fund.'

'That sounds safer than the army, at any rate,' said Harriet.

'Well, I had ten years in, and then a couple of years working on the other side of the street for a private security firm. But now I'm looking for a quieter life.'

'And what a jammy job he has too, Harriet,' said Henry. 'He works for Bilbo Mountwilliam. Do you remember Bilbo? No? Wasn't he at school with us, Eck? A year or two above us? For some reason he pays Eck the most enormous salary just to have lunch or dinner with people.'

'It is real work,' I told Harriet. 'I don't know if Henry could explain how he passes his working days, but mine are pretty full. And as you say, it's safer than the army.'

At that instant, Valerie appeared in the doorway and announced that dinner was ready.

The rest of the evening passed without difficulty. Henry and Harriet got on well enough; they both knew some of the same people in Gloucestershire. It was I who felt on the edge of the conversation. If Harriet had been a client I would have managed well enough. I had never found it difficult to talk to other men, which was one of the reasons Bilbo had hired me – maybe the only reason. I was fluent enough sitting in Wiltons and chewing on a Dover sole, while I asked after my guest's golfing, or fishing, or shooting, and worked him around into a good mood so that I could bring up the subject of Mountwilliam Partners. I sometimes found myself observing my own behaviour at a dinner or drinks party and thinking, I'm the life and soul of the party. How do I do that? It was a little like thinking about riding a bike: everything's OK while you're just getting on with it, but the minute you start to wonder how you stay upright you are in danger of falling off. That was how I felt now: I had forgotten how to talk, how to be easy and amusing, and I simply couldn't work my way back into the conversation. I sat and watched Harriet talking, even laughing once or twice, and found myself wishing Henry was dead, or in Gloucestershire. I wanted her to myself. I wanted her attention to be focused on me, and me alone. Why could I not think of anything to talk about? This was my cousin, someone I had known most of my life.

What I really wanted to say was, 'Harriet, forget about Bob. He's been dead for two years. Stop living in exile and come back and live with me in England.' What I actually said was, 'And how is your mother, Harriet?'

At that moment, I couldn't have cared less about her mother, but Harriet appreciated my interest.

'She's very well, for her age. A bit wobbly on her legs but still as sharp as a tack.'

'Oh, good.'

This was a classic conversational dead end. Why did they not train you to talk to girls at school? I was the victim of single-sex education. Of course, there had been girls at parties and at dances in my teenage years, and one or two brief romances which had blossomed – and withered away almost as soon as they had blossomed – during my army years. I always seemed to be just about to get into bed with some girl or other when my leave was over and I was on my way back to Northern Ireland, or Germany, or the Middle East.

Since leaving the army and settling down in my parents' old home in Teesdale I had managed one or two tumbles with girls I had met. But once the bedroom part of our relationship was over, I seemed unable to concentrate on whichever girl I was with. All they wanted to do afterwards was talk. All I wanted to do was have a drink and switch on the television. It was as if part of me – the adult part – had not yet woken up.

It was quite different with Harriet. I did want to talk to her. I wanted to spend hours talking to her, and listening to her talk. But now that it really mattered, my powers of conversation were not much greater than those of a Speak Your Weight machine.

There was a silence. Henry was gnawing on a lamb cutlet, his mouth too full to speak, so I tried again to think of something witty or memorable to say. What I came out with was: 'Don't you ever get tired of French food?'

Before she could reply, if such an inane remark deserved any reply, Henry put down the bone from which he had now removed every scrap of meat and said, 'But why would she? I never would.'

That was true. Henry's capacity for food – French, Thai, South American, it was all one to him – was legendary. When eating out, he studied menus with devotional intensity and he never skipped a starter or a pudding. He had trained Sarah, and Sarah had trained their cook, to provide him with two courses at lunch every day he was at home, and three at dinner. Despite this, he was not fat: Henry was one of those irritating people whose metabolism coped with almost anything in the way of intake without ever punishing him with an expanding waistline.

Harriet said, 'I do miss some things about home, sometimes.'

'Such as?' I asked.

'Oh, English weather: English seasons, I mean. Seeing friends. Seeing more of my mother while I've still got her.'

'You couldn't miss the English weather,' said Henry. 'You must have forgotten what it's like.'

We did not sit up late. Harriet pleaded fatigue and an early start as she had to drive back to attend meetings with clients the following day. I did not want to stay up after she retired, because I wanted to put off the inevitable interrogation by Henry: why did she live in France; what was known of her sex life; what were my own plans in that regard?

The next morning Harriet was up early, and I only just rose in time to offer her a quick cup of coffee. Henry was still in bed. Her face looked serious again, the brief moments of relaxation of the night before now forgotten.

'I'm so glad you could come over for dinner.'

'It was such fun,' said Harriet, although she did not smile as she said it.

'It was good to see you again.'

'You too, Eck – and it was nice to meet Henry.'

To hell with Henry. I put a hand on her arm and said,

'Harriet – when do you think we might meet again? Won't you ever come back home to England?'

She looked at me, and I could see she understood.

'I don't know, Eck. I don't want to make plans at the moment.'

'Can I write to you?'

'Of course you can write to me. I like getting your letters. Tell me what's going on in your life, apart from games of golf.'

She smiled then, and kissed me for the second time, on the cheek. Then she was gone, a cloud of dust marking the passage of her car towards the road. I went back into the house and encountered Henry, wearing a bathrobe, padding towards the terrace with a cup of coffee. He looked very relaxed as he bid me good morning; I decided to follow him outside with a cup of my own, and to try and bring the conversation around to Mountwilliam Partners and their magical touch.

The following night, because it was the last of our trip, Henry insisted that we go somewhere special for dinner. There was a restaurant we had eaten in before which seemed to fit the bill and was not far from where we were staying. It was in the middle of a small fortified village that clung to the edges of a limestone gorge. The restaurant itself occupied most of the central square – the part of the square not covered in tables and chairs being used as a piste for pétanque. We sat at a table near the edge of the terrace. It was early June and the evenings were warm enough to sit outside comfortably, the heat not yet oppressive. Behind a low wall, what had once been the ramparts of a castle fell steeply away into a dim green darkness, the haunt of bats and swifts. As we sipped our whiskies and Henry read out to me offerings from the menu, I became conscious of someone standing quite close behind me. An aroma, hard to analyse with any exactness, but nevertheless indicating recent consumption of garlic and sour red wine, and the inhalation of many cigarettes, wafted over me. A voice said, 'Evening, gents.'

Henry looked up and I looked around, to see the man who had cadged a light for his cigar from us the previous day.

'Funny bumping into you again like this,' said the new arrival, as if we were the oldest of friends. 'Bit off the beaten track here. Charlie Summers, by the way. Don't think I mentioned my name the last time we met.'

Henry's behaviour in these situations was better than mine. If I had been on my own I might have repaid such an interruption with scant courtesy, suggesting that the newcomer might take himself elsewhere, but Henry rose to his feet and introduced us both, using my full name – Hector Chetwode-Talbot. He would have been no more polite to visiting royalty.

'Call me Eck,' I added. There seemed to be nothing to do but ask the man to sit down and have a glass of wine with us.

'Didn't mean to intrude,' said Charlie Summers, seating himself with alacrity. 'Just happened to be passing through; fellow I met told me about this place, and I thought I'd look it up.'

'Are you on holiday here for long?' I asked him.

'Not on holiday. Not as such. The fact is I've had a misunderstanding with Her Majesty's Customs and Revenue. I thought it better to take a leave of absence while my accountant sorts things out. It's the VAT, you see. I never could understand VAT.'

Charlie Summers accepted a glass of wine with every appearance of surprise, drank half of it down, and accepted a top-up.

'Goes down a treat, this local wine,' he remarked. 'Forget what they call it, but they say it's good for your heart.'

Henry said, 'Well, it goes down all right. Are you staying near here?'

'Oh, I move about,' said Charlie Summers. 'I get a bit restless staying in the same place for too long, to tell the truth. Rather hoping to get back to the UK soon – a lot of unfinished business had to be set aside when these taxmen interrupted my affairs.'

'What sort of business are you in?' I asked. Charlie Summers turned and gave me a smile. The smile was unsettling. It was imbued with considerable charm, yet there was something not quite sane about it. It gave Charlie the look of an engaging, slightly manic schoolboy about to play a prank: like a middle-aged Norman Wisdom. It was odd to sit next to someone who, I had to admit, must look very much like me, even if a few years older – apart from that smile.

'Dog food,' said Charlie Summers.

'Dog food?' asked Henry. 'What kind of dog food?'

'Ah,' said Charlie. He tapped the side of his nose with his forefinger. 'I know what you're thinking. It's a very competitive business, dog food. Cash and carries, farmers' cooperatives, all those people sell it. There's a lot of cut-price food which you can buy by the ton. But that cheap stuff doesn't do the dogs any favours. They do their business everywhere and their coats look like something that's been left out in the rain.'

'And you've found the answer?' asked Henry.

'Japanese dog food, that's the answer. Full of alginates –

that's seaweed, to you and me. Cleans up the digestive tract, particularly good for black Labradors, makes their fur and noses blacker and shinier. But you need to know your way around the market. There are snags.'

'What sort of snags?' I asked. Somehow the conversation seemed to have gained a life of its own. The waitress arrived to take our orders, and before I could do anything about it, Henry had asked Charlie to join us for dinner. Later he admitted he couldn't pass up the opportunity of seeing what to him were two almost identical red-haired, blue-eyed twins, sitting side by side and talking about Japanese dog food.

'I could have waited for ever for that to happen,' he told me.

We ordered our food, and some more wine. When that had all been settled, Charlie said, 'You were asking what sort of snags I found with the dog food business? The fact is, you can be tripped up. That's one of the reasons I'm here at the moment. The first batch I shipped in from Japan turned out to have dolphin meat in it. It didn't say so on the label, of course, but some bright spark sent a sample off to Trading Standards and they found dolphin DNA in it. Nothing to do with me; I was just the importer. I didn't kill the bloody dolphins. But you know what people are like. The next thing I knew it was in all the local papers: I had Greenpeace round my neck, Save the Whale, you name it. It wasn't good for business, I can tell you.'

Henry was laughing.

'Awfully bad luck,' he said.

'Not the sort of image I was aiming for,' agreed Charlie. 'When the VAT problem turned up on top of all that, I thought I'd cool my heels out here for a while, then go home and do a rebranding and a fresh launch.'

'I must buy some for my own dog,' said Henry, to make up for having laughed so much.

'What sort of dog do you have?' asked Charlie.

'A black Labrador: a working dog.'

'Ah, well, you see,' said Charlie, 'this food was developed for Akitas. That's the Japanese fighting dog: used to go into battle on the shoulders of samurai.'

The food arrived and for a while we talked of things other than dogs. I found myself relenting a bit towards Charlie Summers. He had an odd air of self-confidence verging on cockiness, softened by a look of apology he gave from time to time, as if to say, 'I can't help what I am, I'm doing the best I can in the circumstances.' He enquired about Henry and myself; not obviously interested in Henry's description of himself as being involved in 'a little bit of farming', he showed a more lively enthusiasm for my own career in the army.

'I expect you were in Special Forces,' he said to me.

'No, just a regular soldier,' I said, but Charlie wasn't having it.

'I know you've got to say that,' he observed. 'I respect a man who doesn't brag.'

Because of our new companion, we drank rather more wine than usual. Henry poured it freely in order to keep the talk flowing.

'Are you a married man, Henry?' asked Charlie. Henry admitted that he was. 'And you, Eck? You're not, are you? You have that bachelor look, like me.'

'You're right, I'm afraid,' I said. For some reason, I felt as if I had been reproached.

'Can't make up your mind who to tie the knot with?' asked Charlie. He grinned, looking more like Norman Wisdom than ever, then he added, 'I used to be a bit of a ladies' man myself, you know.'

'Really?' I asked.

'I can well believe it,' agreed Henry, 'a chap with your looks.'

'Now you're joking,' said Charlie, but he seemed pleased, and was by no means disposed to deny that he had been, or perhaps still was, something of a Don Juan.

We moved on to cognac and cigars as twilight settled around the square. It was midweek and the place was quiet. Candles were lit, and people talked in soft voices as they watched the last streaks of light fading above the jagged limestone hills.

'Such a beautiful evening,' said Henry, 'candlelight and wine. All we lack is soft music.'

He was not drunk, but had consumed a lot of wine. I had been more circumspect, as I was driving us back.

Charlie said, 'Oh, music; I can provide the music.'

Then, quite without embarrassment, he stood up and put one foot on the seat of his chair, and began to sing in a surprisingly sweet and tuneful tenor. At first his voice was low, just audible to ourselves, but then it gathered in strength until the whole restaurant fell silent and listened to him sing. The tune was familiar from long ago, at school concerts and – later – weddings; the words, in Latin, were less easily recalled: *'Panis angelicus/ Fit panis hominum . . .'*

The performance was as angelic as the words demanded. Where Charlie had learned to sing like that, I could not think. For a moment I forgot everything except the music itself, its emotional impact magnified by the beauty of the majestic hills behind the singer, augmented by the screeching of the swifts as they soared high up into the darkness. When Cesar Franck composed the music he no doubt had in mind the shadowy interior of some Gothic cathedral as the setting for its performance; one felt he would have approved equally of a Provençal hillside in a June dusk.

There was a ripple of applause from around the restaurant when Charlie finished. He bowed slightly, and sat down.

We both congratulated him and asked him where he had learned to sing so well.

'Oh, in the school choir a long time ago,' he said. 'I don't much look like a choirboy now, I know.'

He did not seem to want to say more about his childhood.

Not much later, it was time to go. We paid the bill, including Charlie's share. He thanked us. Then he said he would stay on for a bit and smoke another cigar. Before we left, Henry pulled a visiting card from his wallet. The wine had made him companionable and disposed to think well of everyone, even someone as eminently unsuitable as Charlie appeared to be.

'If ever you're in our part of Gloucestershire,' he said, 'look us up. Bring some dog food with you.'

Two

As Henry remarked to me when we were discussing Charlie Summers one evening, there are sixty million people living in the United Kingdom, and fifty-nine million, nine hundred and ninety-nine thousand of them know very well what is meant by the phrase 'Do look us up some time'. It is a perfectly plain form of dismissal, as used by the English upper and middle classes, indicating that any future crossing of paths would be distinctly unwelcome, if not actively resisted.

Charlie was the exception to this rule.

Henry told me it was perhaps two months after we had been in France together, some time in early August, that Charlie turned up at Stanton Hall. The ancestral home of the Newarks was set amid a few hundred acres of woodland and a couple of thousand acres of pasture. The house itself was Elizabethan Revival, built in the 1840s from the proceeds of successful property dealing by the Stanton family around the centre of Birmingham. In a region where villages were constructed, for the most part, from the honey-coloured stone that warms the hearts of visiting tourists and estate agents, this building had the distinction of being built in red brick. It looked like an early Victorian town hall that had lost its way and ended up in this quiet and hidden valley. Its flat front was relieved by large mullioned and transomed windows, and the roof of the house was punctuated by arrays of tall chimneys and a central spire. The place looked enormous, but did not have extensive living quarters: instead it was set among endless domestic offices and abandoned bakeries and brewhouses that seemed to have sprung up among these woods.

The house was surrounded by formal gardens, which I have always found rather oppressive. Beyond them lay parkland containing a small herd of fallow deer and then encircling woodlands, rich with bluebells in the spring and heaving with pheasants in the autumn and winter. Henry had a very good driven pheasant shoot, and I used to join him for a day most years.

Sarah Newark was kneeling on a weeding mat, deadheading the roses that filled two enormous beds on either side of the front drive. It was a warm afternoon without a breath of wind, and the sky was grey and overcast. Sarah would have been in her element, organising the flower beds safe in the knowledge that the nanny would keep her children out of the way until after tea. Charlie must have arrived by taxi, but she did not hear the car. She suddenly became aware of someone near by – a slight clearing of the throat, perhaps, alerted her – and she looked up to see a man, not smartly dressed by any means, standing diffidently in the middle of the drive. For a moment she frowned, unable to think who this might be, then her face cleared.

'If you go around to the back of the house,' she said, 'and ring the bell, the housekeeper will come and show you where the meter is.'

There was a pause while she and Charlie looked at each other in mutual incomprehension. Then he said, 'Oh, I'm sorry. You must have thought . . . the fact is, I'm a friend of your husband's. I met Henry in France and he suggested I drop in some time. And, well . . . here I am. Charlie Summers is my name.'

He laughed nervously and put down the bag he was carrying on the gravel. Sarah realised then that this was no meter-reader's bag – if indeed they have bags – but a serious canvas holdall that might contain a week's supply of spare clothing. Her heart sank. Henry had said nothing about this.

She rose to her feet awkwardly, brushing dead petals and moss from her clothes.

'I'm terribly sorry, Mr Summers, but Henry isn't in the house just now. He's out and about somewhere.'

Charlie was not sure what to do. Henry's wife did not seem to be rolling out the red carpet for him, but he had been counting on being asked to stay. So he just said, 'Oh.'

'Shall I tell him you called in?'

Charlie Summers looked a little uneasy. He turned about and glanced down the drive, then up at the sky, then back at Sarah.

'Oh,' he said again. 'Well, the awkward thing is, the taxi appears to have gone. I should have made him stay, but it cost a fortune to get here from the station and I didn't want too many more pounds added to the meter. Would I be in the way if I waited somewhere for a minute? I just want to say hello, really, and then I'll be on my way.'

After that Sarah had to ask him into the house. They went in the back way, and she sat him in the kitchen and made him a mug of tea, which is also what he would have been given had he been a meter reader, as Sarah knew the importance of buttering up tradesmen.

'Are you a golfing man, Mr Summers?' she asked. 'That's what my husband normally spends his time doing in France. Is that how you met him?'

'No, I don't play golf,' said Charlie. 'We just met, in one of those little towns down there. I happened to be travelling in that part of the world.'

There was a long silence. Charlie tried to drink his tea without making too much noise while Sarah Newark tried to choke down a rising tide of resentment at this interruption to precious gardening time. She realised she was in danger of being bad mannered.

'Were you there on business?' she asked.

'In a way,' said Charlie. 'I was really taking some time out to think through a new business idea.'

'And what is it you do, Mr Summers?'

'Do call me Charlie. I'm a dog nutritionist.'

He gave her a smile. He reminded her of someone, but before she could think who, the kitchen door swung open and a large black Labrador came bounding in, sniffed at Charlie's crotch, and then went and said hello to its mistress.

'*Oogiewoogiewoogie woo*,' said Sarah Newark. 'And has his daddy come home? Has he had a nice time playing in the woods? *Oogums*.'

A moment later Henry came into the kitchen, started to say something, either to his wife or the dog, and then stopped dead as he recognised Charlie.

'Oh,' he said, in a surprised voice. Then, gathering his wits, 'How nice to see you – what on earth are you doing here? Get to your basket!' This last remark was addressed to the black Labrador, who was investigating Charlie's trousers again.

By this time even someone as insensitive as me, for example – and I regard myself as reasonably thick skinned in most social situations – would have decided it was time to make my excuses and leave. The atmosphere was obviously

31

not one of welcome; there was no rush to kill the fatted calf, or otherwise to celebrate Charlie's arrival. But one of Charlie's great qualities, as we all subsequently realised, was determination; if only it had been applied to more rewarding objectives.

Now he stood his ground and said, 'It was kind of you to ask me to look you up when we last met. I thought it would be rude not to, seeing as I was passing.'

'Will you excuse Sarah and me for a second?' Henry said. 'There is something I need to tell her I don't want to bore you with. Then let's all have a cup of tea.'

Charlie did not feel able to point out that he was already drinking a mug of tea, and that yet more tea was not as high on his list of priorities as, say, an early whisky and soda. Sarah stood up and left the kitchen with Henry, and I gathered from Henry later the gist of their conversation. I like to imagine that Charlie may have overheard whispered fragments: '. . . *can't turn him away* . . . *I did say something to him about looking us up* . . . *I never expected him simply to arrive out of the blue* . . .'

'. . . *quite out of the question* . . . *what on earth do you expect me to do with him* . . .'

A moment later Henry came back into the kitchen and said, 'Sarah's gone to find Lizzie, our housekeeper, to organise some proper tea. You must be hungry, after your journey. We'll have some cucumber sandwiches put up. Where have you come from?'

Charlie explained he had landed at Southampton that morning.

'And you said you were passing through? Are you stopping with people near by? What are your plans, exactly?'

'I'm going to start up my dog food business again,' Charlie

replied. 'This seemed like a good part of the world to do it in: lots of money in Gloucestershire; lots of dogs, too.'

Henry took Charlie by the arm and said, 'Let's walk in the garden until tea is ready. Leave your bag here.'

They strolled amongst the rose beds. Henry had enough sense to see he had a small crisis on his hands, and the time had come for damage limitation. After a few more minutes' conversation, it was established that Charlie might stay for supper, and for one night. Then he had to go. Henry promised to ring the Stanton Arms, in the local village of Stanton St Mary, where they did bed and breakfast at very reasonable rates, to make sure Charlie had somewhere to go on to. Then Henry went inside while Charlie tactfully examined the rose beds for a few moments.

After a short while Sarah Newark came out.

'So pleased you can stay the night, Mr Summers,' she said grimly. 'Do come and have some tea now, you must be famished.'

'Call me Charlie,' said Charlie, but she had already turned her back on him and was striding towards the house.

Tea was taken in the large entrance hall, which doubled as a drawing room. It was served from a low table in front of a coal fire which sputtered and smoked. Despite the fire, the stone-flagged hall was cool and damp. There were two kinds of tea: Indian and China in silver teapots with ebony handles; cucumber sandwiches with the crusts cut off; crumpets with melted butter; and a large and poisonous-looking chocolate cake.

Charlie helped himself. He found he was very hungry. He dropped some melted butter on to his blazer lapel, where he found it later that evening. In the middle of this feast, the conversation, which had been a little slow, was interrupted by the arrival of two small children and their nanny. There was a boy, called Simon, who looked about ten, and a girl, called Arabella, who was eight. Both had beautifully brushed blond hair and pale, innocent faces. The nanny was buxom, wearing jeans and an enormous jersey, with mousy brown hair enlivened by a streak of startling green.

'This is Mr Summers,' said Sarah.

Both the children were presented to Charlie, and shook his hand with immaculate good manners. After a few moments the nanny took them off to a distant nursery.

'Don't mind Belinda's funny coloured hair,' said Sarah. 'She's a very sensible girl on the whole. I'd rather she dyed her hair like that than go in for all this body piercing. That's what some of our friend's nannies do. I wouldn't stand for it here.'

Arrangements were then made to show Charlie his room. This turned out to be a servant's room, a long way from the rest of the bedrooms, and showed no sign of recent use. There was a small bed about five feet long, a washbasin and not much else in the way of decoration. A bathroom with a lino floor across the corridor was thrown in as additional hospitality. It was lit by one of the new low-energy bulbs, which seemed designed barely to register any form of electric current, emitting a glow similar to what might have been produced by half a dozen fireflies.

'I'm so sorry, none of the guest bedrooms are made up at the moment,' said Sarah, as she showed him the spartan room. 'If only we'd known you were coming. Now, I must tell Cook we've one extra for dinner.'

Charlie laid out his sponge bag and a pair of flannel pyjamas with purple stripes that looked as if they had seen too much active service. Then he went downstairs to see whether Henry would offer him a drink, as it was nearly six o'clock.

In the hall, copies of most of the day's newspapers were folded and set out on another table, together with an array of glossy magazines. A bowl of cut flowers sat beside them. Sarah Newark was nowhere to be seen; presumably supervising supper, or the children's bath time.

Henry was an understanding host: as soon as he arrived in the hall, Charlie was pointed in the direction of a side table on which stood decanters and bottles, and invited to help himself to a drink. I imagine he felt he needed one by then: he poured a dark brown whisky with not too much soda.

Henry did the same, and for a while the two of them read the papers. Then Henry said, 'So, you've decided to settle in Gloucestershire for a while.'

'I thought I might,' said Charlie. 'I'm going to look around for somewhere to rent, get to know the locals a bit, spread the word. I'm in touch with the Japanese dog food supplier again; it shouldn't be long before the first shipment comes in. It's just a question of organising letters of credit.'

'And where will you live?' asked Henry.

'Oh, I thought I'd rent a cottage somewhere, if I can find one. Meanwhile I shall put myself up at this pub you mentioned.'

Henry frowned. The possibility of having Charlie as a near neighbour had not really occurred to him before. It seemed a high price to pay for offering a drink to someone on a chance encounter in the South of France. Conversation languished, and after a while Henry looked at his watch.

'I might have a hot bath before dinner. Would you like to go and freshen up yourself? Come downstairs at eight. Don't bother to change for dinner, just stay as you are.'

Charlie agreed to this plan and wandered upstairs. As he ascended towards a landing he encountered the two children, now looking pink and scrubbed and in their dressing gowns. The girl was clutching an enormous teddy bear. They had their backs to him and were discussing something in their pure, treble voices.

'I thought he was simply ghastly,' the boy was saying.

'Too common for words,' agreed the little girl. 'Where *did* Daddy find him?'

A floorboard creaked as Charlie climbed the last stair. Both children turned about and adopted expressions of great surprise.

'Good evening again, children,' said Charlie. The two of them stared at him for a moment longer then, giggling, ran off in the direction of a warmly lit room which he supposed was the nursery.

Proceeding to his own bedroom, he undressed and then, wrapping a towel around his waist, went to the bathroom. Such modesty may not have been necessary: this wing of the house felt as if it had been uninhabited for some years. The water was hot, however, and the bath was a good length. He lay down in it with contentment, even if in virtual darkness. Someone had thoughtfully left a bottle of what looked like shampoo by the side of the bath, so he decided to wash his hair. The shampoo had a strange, but not unpleasant, smell and turned the bathwater an indeterminate colour not easy to make out in the gloom.

Charlie dried himself off and went back to the bedroom, where he dressed, spending some time trying to remove the spot of melted butter from his blazer. Then he adjusted his tie and combed his hair, checking himself in a badly spotted mirror on the dressing table. His hair seemed to have tints in it he had not noticed before.

Must have caught the sun, he thought.

He headed back downstairs. Henry and Sarah were standing near the fire, drinking champagne.

'Ah, there you are,' said Henry. 'Would you like a glass of this stuff? Or would you prefer to stick to whisky?'

He gave Charlie an odd look as he spoke.

'Is that champers you're drinking?' said Charlie. 'I'd love some.'

Henry poured out a glass and handed it to Charlie. The expression on his face was now quite enigmatic. His lips were compressed in a thin line, as if he wanted to say something but could not find the right words. His wife was less inhibited.

'Mr Summers, something seems to have happened to your hair.'

'What?' asked Charlie. He put his hand up to his head. His hair was all there, still slightly damp from his bath.

Henry said, in a choked voice, 'Perhaps you'd better have a quick look in the mirror, old boy. There's one near the door.'

Charlie did not move for a moment. He did not quite understand what was going on. Perhaps this was some elaborate family joke that he would be let in on in a moment or two. He smiled weakly and sipped his champagne. Suddenly Sarah said, 'Oh my God,' and, putting her glass down, she rushed up the stairs. A few moments later she was back, holding a bottle in her hand.

'Did you use this to wash your hair?' she asked Charlie.

'Yes, I'm afraid I borrowed some,' said Charlie. 'I couldn't find where I'd packed my own shampoo.'

'It's not shampoo,' said Sarah. 'It's the nanny's hair dye. I can't imagine what it was doing in your bathroom.'

Charlie decided he had better have a look. If this was a joke, it was a very obscure one. He crossed the hall and inspected his reflection in the large rectangular mirror that stood near the front door. The light was better here than upstairs and he could now see that his hair was a bright, emerald green. There was nothing more one could say about it.

'Well, I'm terribly sorry,' he said, crossing back towards the fire. 'It does look rather odd, doesn't it? I wonder if it will wash out?'

'Don't worry, old boy, it's only the three of us for dinner,' said Henry. He drank some champagne and coughed as some of it went up his nose.

'Not terribly good for business, green hair,' Charlie commented.

At that moment the nanny, Belinda, and her two charges came down the stairs. The children looked angelic as they went over to their father and mother.

'Goodnight, Daddy; goodnight, Mummy.'

'Just a minute,' said Sarah. 'Do you children know anything about how Belinda's hair dye got into Mr Summers' bathroom?'

The children looked at Charlie and Simon said solemnly, 'Mr Summers' hair's all green, Mummy. Just like Belinda's.'

'You haven't answered my question,' said Sarah.

'No, Mummy,' said Arabella. 'Perhaps Lizzie put it there by mistake?'

There was some more discussion, but no solution presented itself as to how the dye might have come to be in Charlie's bathroom. Belinda the nanny, not unaffected by the sight of Charlie's hair, told him the dye would wash out quite easily.

'You won't even know it was there after a few days,' she reassured him. Then she took the children upstairs again and shrieks of laughter could be heard from the landing.

Charlie, Henry and Sarah had dinner at one end of an enormous mahogany dining table, by the light of a three-branched candelabrum. There was spinach soufflé and anchovy sauce to start with; then confit of duck with flageolets and pommes dauphinoise; then an almond tart with crème fraiche. Charlie did not know when he might see another feast on this scale – although for Henry and Sarah, the appearance of pommes dauphinoise for the second time that month was cause for concern about Cook's menu planning – and so he tucked in with relish. The wine was a more than adequate counterpart to the food. Yet still the conversation did not flow, although when Sarah asked, 'What is it you do, Mr Summers?' and he explained again that he was thinking of introducing a new line in dog food, he imagined she became a shade more friendly. It helped that the black Labrador chose that moment to push the dining room door open with his nose and, after investigating Charlie, went and said hello to his master and mistress.

'*Oogums*,' said Henry Newark.

'*Oogiewoogie woo*,' said his wife. Charlie never did find out the dog's proper name.

It was not an easy evening, either for Charlie or Henry, for I had an account of it from both of them at different times. As for Sarah, she showed considerable tactical skills in using the occasion as a bargaining chip. She later extracted from Henry a commitment to take her to Thailand for three weeks, a holiday for which she had been angling for some time.

'After all,' she said to Henry later, '*what* I had to put up with entertaining your ghastly little friend, heaven only knows.'

The next morning Charlie was given breakfast in the kitchen by Henry.

'Sarah's out riding,' he said. 'Horses need a lot of exercise at this time of year.'

'Oh, do they really?'

'Still, it means I can cook us some fried bread if she's out. Like an egg on top of yours?'

The two of them breakfasted well and then Henry drove Charlie down to the Stanton Arms in an old Land Rover, dropping him off outside. By this time Charlie's hair, although still rather a strange colour, was not quite as glaringly green.

'Won't come in, if you don't mind,' said Henry. 'I've got a lot to do. We're going up to London this afternoon. It was so nice of you to call on us. Perhaps we'll see you around the county once you get settled in.'

He drove away at some speed.

Charlie pushed his way into the pub. It was quite dark in the bar and the air smelled of stale beer. A man in his shirtsleeves was polishing the counter.

'Lord Newark drop you off, did he?' the man asked Charlie. 'He said you was coming.'

Charlie tried not to show his surprise at this addition of a title to his new friend's name.

'Yes,' he said, in an offhand way. 'I've been staying with them, but they're off to London now.'

'Old family friend, are you?' asked the man. His expression seemed to Charlie to say, *I think not*. Charlie ignored the question.

'Henry said he had asked you to keep a room for me.'

The man laughed.

'Not much demand this time of year. There's plenty of rooms. Go up the stairs outside this door and pick one, and it's yours for thirty-nine quid a night, breakfast not included. I'm too busy and too old to carry your bag, so you'll have to manage yourself.'

'I don't mind,' said Charlie, and picked up his bag.

'Cash, payable in advance,' said the man. 'We don't take no cheques or credit cards. *If* you don't mind.'

Three

Charlie was given the registration book to sign. He wrote: 'Charlie Summers' in the column headed name; and under the column headed address, he wrote 'Stanton'. His domestic arrangements were in a state of some fluidity and Stanton seemed as good an address as any to give.

Once he had unpacked his things, which did not take long, he took the first steps in a plan he had been formulating for some time.

Charlie had long experience of starting new businesses. One might add he had an equally long experience of watching them fold, but with each new venture he set out with the enthusiasm, attention to detail and diligence of an accomplished entrepreneur. It is true there had been failures in the past. He had worked as a salesman for numerous companies, selling household products door to door. There had been a scheme to recycle ink cartridges for computer printers, which had been a franchise that Charlie had signed up to: the secret formula involved pouring some water and a small amount of green powder into the used cartridge, producing an evil-smelling goo that clogged up most printers within minutes. That business was not a success and he had moved on to other things. He was for a while a travel courier; a time-share broker marketing unoccupied holiday homes in Sicily; he had distributed a special formula that reduced the fuel consumption of your car by half (or in some cases altogether, when the engine seized up); he ran loan books for sub-prime lenders who paid you in advance on the promise of receiving your pay cheque, after certain necessary deductions for interest and service.

The Yoruza dog food scheme had a number of admirable features peculiar to itself: appealing to the warm-heartedness of the English dog lover, it promised health and long life to the lucky animal that was fed on it, and benefited, so the literature explained, from the many centuries of experience in dog nutrition of the warrior-monks of Yokohama.

Re-establishing the business in its new form in Gloucester-shire involved a series of bus journeys to Gloucester. On the first day, Charlie made a close study of classified ads in the local press, together with a number of phone calls on the pay-as-you-go mobile he had purchased. On the second day he found what he was looking for: small premises that had once been somebody's garage and were now a lock-up. A friendly local printer agreed to supply some bags and prepare the artwork for the labelling; and Charlie arranged for the delivery to the lock-up of some industrial weighing scales and other equipment familiar to those whose life's work involves filling paper sacks with dog food.

These exertions occupied the best part of a week. In the evenings he returned to his new home at the Stanton Arms. The pub, like Stanton Hall, was distinguished from its neighbouring stone cottages by being built of brick – in this case, the bricks were not red but of that yellowish tinge much favoured by architects charged with the construction of public urinals. There was one long room that served as the lounge bar, elegantly furnished with veneered chipboard tables and chairs. This, the more distinguished of the pub's two public rooms, was the setting for quiz nights and meetings of the local horticultural society. The tables were graced with menu cards, not unstained by tomato ketchup and brown sauce, that offered a selection of dishes ranging from lasagne to breaded haddock and jumbo-sized chips. To one side of this room, separated by a swing-door, was the public bar, where a more agricultural clientele was likely to be found in the evenings. Upstairs were four bedrooms, two described as en suite and graced with a shower cubicle and loo, and two others that shared a bathroom, but as there were never any other guests while Charlie was there, he had the luxury of the bathroom to himself.

The Stanton Arms lacked some of the charms of the traditional English coaching inn. There were no roses round the door; no quaintly painted swinging pub sign. Inside were no polished brasses, no fox masks on the wall, no hunting prints or reproductions of cartoons by Rowlandson or Hogarth. The utilitarian nature of the premises reflected the personality of the landlord, described over the lintel as 'Mr Robert Henderson, Licensee'. Known in the village simply as 'Bob', this individual in no way corresponded to the image of the genial country pub landlord: one's first thought on meeting him was to wonder whether he might recently have been detained as a guest at Her Majesty's pleasure.

In the evenings Charlie killed time in the lounge bar and at 7.30 exactly he ordered his supper – microwaved scampi and chips, or lasagne, or whatever else was on the evening menu – and then he nursed a pint of beer for an hour or so. Charlie knew the importance of frugality at this stage of a new business venture. Like all imaginative entrepreneurs, he understood the value of credit, when to stretch it to the limit, and when not to. His budget for the evening consumed, he would retire upstairs to his room and try to make out the ten o'clock news through the snowstorm on the television screen in his room.

Stanton St Mary was a quiet village, not especially on the road to anywhere. It lay among water meadows, surrounded for the most part by the Stanton woods. It was the sort of village that, had you been on a motoring holiday, you would have driven into with a sense of delight and discovery; and then driven out of five minutes later. The village sat astride a small stream that wound its way through marshy pastures and on down to the Severn some miles off. Most mornings and evenings, a damp mist rose from these meadows, lending the village a disembodied, mournful aspect. The houses, for the most part, were built in Cotswold stone and had all been put up some time in the eighteenth century to house workers from the Stanton estate. Now they were owned by more prosperous occupants, with Audis and Range Rovers parked outside some of them. There was a row of smaller brick cottages at one end of the village, and beyond them a slightly larger stone house, known as Stanton House, standing in its own few acres of grass park, that belonged to Mrs Bently. Beyond that was Stanton Hall.

Apart from the village shop, which sold newspapers, groceries, sliced white bread, tins of peaches and Bulgarian white and red wine, there was not much commercial life. A scrapyard behind one of the brick cottages did bodywork repairs; another cottage usually had a hearse parked beside it, announcing the presence of the village undertaker; apart from that, entrepreneurs were thin on the ground in Stanton St Mary before Charlie arrived.

*

The pub was not busy. It was still high summer, but the tourist trade, such as it was in Stanton St Mary, had already fallen away. The locals tended to come in at weekends or if the pub was holding a quiz night. Otherwise the landlord was not overstretched in his duties, so Charlie used the opportunity to find out what he could about the area: in particular, potential future customers for his range of Japanese dog food. Bob, the landlord, was neither communicative nor friendly; but he was trapped behind the bar most evenings, and Charlie sat on the other side, making it impossible for Bob to avoid discourse with him altogether.

Charlie learned that Stanton was the family name of Henry and Sarah and that Newark was a title conferred on an earlier Stanton by Queen Victoria; he learned the name of several other families in the area who might be expected to ensure that their dogs had the best of everything. He went and looked at the names of former Stantons in St Mary's Church, engraved on tombstones laid down among the stone flags of the church floor or else mounted on tablets of marble set into the church wall. It was obvious that the Stantons were still a power in the land; or at least in this corner of it.

Friday night was quiz night, and Charlie decided to attend as a spectator. The quiz, once it started, was a lively affair with much banter from the audience. The vicar was by far the strongest member of the home team, and a handsome lady no longer in the first flush of middle age, who was addressed by the quizmaster as 'Mrs Bently', the weakest. The quizmaster was more democratic in his address to other members of the team: even the vicar, the Reverend Simon Porter, was called Simon, and others were Bert, or Dave, or Kevin. Charlie deduced that Mrs Bently did not like too much familiarity. She was dressed with rather more care than most other people in the room, wearing black trousers, a cardigan over a white blouse, and a silk scarf. Spectacles hung around her neck on a black cord. Charlie thought she looked rather elegant: 'lady-like' was the term he used to himself. She carried herself with a certain poise.

'What is the capital of Peru?' asked the quizmaster, announcing the next question. Then he read out various answers supplied by the team players. Mrs Bently's answer was 'Alpaca'. There was some laughter when this was read out.

'It's "Lima", I'm afraid, Mrs Bently,' the quizmaster said.

'Oh, what can I be thinking of, then? I'm sure alpaca has something to do with Peru. That's where this cardigan comes from.'

It was then explained to her that an alpaca was an animal that looked like a cross between a sheep and a camel.

'Oh, of course,' said Mrs Bently, laughing. 'How silly of me! But alpacas live in Peru, don't they? That must have been what I was thinking of.'

Charlie wondered whether Mrs Bently was a dog owner.

The quiz came to an end and, in the cheerful scrum that followed as people got up from chairs and replaced their drinks with fresh ones, Charlie found himself standing next to Mrs Bently. He smiled at her and was surprised when she smiled back.

'Are you Mr Summers-Stanton?' she asked. 'Forgive me, but I saw your name in the hotel guest book. The Stanton Arms has so few visitors we tend to notice the ones who come.'

Charlie realised she must have misread the entry in the book. He had written, or rather scrawled, his name and then the name of the village as his address. She had assumed a hyphen between the two. He did not, however, correct the error.

'Charlie Summers, I'm known as,' was all he said.

'But you must be related to Henry and Sarah Newark. Stanton's their family name too, as you may know.'

'Yes, I was staying with them before I came here,' said Charlie, avoiding a more precise analysis of his relationship to the Stanton family.

That was all the conversation there was on the subject at the time, but from then on Charlie became aware of a revision of his status in the village. His account at the village shop was addressed to 'C. Summers-Stanton Esq.', and in general he found that more people were ready to stop and exchange a word with him than before.

The following week Charlie moved out of the Stanton Arms to a very small cottage which was available by the month, rented for a good deal less than he was paying at the pub. Charlie felt a residential address was important. One could not run a major pet food business from the top floor of a public house. He had some headed notepaper and business cards designed:

Charles Summers-Stanton
Piggery Cottage
Stanton St Mary
Glos.

This didn't seem quite right, and he was a bit worried about the addition of Stanton to his surname, which he felt might be drawn to the attention of the Stanton family themselves. Far better to be known simply as Charlie Summers; he could always drop hints about grand relations from time to time. The next revision was more satisfactory. It read:

Charles Summers Esq., FRSDN
Dog Nutritionist
Piggery Farmhouse
Stanton St Mary
Glos.

The initials after his name added a touch of class, Charlie felt: they stood for 'Fellow of the Royal Society for Dog Nutrition', an institution that, if it did not yet exist, certainly ought to have done.

By this stage, Charlie was ready to start his new venture. It was time to earn an income. His outgoings had been modest so far, but some investment, as with all new businesses, had been unavoidable, and not all of it could be obtained on credit.

A card appeared in the window of the village shop. It said:

Coming Soon!!
Yoruza
Balanced Nutrition For Dogs

This was followed by advertisements in the local newspapers, which were reproduced as a single-page direct mail-shot sent to every manor house, farmhouse and cottage that Charlie could find the address of, within twenty miles of Stanton St Mary. The advertisement showed a picture of a black Labrador, absolutely glowing with health and good humour. Underneath were the words:

Feed him on Yoruza –
Because he's worth it!

Charlie was particularly proud of the slogan. He had heard it or seen it somewhere in a different context, but felt that this was the first time it had been used in reference to dog food – certainly dog food that came from Japan. Beneath the heading were some statements, suitably vague, about a secret formula concocted by the monks of Yokohama, involving kelp and other alginates, and rich in potassium and a number of other minerals essential to the health of dogs.

With what headroom remained to him on his credit card, Charlie rented a pick-up truck. He had a transfer created for the door and side panels with the words 'Yoruza', 'Balanced Nutrition for Dogs' and a mobile phone number prominently displayed.

Charlie Summers was back in business.

Charlie bagged up the food in his rented premises in Gloucestershire. I doubt that any of it originated in Japan. Charlie was wary, he later told me, of any repeat of the dolphin-meat fiasco. Besides, someone had told him that in Korea, if you asked for dog food, what you got was food made from dogs. Charlie remembered from school that Korea was quite near to Japan. He felt that, rather than run any risk, and bearing in mind the problems with minced dolphin he had experienced with previous shipments, it would be better to mix the food himself from locally available ingredients, and present it in the Japanese manner. As a result, it looked very much like all the other dog food you find in your local cash-and-carry at the less expensive end of the range, but it was mixed with some scraps of dried vegetable that were described on the label as 'specially selected alginates from the Sea of Japan'. The profit margin, even with these cost-saving measures, was exiguous.

The bags, which Charlie weighed and filled himself, were a masterclass in marketing. The familiar slogan and the brand name 'Yoruza' were prominent; smaller script declared that the product was 'manufactured in Yokohama for Summers Pet Food Industries', and there was some Japanese script on one corner of the bag that Charlie's printer had copied from somewhere. He wasn't sure what it meant. He loaded the bags into the back of his pick-up, and drove around the county fulfilling the orders that were beginning to roll in.

Henry Newark met Charlie outside the Stanton village shop a week or two after Charlie's career as a dog nutritionist had been renewed. It was the first time they had met since Charlie's unannounced visit to Stanton Hall. Henry told me he had been quite careful not to meet Charlie, but it was inevitable they should bump into each other sooner or later.

After a preliminary greeting, Henry asked, 'And how's the dog food business going?'

'Very well, Henry,' said Charlie, 'people are being very supportive.'

'Why's it called Yóruza?'

'Oh. Well, Yoruza was a samurai's dog who starved to death on his master's grave. The Japanese rather admired him for his loyalty,' explained Charlie.

'It seems a bit odd to name a dog food after an animal that starved to death,' said Henry. Feeling he might have been a trifle unkind he felt compelled to add, 'You'd better let me have a couple of bags, then. What will that set me back?'

Charlie told him. Henry winced, but pulled a handful of twenty-pound notes from his wallet and counted out what he owed Charlie.

'Not cheap,' he said.

'It's the shipping costs from Japan,' Charlie explained.

'But you'll find your dog has never looked better. Give it a week or two, and then you'll see a difference. After all, you get what you pay for in this world, don't you think?'

That evening Charlie went to the pub, feeling he could afford a night out. Cash flow had improved recently. He had even been able to make a small payment to reduce the balance on one of his credit cards.

He was greeted by a number of people as he entered the Stanton Arms. By now Charlie had become an accepted part of the local landscape. Wearing either his shiny blazer, or a very old wax jacket that looked as if it had been recovered from the corpse of a poacher, or – for pub evenings – a rather tight-fitting beige cardigan, he was always cheerful, and took in good part a certain amount of the teasing that came his way. He was prepared to stand the occasional round of drinks, too, and did so this evening.

'You mus' be a millionaire by now, I s'ppose,' said Kevin, as he accepted a pint of bitter. Kevin worked as a butcher's boy selling sausages and chops from the back of a van.

'People seem to like the stuff,' said Charlie.

'Or their dogs do,' said Kevin. 'It's not *people* what has to eat it, is it, Charlie?'

There was some laughter at this; it was felt that Kevin had scored a point.

'You're in the wrong business, mate,' continued Kevin. 'Now, the way to make money these days is buy-to-let.'

There were expressions of interest from Kevin's immediate entourage. Charlie listened with an expression of polite in-difference. Sufficiently encouraged, Kevin continued: 'All you have to do is find a property what's a little run down – a student flat, like that. You goes to the bank or the building society. They have these special buy-to-let mortgages. They'll give you the full price of the flat without a deposit, or not much of one. You add a lick of paint here and there, put an ad in the papers, get a tenant, and that's all there is to it.'

'Simple as that?' asked Charlie doubtfully.

'Simple as that, Charlie: you pays six per cent on your mortgage, interest only. Your rent pays your mortgage, the value of the flat goes up by ten or twenty per cent per year, and there you are. I know people what don't do anything else. That lad that owns the paper shop in Stanton St John, Mohammed, he says he owns five flats in Cheltenham now.'

'Does he?' said half a dozen admiring voices from around the bar.

Dave, who was apprenticing to be the village undertaker, said, 'Of course, Kev, if you want to pay six per cent on your mortgage you can do, but I've heard it's better to borrow in euros and that only costs three per cent, and a bit.'

'I'm getting my Single Farm Premium in euros,' said Cleggie, who had five hundred acres of wheat and barley a mile or so from the village. 'I reckon the pound is going to fall against the euro. Stands to reason, doesn't it?'

No one quite knew what the reason might be, so this remark was accepted as being the last word on exchange rates.

There was a lively discussion around the bar for a moment concerning interest rate differentials, currency futures, hedges, and the like. If the Governor of the Bank of England had been in the bar, he would have struggled to keep up with some of the more technical observations. At length Charlie broke in and said, 'If it's that easy, Kevin, why aren't you doing it now? Why are you still selling sausages from the back of a van?'

Kevin looked hurt.

'I'm laying me plans, Charlie, laying me plans. You just look me up this time next year, and you'll see how easy it is to make money for them what knows how. Watch and learn, Charlie; watch and learn.'

Charlie excused himself, saying he was going outside to have a smoke. On the doorstep of the pub he met Mrs Bently, who was puffing away at a cigarette in a long ebony holder. It was a sight that would have been more congruous in the lounge of the Ritz Hotel thirty years ago, rather than outside the Stanton Arms in rural Gloucestershire. Whatever she was smoking was fragrant, and reminded Charlie of his childhood.

'Good evening, Mrs Bently,' said Charlie. 'What a nice smell your cigarette has.'

'Oh,' said Mrs Bently. 'Mr Summers-Stanton. I didn't realise you were in the pub tonight. Do you like the scent of the tobacco? It's Egyptian.'

'Please call me Charlie,' said Charlie. Once back inside the pub, matters arranged themselves so that Charlie found himself sitting at a corner table with Mrs Bently, having bought her a fresh gin and tonic (large), and another pint of bitter for himself.

'How is your dog food business going?' asked Mrs Bently.

'Surprisingly well,' said Charlie. 'People in this part of the world obviously care enough about their dogs to spend just that little bit extra to make sure their pets have a proper diet.'

'So brave of you to come and start a new business in a new place,' said Mrs Bently. 'Have you always been in dog food?'

'No, not always,' said Charlie. He could not think of an acceptable way to summarise the last twenty years of his varied career, so he said, 'I was in the army for a while.'

This was a complete lie. Charlie was no more of a soldier than I was a brain surgeon.

Mrs Bently looked at him with a trace more enthusiasm in her gaze. Not only was Charlie a relation of the Newarks, but he was clearly a member of the officer class as well.

She said, 'My ex-husband was in the Coldstreams for a while. What regiment were you in? We used to meet a lot of soldiers at one time; although that was many years ago.'

Charlie had thought, until then, that Coldstream was the name of a river, or a town. He temporised.

'I was in Special Forces. We're not really supposed to talk about it, even after we've left.'

Mrs Bently now looked at him with frank admiration.

'I imagine you could tell some tales if you were allowed to, Mr Summers-Stanton.'

Charlie shook his head modestly, and sipped his glass of bitter. There was a pause. Then he said, 'Do you have a dog, Mrs Bently?'

'No, I've never thought about it,' she admitted.

'They are such good company,' said Charlie. He had never personally owned a dog, but felt confident enough in making this assertion. His acquaintance of local dogs was widening by the week

Conversation over a drink led to an invitation to call on Mrs Bently for a cup of tea a few days later. It might be more truthful to say that the suggestion had been Charlie's, and that Mrs Bently had not felt able to turn him down flat.

Stanton House was approached by a short drive with grass pasture on either side. At the end of the drive was a large farmhouse, adorned with bay windows and Virginia creeper, with a stable block at the back around three sides of a cobbled yard. Though not in mint condition the house was well looked after, the yard was free from weeds and there was an air of money somewhere in the background which warmed Charlie's heart.

He was welcomed by Mrs Bently at the door. He thought he detected in her expression some hesitation, as if she might have forgotten he was coming or, perhaps more likely, was now wondering why she had agreed to the idea.

'Do come in, Mr Summers-Stanton.'

'Please call me Charlie,' said Charlie.

He followed his hostess into a small hall where a long-case clock ticked away. A bowl of autumn crocuses was flowering on top of a polished oak chest. They passed on into a drawing room, which was large and filled with afternoon sunshine. Through the windows was a view of a well-tended garden. Charlie was offered a seat, and sat down on the edge of a sofa. Mrs Bently disappeared for a moment and Charlie looked around him. The walls of the room were hung with small oil paintings, and a few watercolours with floral themes. The furniture was good and smelled of wax polish: there was a small breakfront bookcase, a tallboy and two mahogany side tables. Mrs Bently returned with a tray of tea things, and poured Charlie a cup.

'It's Earl Grey,' she said, 'I hope that's all right.'

'My favourite,' said Charlie.

'Men so often like Indian tea.'

'We always used to drink Earl Grey at home,' said Charlie, inaccurately.

'Oh? Where was home?' asked Mrs Bently.

'My people came from Middlesbrough,' said Charlie. He did not offer any further elaboration but dropped four lumps of sugar into his tea and stirred it vigorously. 'Have you always lived here, Mrs Bently?'

'It was my parents' home,' she said. 'My father bought it from the previous generation of Newarks just after the war, when they had to sell off some property to pay death duties. I grew up here and, when my husband and I were married, we moved to Stanton St Mary after my mother died. Now I live on my own except when my daughter and her husband come to stay, which I'm afraid isn't very often. He has a large estate in Scotland, you know. It keeps them very busy.'

'Is your husband still alive?' asked Charlie.

'We were divorced a long time ago. He lives in France now. He remarried.'

Mrs Bently sounded bitter. Time had not healed all, thought Charlie. There was a silence.

'Do you really think it would be a good idea to have a dog?' said Mrs Bently in a brighter tone, changing to a more cheerful topic.

'I don't know anyone who has ever regretted it,' said Charlie. 'And I meet a lot of dog owners in my business, you know.'

'What sort of dog would you recommend for someone like me?' asked Mrs Bently.

'Ah, well . . .' said Charlie. He tried to remember what sorts of dogs there were. He had come across so many in the last few weeks. Big ones, small ones; brown ones, black ones; all had tails that wagged, or else they had barked at him. But what kinds of dogs they had been he could not for the life of him remember, apart from the Labradors.

'I don't think I'd like a very big dog,' said Mrs Bently.

'No,' said Charlie with authority. 'I'm quite sure a big dog wouldn't do.'

57

'A terrier, do you think? A sweet little Jack Russell? Or a chihuahua?'

Mrs Bently smiled at Charlie as she said this; the smile suggested they might become friends, if Charlie could help to find her a dog.

'I tell you what I'll do,' he said. 'I'll keep my eyes open. Something might just turn up.'

'Oh, *would* you?'

Charlie thought that Mrs Bently would be very grateful if he found her a dog; very grateful indeed.

Four

The dream was always the same.

It is late at night, in the hour before dawn. The place is a dry, shallow wadi in south-eastern Afghanistan, in the hills above Gholam Khot, where a mule trail winds its way south towards the border with Pakistan. I am lying up among some rocks with two other soldiers. We are regular soldiers, seconded to work with an American special operations unit. None of us is meant to be here. It is the millennium and we are not at war with Afghanistan or the Taleban, at least not officially. But here we are anyway, cold, uncomfortable and a little frightened.

Nick Davies, whom I have known since I joined up, is operating the laser designator.

In the army, as in other walks of life, one meets plenty of people who talk the talk: men who try to project themselves as hard bitten, afraid of nothing, ruthless in their disposition. Nick was one of those rare people who didn't pretend to be anything: he was born with the constitution and, as far as I could tell, the emotional register of a slab of granite. He never worried; he was cautious but unafraid in circumstances that had me shaking like a leaf. He was easy enough to talk to, but despite all the years I knew Nick, when I last saw him I still didn't know much more about him than on the first occasion we had met.

The other man, whom I never saw again after that night

and who was later killed by an IED outside Basra, is watching Nick's back, and in general trying to make sure that none of us is seen and killed. We have been waiting in this place for several hours, and the temperature is minus nine degrees Centigrade. I am so cold I can scarcely think: forty-eight hours ago I was on the base at Thumrayt in the Oman, perspiring in the hot wind blown in from the Empty Quarter.

Despite the low temperatures, there are no fires in the encampment across the valley, nothing that would attract attention. With night vision we can see the huddles of men sleeping, a few makeshift tents, three Toyota pick-ups parked beside some rocks and partially covered with tarpaulins. This is a group of Taleban – the reason we are here, in this strange and dangerous country, on a clandestine operation. Without the night vision, they would be invisible: just grey shapes on a hillside littered with grey rocks and larger outcrops of grey stone. We wait in silence, as we are trained to wait.

The air is so cold and clear I feel I could reach out and touch the ridges of the low line of hills that define the far edge of the wadi.

The AC-130 Spectre gunship pops up over the range of hills to the south just as the first tints of rose are appearing along the stone ridges. Our laser shines on the target, which is picked up by the gunship's systems: within a few moments the 20mm Gatlings on the front end of the plane open up, firing six thousand rounds per minute at the men on the hillside. As the plane passes over the encampment, the rear-mounted 105mm howitzer starts dumping ordnance. The noise is horrendous: the howling of the aircraft as it flies overhead, very low; the burping of its guns; the secondary sounds of impact on rock and stone and perhaps flesh.

'Wake-up call,' says Nick.

A few seconds behind the AC-130 are two Apache heli-copters and a Chinook. They too pop up over the brightening range and each of the Apaches fires a Hellfire missile into the hillside, followed by short bursts from 30mm cannon. After two more sweeps across the hillside, the Chinook settles on the ground, dust swirling all around it. The other two helicopters circle overhead, providing top cover in case they've missed anyone, or in case anyone else tries to crash the party. The AC-130 has either gone home or is off to disturb some other group of travellers. Six men in desert camouflage and body armour jump out from the Chinook to check the scene and do a headcount. After a few minutes one of them fires a shot in the air.

'Time to go home,' I say to the other two soldiers with me. The Chinook is our ride out.

We break cover and move as quickly as we can across the rock-strewn hillside towards the attack site. It is still not too late for someone to take a shot at us, but no one does. The area around the helicopter is carnage. I can see at least eight human corpses, mostly with their clothes blown off by the force of the explosions. It is hard to tell what colour their turbans might once have been: the Taleban wear black. There is no doubt that these people are all dead. There are no signs of any weapons. A young camel, which had been tethered in the back of one of the pick-ups, has miraculously escaped all the gunfire and is now hobbling about on the slopes above us, looking worried, as well it might.

I wonder if we have identified anyone special: as usual, we haven't been told who we are after, and as usual, there's a rumour it is Mullah Dadullah.

We climb on board the Chinook and the American soldiers climb in with us. A combined operation; they don't always work. As the helicopter lifts off I give an interrogative thumbs-up to the American officer who now sits in the jump seat next to me. He shouts something above the sound of the rotors.

'What?' I say, cupping my hand over my ear to show I can't hear. He leans in and I can smell a minty gum fragrance over the sour breath of someone who hasn't been near a toothbrush for a while.

'The wrong target,' he shouts.

'What!'

'Eight guys we don't know, can't ID any of them.'

'We've killed eight people and we don't know why?' I yelled, above the rising note of the engines as the Chinook rose, tilted, and flew low and fast towards the south.

'Just some guys in the wrong place at the wrong time: bad intel. Ragheads, anyway,' he shouts. 'What does it matter – they're dead now.'

I look at Nick, to see whether he has heard this exchange. He has. He shrugs.

Not long after that operation, I came back to the UK. There had been a debriefing back at the base we shared with the Americans at Thumrayt. I was never clear why we had been given wrong intelligence, or whether it was us, or the Americans, who had screwed up. No one seemed to be very interested in eight dead Pashtuns. Maybe they were innocent tribesmen, maybe they weren't. They might have been going somewhere to buy and sell camels or goats. They might have been on their way to a terrorist training camp near Quetta. Who could say? The good thing about it, as Bilbo observed when I told him the story later, was that we hadn't shot up eight of our own side, which happened more often than one might think.

You don't work for the army without running the risk of seeing a few dead bodies. You might even be in a few firefights yourself. That goes with the job. But the fact was that I had been – at least in part – responsible for the deaths of eight human beings who were probably quite undeserving of the rain of bullets and missiles I had brought down on them. That, and a general feeling that my luck had run out, was what made me decide to leave the army. I left, and the dream came with me.

Except it isn't really a dream. It is a slow-motion flashback that comes to me as I lie somewhere between sleep and waking. Once it starts, there doesn't seem to be a 'Stop' button I can hit. I have to let it loop around and around in my head, while I lie awake, shaking. This happened to me quite a lot in the weeks after the event. Since then I have still had the dream, although less frequently than before, thank God.

I had joined the army for all sorts of reasons, none of them particularly well defined. My father had been in the army all his life, retiring as colonel; his cousin, Harriet's father, had reached the rank of brigadier general. The family view, mine included, was that it was a straightforward enough answer to the awkward question of what to do after leaving school. Beyond that, I will admit to feeling that I might do something worthwhile; serve my Queen and Country; make the world a better place. Of course, one never puts it quite like that, but that is what I believed at the time.

I left the army with different feelings altogether. I felt displaced and purposeless. It was impossible to talk to anyone about what I had been doing with my life for the last few years. To talk about operations was discouraged by my former employers. In any case, I don't think anybody was particularly interested. The wars I had been involved in were of little concern to anyone but the participants, and most of my friends at home probably couldn't even have found the places on the map. Above all, I left the army with a feeling of moral blankness: after what had happened, it was hard to see what I could do to move on.

Returning home to England was a cold dose of reality. Both my parents had died young, in their sixties. I had inherited from them a rambling stone farmhouse dignified by the name of Pikes Garth Hall, on the edge of the moors not many miles from Middleton-in-Teesdale in County Durham. It had been a romantic speculation of my father's when he had retired from the army, at a much older age than I was when I left. I think he had a vision – never fulfilled – of becoming a gentleman farmer. The house was stone built, with slate roofs, spacious, and very cold in the winter. At the bottom of the lane that led up to the farmhouse was a cottage which was also part of the property: this was let to an elderly couple, the Pierces. The rent was paid in kind, not cash: Sam Pierce cut the grass, repaired the dry-stone walls and did other odd jobs about the place. His wife Mary did occasional housework and ironing for me, and made sure there was something in the fridge on my weekend visits. The whole property was a smallholding of about one hundred and fifty acres: too big to be easily managed, far too small to be economical, for the land was poor grazing.

When I came back home the house had been let to tenants who had not been too fussy in the way they treated other people's property, and it took some time and a painful proportion of my savings to put it back in order and make it more or less habitable. It was in a wonderful situation, on the edge of the green dale and at the foot of the moors. The views of the dale went on for ever. In the spring the hillside above Pikes Garth was the haunt of lapwing and curlews. In the summer it became purple as the heather flowered, and one could hear the cackle of grouse. The Pike Beck flowed almost past the door, and its stony voice lulled me to sleep at nights.

All of this was very well, and for a while just being there and going for long tramps along the footpaths and bridleways that criss-crossed the moors was reward enough. I got back in touch with a few of my childhood friends and for a while it was as if we had never been apart. I was asked out to lunch and dinner and for a few months was fêted as if I were a returning hero. But then my novelty wore off and I began to wonder what on earth I was going to do with myself. I didn't want to farm; I had no idea what other forms of employment might be open to me. The other people who had come out around the same time all sailed into jobs. Nick Davies was recruited by a private security contractor, working on the other side of the street, as it were. Nick was always a high-flyer. He was tough, very focused, not really a social animal. Whatever he did, I used to think, he would do it well. He got in touch with me from his new firm and offered me a temporary contract, which I accepted with alacrity. I would be working with people I knew, doing a job I more or less understood.

The pay was very good, the conditions were not. I started out doing close protection work – what was known, not inaccurately, as 'bullet-stopping'. We worked in Iraq, Kosovo, Colombia and other places where wars were being fought, some in the public eye, others more obscure. We organised security for contractors and VIPs; then I was moved on to what was known as 'hostage resolution'. That was a lot more interesting, and a lot more complicated, and for a while I almost thought about making a permanent career of it. But then, on a job in Colombia, I had an unpleasant near-miss – about as near a miss as one ever lives to talk about – and I decided to pack in the military life for good, and come home.

Come home to what? was the problem. Neither my training nor my inclination fitted me for the jobs on offer, and those were few: working as secretary for a local charity, or else lying up in the moors watching a hen harrier's nest in case somebody's gamekeeper had a go at the eggs; working for a firm doing security surveys for Lloyd's of London. None of these appealed to me at all. So when Bilbo Mountwilliam rang, I was ready for any suggestion as to what to do with my life.

I remembered Bilbo from school. He had been three years above me: a large, silent boy, excelling neither in sports nor in the classroom. Nevertheless, he was treated with respect: caution might have been a better word. He was known to have a temper. A boy in his year broke both arms falling out of a tree on a walk with Bilbo. That was the official story. Another version, current in the lower years of the school, was that Bilbo had beaten up this boy for some affront, real or imagined. I had no special reason to follow his career with any interest after he left school, although I was aware that, like me, he had joined the army. I later heard that he had gone into the City. Then, it seemed, he had started up an investment company, based somewhere in Bloomsbury.

Bilbo still had a reputation of being a hard man who had been fond – some said too fond – of his job in the army and as a bon viveur. Now he ran a hedge fund from which he was said to earn an enormous amount. I had not heard who the other investors were, but was told Bilbo had partners. The proceeds allowed him to maintain an expensive house in London and a large house in Yorkshire. The Mountwilliams were a well-known Northern family who had once been very wealthy: the money, originally dug out of the ground in the form of coal in the nineteenth century, had long since been spent. Before Bilbo made his fortune, the Mountwilliams had sold up most of their property. Bilbo had been able to buy back the family home a couple of years ago, and had it re-modelled, redecorated and refurnished at enormous expense. He almost never went there but on his very occasional visits neighbours would be invited in to dine, to admire the house, to drink the expensive claret, and – for all I knew – eat off gold plates. News of these excesses travelled all the way to County Durham. It sounded as if Bilbo had restored the family's former glory.

I gathered he'd got hold of my number through a mutual acquaintance.

When he had introduced himself and reminded me where we had last met, he said, 'Are you ever in London? I want you to have lunch with me.'

'Well, I . . .'

'Don't be shy. You probably know what I do. I want you to consider coming to work for us.'

I wasn't planning on being in London, but this sounded like a good enough reason for going. Any job offer, by this stage, deserved serious consideration.

'I could come down any day next week,' I said cautiously. As a matter of fact, I could have come down to London in the next twenty minutes if necessary, but I didn't want to seem too desperate.

'Good man: next Wednesday at one o'clock, then. Now, where shall we eat?'

There was a pause while I wondered whether he was expecting me to offer a suggestion. Given the distance of my journey and the expense involved, I thought I deserved somewhere with a reasonable number of stars and a good wine list. Claridge's, the Ritz, the Connaught all crossed my mind. I was about to suggest one of them when Bilbo said, 'I know. Meet me at the Pizza Parlour in Wardour Street. It will be such fun to go somewhere a bit different.'

When I came to know Bilbo better, I realised that his choice of restaurant for that first meeting was not for reasons of economy, nor some calculated gesture aimed at moderating my expectations. He was whimsical about his likes and dislikes. At the precise moment of his telephone call, he had decided he felt like eating pizza, so that was what we would do.

'They serve excellent pizzas here,' said Bilbo when we finally met. 'I'm sure you're bored with expensive restaurants. I know I am.'

Bilbo was a large man, with a bland, pale face and a small mouth. I could just discern in him the boy I had known at school. His most distinguishing feature was a pair of heavy black eyebrows, underneath which were small hazel eyes. His hair was black, tightly curled and receding. The backs of his hands and wrists, protruding from snowy-white cuffs fastened by gold cufflinks, were also covered in black hairs. He wore a dark blue suit of immaculate cut and he radiated a mixture of prosperity and menace – rather like a successful barrister.

I had talked to one or two friends still in the army before

coming down to London. One of them told me: 'You know he used to be called "Tent Peg Mountwilliam" in the army?'

'Don't tell me why – I'm sure I'd rather not know.'

My informant told me anyway, with obvious relish: 'He was such a bad shot he decided to specialise in close-quarter work. His weapon of choice was a sharpened tent peg. It's the one thing the Ministry of Defence makes sure we never run out of. Body armour, ammunition, helicopters: none of them are ever there when you need them. But you can always rely on a supply of tent pegs. That's why Bilbo liked them.'

Now I had met Bilbo it was hard to imagine him at work with tent pegs, either setting up camp or in more sinister applications. For the time being, he was charm itself.

'I wonder if you've found yourself a job since leaving the army?' he said, after we had reintroduced ourselves and sat down at a table. 'It isn't easy, is it? They spend all that money on training us, we have to learn to take split-second decisions in circumstances that would render most chief executives speechless, and then what do we find is on offer? Underpaid jobs working for a charity or a boy's club. That's what the general population thinks we're capable of, isn't it?'

'I'm still looking for something,' I admitted.

'Quite,' said Bilbo. 'Unemployed and unemployable. It's a very unfair world. Once you've done your time in the services, people just don't want to know. I'm told you were good at your job as a soldier until that friendly-fire incident. Why the hell did you quit: because a few Pashtun were shot up? Christ, they wouldn't have lost sleep over it if it had been the other way around.'

'Well, I wasn't proud of what happened,' I said.

Bilbo poured a glass of white wine for each of us.

'There never was an official inquiry, was there? It never made the press, did it?'

'No, thank goodness. Anyway, all we know is that they weren't the people *we* were after. That doesn't mean that they were innocent civilians, not in that part of the world.'

'Ah well,' said Bilbo, 'the presumption is that if they aren't obviously against us, they must be for us. These things happen. Have some more wine?'

We sipped our wine and Bilbo smiled at me in a fatherly sort of way.

'When I left the army, I was lucky enough to be offered a helping hand by a friend from my regiment who had family connections in a merchant bank,' Bilbo told me. He seemed to be leading up to something. 'Now I run a hedge fund,' he explained. 'A hedge fund is just a high-performance in-vestment fund, but we're not as tied down by rules and regulations as the big mutual funds. We can invest in more or less anything we like: bank debt, high-yield derivatives, fixed-income straddles, all that sort of thing.'

I knew Bilbo was speaking to me in English, but it might as well have been Korean.

'I know none of this means anything to you at all,' said Bilbo. 'I was the same a few years ago. When I came out of the army, I hadn't any idea what to do. Then my friend rang me up – just as I got in touch with you – and offered me a job. The pay wasn't much, but it was a start. Banks in those days were always looking for "good chaps" like me: presentable, decent background, someone who might know the right way to hold a knife and fork. So I joined up. It turned out to be much more interesting than I had expected. After a while I saw that for every ten people who worked there, one made the money and the other nine sat around writing reports about it. Once I saw how it worked, I borrowed some money, lured a couple of particularly bright young traders with MBAs to join me, and set up on my own. That was five years ago. Now we've got several hundred million pounds under management.'

Bilbo poured some more wine. I wondered how his friend had felt about his new employee walking off with his best and brightest staff. I thought I had better try to find out why Bilbo was interested in me.

'What could I do for you?' I asked. 'I know nothing at all about investment. I've never had any spare money of my own to invest.'

'Oh, it's not very complicated. The back office does all the technical stuff. But we need people with some personality and what my mother used to call "background" working in the front office. Our clients need to be kissed and cuddled before they'll part with their money. That would be your job: introducing us to high-net-worth individuals you might know, or you might get to know, giving them lunch and dinner and taking them to the races and so on. You know lots of people, Eck. Even at school, you knew everyone and everyone knew you. People seem to trust you. We need someone like you to be the public face of our little firm. We're concentrating on developing the private-client side of the business at present. And it's not exactly work.'

'What's the catch?' I asked.

'You have to take a few exams. Don't worry: we'll help you through them, and we'll put you on a salary from Day One, as long as you pass them. That's just to make you legal. After that, your job is to make people feel good about Mountwilliam Partners. Get them in front of me and some of my traders – we know how to get their attention. They don't really care about the detail. They've all heard about hedge funds. They *want* to believe we'll make them richer than anyone else can.'

'And can we?' I asked Bilbo.

'Oh, yes,' said Bilbo. 'It's all about trust. Once you get them through the front door, they'll be happy to part with their money when they see our returns.'

The pizzas arrived and Bilbo attacked his with gusto.

'I remember your parents. Are they still alive?' he asked.

'No.'

'So you've got that nice house near Middleton-in-Teesdale all to yourself. Won't you rattle around in it on your own?'

'No.'

'I'm sure you will, you know. That's why you ought to come and work for me. What else are you going to do with your time? Learn flower arranging?'

Bilbo put down his knife and fork. The pizza in front of him, which had started out the size of a mini-roundabout, had now been cut down to manageable size. I chewed on a corner of mine. He said, 'You need to have money in this world. When I bought back my family home it had practically fallen down. You might know of it?'

I nodded.

'My ancestors were coal miners in the eighteenth century. Their children became mine foremen. The third generation had its own collieries. After that, no one did a stroke of work for the next century. All the money was spent by the time I came along. We had our own crest by then, and family plate, but absolutely no cash at all.'

Bilbo held up the little finger of his left hand, and showed me the signet ring he wore there. It was hard to make out the engraved figure on it, but it looked like a cat, or dog, sitting and licking its paw.

'What is it?' I asked.

'The cat that got its cream,' said Bilbo, 'and we had a family motto to go with it. *Semper Plus*: "always more". It's my motto, too.'

That is how I started working for Bilbo and Mountwilliam Partners. The company was co-owned by Bilbo and a group of investors, and had modest offices in a maze of anonymous streets somewhere south of the British Museum. The registered head office was in the Cayman Islands. The converted terraced houses that contained Mountwilliam Partners were located next door to a Greek restaurant, and there was a café a few yards farther down the street, which ran to all-day breakfasts and quite good cups of coffee. It was not a bad place to work: inconvenient but with an eccentric charm of its own. I think I would have liked working in a large, soulless office block much less.

Beside the front door, a brass plate bore the legend 'Mountwilliam Partners'. When you rang the bell, you were inspected by a small remote camera, and then buzzed in. Through the front door one was confronted by a steep staircase, with doors off to the right and left of the minute entrance hall. On this floor were the trading desks: soft commodities, gold, oil, fixed income, distressed debt – those were some of our specialities. The traders started work at six or seven in the morning and were often at their desks until eight or nine at night. They were expected to keep their mobiles beside their bedsides in case Bilbo wanted to reach them. If Bilbo rang, you talked to him. That was the house rule.

When you entered the trading room, there was always a buzz about it, a sense of adrenalin flowing, a hum of raised voices that could be heard even before you opened the door. Inside were two rows of desks, each with its own set of screens: a Bloomberg terminal, a couple of trading screens, a PC linked to the network. Over the entrance to the room was a printed sign that read:

RULE 1: We are here to make money
RULE 2: We are here to make money
RULE 3: Don't forget Rules 1 and 2

The top floor was accessed only through a door with a keypad: this was where the rocket scientists lived, the people who developed the strategies, expressed in complex mathematical language, that were the lifeblood of the trading department. I didn't know any of this elite except by name, but I had a few friends among the traders: Doug Williams, a thin, cynical man who traded in commodities; Alan Mc-Nisbet, who bought and sold bank debt; and one or two others. There was not much time for socialising given the hours everyone worked – except for me – but occasionally Doug and I might have a drink together. I don't suppose most of the traders thought much of me: I was just the man who walked the clients through the front door; they were the people who made them rich.

The people who worked at Mountwilliam Partners were an interesting mixture. I was the only other person apart from Bilbo with an army background. There were a few ferociously bright graduates with degrees in mathematics or economics; and a number of slightly older, hard-bitten-looking traders, with nails gnawed down to the quick and nicotine-stained fingers. There was, of course, no smoking in the offices and therefore everyone met on the pavement outside during fag breaks, where traders and salesmen happily shared information they would never have been allowed to talk about upstairs.

The first year or so was a challenge: going to the office for several hours and then, in the afternoon or early evening, attending lectures, or nodding off over textbooks. But I managed it, somehow. I was not paid much to start with but I knew my salary would be on a steep upward curve as soon as I was qualified, and that was sufficient incentive to keep me at it. In retrospect, the work was not so hard, considering I was now licensed to take people's money away from them.

Once I had passed my exams, my new career started in earnest. I found that the job suited me. The present and future clients I mixed with were people I sometimes already knew, and even liked. My job involved organising endless drinks parties and receptions, sponsoring various minor sporting fixtures where potential clients might gather, and taking investment roadshows around the country. More often it was simply a question of spending time with the right sort of people. I was paid to entertain potential clients and if they ever asked me any difficult questions about what Mountwilliam Partners actually did, I simply arranged for them to meet Bilbo. I could not really believe my luck. The principal disadvantage of my new life was living in London during the week; but I reasoned, if ten million other people could put up with that, so could I. So I bought myself a small service flat in West Hampstead with the remains of my capital and a large mortgage, and became used to the weekly commute: catching the six o'clock to Darlington from King's Cross on Friday nights, the train known by habitués as 'the Vodka Special', and commuting back down on Sunday evenings.

Of course, we were all encouraged to invest our substantial earnings in the firm. Bilbo called it 'putting your money where your mouth is'.

'You have to be able to tell people *you've* bought into the story,' he told me. 'We'll help you take some equity out of that flat of yours – you could raise fifty thousand from that without any problem, couldn't you? And there's an investment savings scheme we invite you to contribute to from your salary.'

If I had any doubts about investing in things I still didn't quite understand, it was made easier for me when I was told that an investment in the firm's funds was automatically deducted from one's monthly pay cheque. But I couldn't complain about this additional taxation: I was grateful to Bilbo for setting me up. I had no need to think too hard about my life, or what I was going to do next. I saw Bilbo himself most days, but less of the other people who worked for him. He liked to keep us in different compartments, I think. He – and, no doubt, his partners, whoever they were – were the only people who knew everything that was going on.

And so my new career as a junior financier was launched. I was interested, even absorbed by it all. The work was sufficiently demanding that I didn't mind the absence of any social life outside it. Too many evenings were spent entertaining people anyway, and the little free time I had during the week was spent mostly in my flat, catching up on my sleep. I had achieved peace of mind at last, after Afghanistan. Except that it wasn't peace of mind: it was numbness of mind. The dream of Gholam Khot stayed with me: perhaps once a month I would awake perspiring and moaning, the sound of gunfire in my ears.

*

For a while this numbness of mind suited me well. I did my job, and earned money, and spent it as fast as I earned it, because the following year I was expecting to raise even more. Spending money is a good way of avoiding thinking about anything, I have found. Then, one day, I had to go to Bob Matthews' funeral.

It was in the middle of an intense phase of the war in Iraq and I was concentrating very hard on shutting out painful memories of my own. Bob Matthews' funeral was when I saw Harriet for the first time since her engagement party a few months earlier. When I saw her, I was struck by how ill she looked. Never very substantial, she had lost weight, and her skin was the colour of parchment. Dressed in a dark coat and black hat, she was the living embodiment of mourning, a testament to the power of grief. One could see that she had once been a very attractive girl: or perhaps I was superimposing over her strained features the image of a remembered Harriet, Harriet at her engagement party. Whatever it was, as I looked at her I became conscious of a lump in my throat so big I could scarcely swallow. I spoke a few words to her after the service. She touched my arm and said, 'Thank you so much for coming. Bob would have appreciated it.'

I'm not convinced she even knew to whom she was speaking.

'Of course I had to come, Harriet. Please let me know if there is ever anything I can do for you.'

She focused on me then and said, 'Thank you, Eck. It was good to see you.'

I was dismissed, in the most kindly fashion, as she moved away from me to thank some of the other mourners.

From that day, my peace of mind – or the numbness I had become accustomed to – was gone. I started to think about

Harriet and, once I'd started, I forgot to stop, as they say in my part of the world. I began to imagine what I knew would never happen: a life together with Harriet. I knew it would never happen because I felt that she was one of those girls for whom there is only ever one man: they still exist, even in this polygamous age. And the more I told myself it would never happen, the more I thought about it happening.

The odd thing was that I started to think about the relevance of my present mode of life in the context of that imagined world. I couldn't quite see myself standing at the front door of my flat in West Hampstead and kissing Harriet goodbye in those fond daydreams of some improbable connubial bliss. I couldn't imagine Harriet accompanying me to the jolly lunches and dinners and race meetings that constituted much of my daily life. If we had a future together, which of course seemed unlikely, it wasn't in the world of Mountwilliam Partners.

As a consequence of these thoughts, bit by bit I began to realise that working for Bilbo was not as desirable a way of life as I had first thought. The money was good; if I was honest, I was being paid much more than I thought I was worth. My investments in various Mountwilliam funds were doing well. When we received the report sheet, twice a year, it looked to me as if my money had gone forth and multiplied, although how or why was harder to say. If you read the papers, you might be forgiven for believing that the most demanding part of making money these days was remembering to get out of bed each morning. House prices were going up by ten per cent or more a year, so if you owned your home, perhaps you didn't even need to get out of bed. The stock markets around the world soared. The newspapers published a story nearly every week about some new entrepreneur, or fund manager, who had made an unimaginable amount of money, all because he had the foresight to go and borrow an amount from the bank.

Even I, good old Eck, was on this new, unstoppable, global gravy train. I couldn't imagine why I was paid to do what I did, but somehow, once I started to have money, it was never quite enough. One discovered new needs. Once I had got by with one pinstriped suit for funerals, regimental reunions and drinks parties; and one tweed suit for racing or Sunday lunch in the country. Now it seemed important to have at least a dozen suits, run up by a tailor in the City whose address had been given to me by Bilbo, and an infinite number of shirts and ties from Jermyn Street. One had to look the part: prosperous, natty, smart – but respectable. Bilbo, I knew, had innumerable suits hanging in a walk-in wardrobe at his London home in Kensington Gate. He had shown me his dressing room on one occasion when I had brought him some documents just after he moved into his new house. You might have seen fewer clothes in the men's department at Harrods.

I had also bought my Audi sports car, when once an old Land Rover had been all that I needed or owned. The only thing this purchase achieved was to accumulate parking fees. I drove about ten miles a week in it, but still, I had to have it. I joined a couple of clubs, to amuse myself while I was in London. The firm helped with my subscription, because men's clubs were where you met friends, and brought up the subject of Mountwilliam Partners' stellar performance as you stood at the bar chatting. I bought expensive wine and ate in expensive restaurants, even when I was on my own. No matter that I was being paid more than I had ever been paid in my life, I still spent most of it.

*

One day, a few months after I had been to France with Henry Newark, I received a phone call. To my astonishment, it was Harriet. After a few polite greetings were exchanged she said, 'Have you heard about Aunt Dorothy?'

'Aunt Dorothy' was Dorothy Branwen, Harriet's maternal aunt: a spinster, reputed to be well off, who used to turn up at family weddings and funerals. She had been a great friend to my parents when I was very small, and I had distant memories of her staying with us from time to time. These visits had stopped when I was still quite young, although I'm not quite sure why. I don't remember that there was any falling out: I think Aunt Dorothy simply became more reclusive.

'No, what about her?' I asked, although I knew what the answer must be.

'She died in her sleep a couple of days ago. It was quite unexpected: she was not ill, as far as anyone knew.'

'Oh, Harriet – I'm so sorry,' I said. I just managed to stop myself from uttering that well-worn remark, 'she was a good age'.

Harriet continued, in a practical tone of voice, 'Well, I hardly ever saw her. I can't say that we were close. Did you know she left everything she had to the two of us?'

Although I had always hoped there might be a *pourboire* for me in the will, as a token of my aunt's former friendship with my parents, I had not expected more. The idea would take some time to digest.

'I'm flying back home tomorrow morning,' said Harriet. 'The funeral will be in Cirencester on Friday. Can you be there?'

Five

I decided to invite myself to stay with Henry and Sarah the night before the funeral, and then drive on to Cirencester the following morning. I drove down from London, timing my journey to make sure I arrived in Stanton St Mary for drinks. Henry was in the hall when I arrived, waiting for me. He took my suitcase from me and set it down.

'Have a drink first, and then I'll show you your room.'

We settled down beside the fire and over whiskies Henry, after first asking a few questions about my trip, told me all about Charlie Summers and his arrival in Stanton St Mary. It was the first I had heard of it, and Henry had to remind me who Charlie Summers was.

'Do you know that man is going around telling people he is some sort of relation of mine?' said Henry.

'Well, you told me you thought I was his twin, so I'm afraid I haven't much sympathy.'

Henry related what he knew of Charlie's new career as dog nutritionist in residence in Stanton St Mary.

'Have you bought any of his dog food?' I asked.

'I had to. I met him outside the village shop and it seemed the only way to get away from him was to purchase a couple of bags.'

'Did it do any good?'

'It has some fairly powerful emetic effects,' said Henry.

'The dog has certainly lost some weight, and is the better for it. But the state of the kitchen floor the morning after we first fed him on the stuff was indescribable.'

Sarah Newark came into the hall at that moment, followed slowly by the black Labrador, which seemed more subdued than usual. I had always been a little frightened of Sarah: of medium height and quite thin, she was good looking but on occasion she could seem a trifle severe with those of Henry's friends with whom she came into contact. She conveyed an impression, whenever one met her, that she had expected better things of life; most people would have considered Sarah very well situated with her fifteen-bedroomed house, full-time cook-cum-housekeeper, nanny and gardener. Yet it often appeared as if she found her surroundings, her husband and the person she was talking to barely adequate. I stood up when Sarah arrived and she pecked me on the cheek.

'I suppose Henry's been telling you about our new neighbour, Mr Summers?'

'Mr Summers-*Stanton*,' Henry corrected her.

'Too dreadful for words: apparently he's renting a tiny lean-to that used to be part of the estate piggery, in the days when pigs made money. We sold it off years ago. Now he calls it "Piggery Farmhouse". I simply don't know where to look when friends ask me about him. People feel we brought him to the village, but really it's all Henry's fault. Yours too, Eck, I shouldn't wonder.'

I began to feel a little sorry for Charlie Summers.

'As for our poor *Oogums*, that man's dog food might have killed him. I almost called in the police, but we put him back on the old food he used to have and he's getting better.'

After dinner Henry and I sat in the hall, drinking a glass of port, while Sarah watched television next door in the sitting room.

'I've been thinking about that investment fund you work for, Eck.'

'Oh yes?'

'Quite a few chums seem to be putting money into these private-client hedge funds.'

'Well, it's one way of ensuring you make money whether the markets go up or down,' I said. This was our mantra, and we were taught to repeat it in every conversation we held with potential clients. 'This is very nice port, Henry,' I said. 'What is it?'

Henry told me and then returned to the subject in hand.

'The trouble is, one always seems to need more money. I own a bit of land, of course, but I'm not exactly awash with cash. Sarah likes her hot holidays and a reasonable standard of living. Then there's the children's education to think of; the worst of that expense is yet to come. And one's income isn't what it might be. I mean, I have a small investment portfolio and we still own a few cottages that provide us with a decent rent. But this place,' said Henry, gesturing at the hall around us, encompassing in the sweep of his hand all the red-brick elevations, and oak staircases, libraries and billiard rooms, 'this places eats its head off. The rest of the estate is mostly grazing land, and that's never going to make me rich. You know what lamb prices are like nowadays.'

I didn't, but I gave a sympathetic grimace.

'I mean, there seems to be so much money about these days. You get people from London, coming down here and buying up old estates like this one, who barely know how to use a knife and fork. I met a couple the other day, Jasper and Suki, they call themselves.'

Henry shook his head, as if he could hardly credit anyone would give their children such names. 'Jasper told me he worked in financial public relations. He drives a brand new Porsche Cayenne with the number plate JAS 1 and his wife has a Range Rover with the number plate SUK 1.'

Henry shook his head again.

'Financial public relations! I mean, for God's sake, what is happening to the world? Who are these people coming to live here? Where does their money come from? Suki buys eventing horses by the dozen, and Jasper is putting in a second swimming pool at the farm they bought, so that the children can play in their pool without disturbing the grown-ups when they want a swim.'

Henry drained his port, as if he needed every drop to have any chance of restoring his mental equilibrium. Perhaps he did.

'Everybody's rolling in money, these days,' he commented. 'It's only people as slow witted as I obviously am who haven't geared up, as I believe you call it, and put their assets to work.'

I made some neutral remark, implying neither faith in Henry's financial judgement nor the opposite, and waited for him to continue.

'The point is, it seems like a good idea to invest in one of your funds now, to help pay for the children's education later on. And it isn't just that. Sarah likes to do things properly, as she calls it, and I'm never quite sure how we manage. But where I would raise the cash to invest with, I don't know. Have some more port?'

I stretched out my glass and Henry refreshed its contents.

'Well, as you say, you've got land, and this house. We

could help you take some equity out of that, you know. Land is very good collateral, especially in this part of the world.'

We talked some more about the hundreds of different ways of making money that seemed to be available to the astute investor, and then Sarah came back into the hall and the conversation drifted towards children and horses.

The next morning I drove down to Cirencester to attend my aunt's funeral and parked in a car park on the edge of the town centre. Harriet was waiting for me in the porch of the church, and greeted me with a kiss. Once again she was in mourning, but the effect this time was to make her look subdued rather than tragic. We walked together into the Cirencester church, which was grander than some cathedrals, a testament to the vanished wealth of wool merchants from the days when sheep were still the thing to invest in. The funeral was sparsely attended and the service was interrupted from time to time by the distant sound of tourists coming in to gaze at the interior of the church. The mourners barely filled a couple of pews in one corner. Aunt Dorothy had few living relations apart from the two of us, and none of the others was there, confined to home by age and frailty, as in the case of Harriet's mother, or simply not sufficiently motivated to attend. Perhaps news of the will bequeathing everything to Harriet and me had discouraged a more general enthusiasm for the reliquaries of a reclusive maiden aunt. There were a few neighbours; an elderly solicitor, Mr Gilkes, who had looked after Dorothy's affairs; and of course the two of us. Mr Gilkes came up and shook our hand when the service was over, and offered us a glass of sherry back at his office. When we declined, he tottered off, leaving Harriet and me alone.

'Let's find somewhere to have lunch,' I suggested. Harriet agreed.

'I've had enough of funerals,' she said. 'A glass of wine and something to eat is just what I need.'

We managed to find a table at a nearby wine bar and I procured a bottle of white. The place was busy and noisy and the chill that had come from sitting in the church listening to the funeral rites gradually wore off. When we had both ordered our lunch, I asked Harriet, 'How long are you staying in England?'

'Not long this time. I want to go and see my mother this afternoon. She isn't steady enough on her feet to come out much, and had to miss the funeral. It was a pity because she was fond of Dorothy.'

'I suppose it will take months before the will is probated,' I said. 'Will the money make a difference to you?'

'I don't know exactly how much there is,' said Harriet. 'And then there's that gloomy house Aunt Dorothy lived in. I suppose that will have to be sold. It must be worth something. And all her furniture needs to be dealt with. Do you want it, Eck? Mahogany dining-room tables don't work well in the South of France.'

For a while the conversation dwelt on the mechanics of inheritance. Then Harriet asked, 'Will the money make a difference to you, Eck?'

'It might. Depends what I'm left with after tax.'

'Would you give up your job?'

'I don't know. No, I don't think so. I'd probably put the money into one of our funds.'

Harriet sipped her wine. 'It's so strange to think of you as a stockbroker, Eck. It's the last thing I'd have imagined you would end up doing. You are a stockbroker, aren't you?'

'Well, it's that sort of idea,' I said. 'What would you have imagined me doing?'

'I thought perhaps you might become a farmer. You're an outdoors sort, aren't you? Do you really enjoy working in London?'

'Well, it's a living,' I said defensively. 'In fact, it's a better living than anything else I could think of.'

In fact, at that moment I was thinking that this was the first time Harriet had really expressed any interest in me, or what I did. It seemed an encouraging sign.

'What about you, Harriet?' I asked. 'Will you give up working if you can afford to?'

'I don't know. It's something to do.'

'You used to have a high-flying job in London, didn't you? What is it you do now: help expats choose the colour of their bathroom fittings, and bribe French planning officials?'

Harriet laughed. It was the first time I had heard her do that in years. The laughter lit up her whole face, and made her look younger, quite different from the sombre-looking girl I had become used to.

'I did have a high-flying job, as you call it. I'm not sure I miss it much now. Perhaps I've found my real vocation: pottering about, helping people to choose their bathroom fittings.'

The food arrived. I returned to the matter close to my heart.

'Seriously, are you going to live in France for the rest of your life?'

'Why not?' asked Harriet. 'The weather's better, and the food's better, and the work isn't too hard unless I get a tricky client.'

'What about your friends here?' I asked. Harriet put down her knife and fork.

'I don't really have many friends here nowadays. I've lost touch with a lot of people.'

'There's me,' I pointed out.

Harriet was silent for a moment, and then she said, 'Of course there's you, Eck.'

My mobile rang. I swore to myself, pulled it from my pocket and looked at the screen. It was Bilbo. He wouldn't be pleased if I didn't take the call: standing instructions were that, if Bilbo rang, you spoke to him. I answered but before he could say anything, I said, 'I'm with someone in a restaurant in Cirencester.'

Bilbo was unimpressed by the news.

'My dear boy, I'm devastated to think that I might be inconveniencing you in any way. But I want you to look in at the office this afternoon. Something has come up.'

I looked at my watch.

'It might not be until around five,' I said.

'Don't be any later,' said Bilbo. 'I have an engagement this evening. So have you.'

'I've got to go back to London,' I said to Harriet, shutting my phone.

'When?'

'Straight after lunch.'

'Oh, Eck, how disappointing. We won't have any time to talk.'

'I could come back here last thing tonight, or early to-morrow. Won't you be around then?'

'No, I'm flying to Nice in the morning,' Harriet replied. 'I'm in the middle of a couple of big jobs.'

I reached across the table and put my hand on hers. It wasn't a calculated move.

'When do you think we will meet again?'

She didn't withdraw her hand, but at the same time I felt that she had frozen at my touch. I withdrew my hand and repeated, 'When will I see you again?'

'I suppose when probate is complete: then we'll have to decide what to do with everything. The house will have to be sold. I can't see either of us wanting to live in it.'

'But that could be months away,' I said. Even to myself I sounded like a spoiled child and I cursed myself. This wasn't the way to gain Harriet's trust and affection, if that was what I was trying to do. For the last minute or so Harriet had been avoiding my gaze, staring down at her lap, but now she raised her eyes and looked directly at me.

'Eck, we'll meet again in a few weeks or maybe a few months. I can't give you what you want, you know.'

She said this softly, but the words were chilling.

'How do you know what I want?'

'You want me to think of you in the same way I thought of Bob. I don't believe that's ever going to be possible.'

I stood up. The conversation was getting out of control, moving at a terrifying speed in the wrong direction.

'I'd better go now, Harriet, I need to get back to London. Bob's dead. I'm not, and neither are you. Everything is possible, if we both want it.'

I bent down and kissed her on the cheek.

'Goodbye Eck,' she said.

'See you in a few weeks,' I replied, as cheerfully as I could. I went to the counter and paid. When I looked back to wave goodbye Harriet was sitting with her head bent, not looking in my direction, as if she had not moved since I stood up to go. I walked out of the restaurant and went in search of my car, calling myself every name under the sun. What had I said all that for, then? Was that the way to win Harriet over? 'Bob's dead; I'm not.' Was that smooth? Was that the most flattering comparison I could think of between myself and Harriet's former fiancé? No, and no again. I cursed myself all the way to Swindon, and then I cursed Bilbo all the way to London.

I managed to find a parking space outside the office, went straight to Bilbo's room and knocked on his door. He called for me to come in. He was tying a bow tie in the looking glass and had already changed into evening dress, although it was just after five. He looked at his watch as I came in.

'You took your time,' he said.

'I had to get here from Cirencester. I've been at my aunt's funeral.'

'Anyway, you're here now. I need to talk to you.'

I sat down and said, reasonably, I thought, 'Couldn't we have talked on the phone?'

'Silly boy,' said Bilbo. 'You never know who is listening in, do you?' He finished knotting his bow tie, and then walked across to a filing cabinet on which stood a decanter of sherry and some glasses. He poured us both a glass, brought them back to the desk and then sat down. His large hands lay flat on the surface before him and as I looked at his hairy knuckles I thought for a second about sharpened tent pegs. Then Bilbo grasped his glass.

'Good health,' he said, raising his drink. I was wary. Bilbo was being nice to me, which was not necessarily a good sign.

'Come on, Bilbo, you haven't dragged me all the way from

Gloucestershire to drink second-rate sherry with me, have you?'

'There's nothing wrong with the sherry,' said Bilbo. 'It's a lovely fresh manzanilla. My wine shipper gets it for me especially. You're lucky to be offered anything. I felt like a glass myself, that's all.'

He paused and looked at me with his cold brown eyes. Bilbo always made one uncomfortable when he adopted that look, as if he were sizing you up, deciding on the best way to carve up the carcass before selecting a joint for the roasting tin.

'What do you think of working for Mountwilliam Partners, Eck?' he said finally.

Had Bilbo made me leave Cirencester in the middle of lunch with Harriet for some kind of appraisal?

'It keeps me busy,' I said cautiously. Feeling that this might sound a bit lukewarm, I added, 'I mean, the firm seems to be doing very well.'

'Yes,' agreed Bilbo. 'We're doing well. Unfortunately, in our business, doing well is never enough. It's like being in the top one hundred tennis players. Very nice to be able to tell your friends about it, but unless you are in the top ten it barely pays your air fares. You have to be in the top ten – better still, in the top five.'

'I don't really follow tennis,' I said. Bilbo knew I was winding him up, but although he looked nettled for a moment, he kept his temper.

'Mountwilliam Partners is still very much an also-ran operation. You are right: we are doing well. But our performance isn't outstanding. We lack scale to make the really big bets. And the bigger you are, usually, the better the chance that others will put their money down where you put it down, and move the market in the direction you want it to go.'

'I don't see how I can help—' I began, but Bilbo cut me off.

'If you will keep quiet for a moment longer, I will explain it to you. What we need is fresh capital.'

He picked up the decanter and poured himself more sherry, saying

'I won't offer you another glass – you're taking someone out to dinner.'

'Who?'

'There's a man – a former Middle Eastern contact of mine – who represents various family interests in the Gulf. He's not a conventional banker, and his clients aren't conventional investors. They are able to take a very long-term view. Think of him as a kind of sovereign wealth fund manager.'

I pondered this.

'If you already know him, why aren't you taking him out to dinner?'

'Because I want *you* to take him to dinner. I recruited you because you and I come from similar backgrounds. Sometimes it's important to have someone you can trust, someone who will keep their mouth shut when necessary. I feel sure I can trust you, Eck. Can't I?'

I nodded.

'By the way, this man's a strict Muslim. He doesn't drink alcohol. Bear that in mind. The other reason I'm not available tonight is that my daughters are coming up to town from school. They are singing in the school choir and I have to attend. It is more than my life is worth not to. The concert is in that nice church in Smith Square. I do adore music in churches.'

'How nice for you, Bilbo,' I said.

Bilbo ignored me and went on, 'His name is Aseeb. He's originally from Afghanistan, but I understand he now spends most of his time in Dubai.'

'What are we supposed to talk about?'

'I hope that he will want to invest money in Mountwilliam Partners as an equity partner, not as a punter. We need money. We need to increase our capital base. The scale of our industry is increasing. Ten years ago the hedge fund industry had about forty billion dollars under management, now it's a trillion. We have to compete and we need to be able to do bigger deals. Aseeb might help us to achieve that. He'll have some questions, no doubt. Answer them to the best of your limited ability . . . he's not expecting you to know all the answers. He only wants to know if he can trust us. Give him a good dinner. Oh, and give him this.'

Bilbo handed me a small silver memory stick.

'What's this?'

'Some information about our firm: it's encrypted, and he has the pass-code. But it's nothing too sensitive.'

'That's it? Take a man out to dinner and give him some files? That's the reason I've raced up to London? Couldn't someone else have done this?'

Bilbo smiled at me fondly.

'I told you, I needed someone I could trust.'

Did Bilbo trust none of his other employees, some of whom, like Doug and Alan, had been with him since he started the business?

'Anyway,' he added, 'he's from Afghanistan. You can chat about old times.'

Sometimes I resented the demands Bilbo made on my life, and this was one of those occasions: I had broken off my lunch with Harriet, someone I very much wanted to spend time with, just because Bilbo had a school concert to attend. He stood up, patted me on the shoulder and said, 'He's staying at the Berkeley in Wilton Place.'

'Under that name? They don't use surnames, do they? Shall I just ask for Aseeb?'

'Show some initiative,' said Bilbo cheerfully, 'ask for whoever you like. Just make sure you meet him. He's in Room Twenty-nine. He's expecting you at eight o'clock. Take him somewhere decent. He doesn't touch alcohol, as I said, so at least the drinks bill should be cheap. Listen to his questions. Do your best. In the morning you can tell me all about it.'

The phone buzzed. Bilbo picked it up and listened to it for a moment, then said: 'I've a taxi outside. Can I drop you anywhere?'

'No thanks,' I said.

'They're singing Panis Angelicus tonight. Do you remember it from school?'

Aseeb was a tall, dark-skinned man, wearing a beautiful suit made of shiny deep grey cloth. His white shirt was buttoned all the way to the collar, but he wore no tie. It was hard to guess his age: he may have been in his forties, but then again he may have had a hard paper round in Kabul when he was a child. His eyes were close set, dark and hooded, his nose aquiline, and his black hair was brushed straight back from his forehead. His chin was covered in a neatly clipped beard. He was quiet and unsmiling, giving me the briefest of handshakes when we met. He was one of those people – and I have met one or two – who, perhaps without any intent on their part, make you wary of them. There was a stillness about Mr Aseeb I did not quite like. He did not look in the least like any fund manager I had ever met.

He said nothing during the taxi ride to the restaurant I had chosen in Kensington. As soon as we had sat down at our table, he took out a cigar case, removed a large cigar, trimmed it and lit it. I had no time to stop him.

'Mr Aseeb, I'm afraid they won't allow smoking in this restaurant.'

He did not seem to understand me, or else chose not to.

'You would like a cigar yourself, Mr Eck? Please take one.' He held out the case.

Before I could say any more, the head waiter rushed over. I would not have been surprised if he'd produced a fire extinguisher. There was some discussion between the waiter and my guest and finally Aseeb said, 'What a pity. But if you insist.'

Looking around and seeing no ashtray, he extinguished the cigar in a pat of butter. After a moment, the butter dish was removed and a new one brought, together with two glasses of Diet Coke. Aseeb raised his glass in a toast and then began to question me.

His English was good and his knowledge of the world of finance much greater than my own. I don't know whether he expected to learn much from me. If so, he must have been disappointed. After only a couple of years in the hedge fund business I was far from being an expert. My job didn't need expertise, just good table manners. All the same, I had met a lot of people in the financial community in the course of my work. As I sat opposite Aseeb and we talked I kept thinking: 'You're no banker.'

When he decided there was no more he could learn from me about hedge funds and debt markets, Aseeb took me by surprise by asking: 'You were a soldier before this job, I think, Mr Eck?'

'Yes, for ten years.'

'That is good. You come from a family of soldiers?'

I had the odd impression that Aseeb was not so much asking questions, as checking off points against a file he had read.

'Yes,' I said again, then tried a question of my own: 'What part of Afghanistan do you come from, Mr Aseeb?'

'Ah,' he said. 'You know that I am an Afghan?'

'I was told you were.'

'My family is from Kabul, but I am a citizen of the world. I have houses in Dubai, Beirut and Palermo. Do you know Afghanistan?'

'I have been there.'

Aseeb gave me a speculative glance. His gaze was very direct.

'And you have happy memories of my country?'

'If you want the truth, no, I don't, Mr Aseeb. With respect, I'd rather not talk about it.'

'Ah,' he said, meditatively. Then he changed the subject abruptly and began to quiz me about Mountwilliam Partners: how it was run, what sorts of clients we had, our reputation. I felt as if I were being put through a rather testing examination, and not doing very well. At the end of the interrogation he pushed away his plate with the half-eaten remains of some lamb and said, 'You will forgive me. I do not enjoy European food. Please tell them to bring me some whisky to take away the taste.'

'I'm sorry,' I said, 'I did not think you would want to drink alcohol.'

'Not often, but tonight I will do so.'

The whisky was brought, and I ordered a glass to keep him company.

'Now,' said Aseeb. 'Do you have something for me?'

Without a word I reached into my pocket and extracted the USB stick. Aseeb took it, nodded and put it in his pocket. Then he said, 'We will meet again, Mr Eck. But now, please take me back to my hotel.'

In the morning I reported back to Bilbo.

'It was like having dinner with the Godfather,' I said. 'Are you sure he's a fund manager?'

'We're not all from the same mould,' said Bilbo crossly.

He looked in poor form, without his usual ebullience. Perhaps he had a hangover. He must have gone on somewhere after the school concert.

'Who exactly does Aseeb represent?' I asked. 'Is it the Qataris? Or someone in Sharjah? Or Abu Dhabi?'

'You don't need to know just at the moment. He has asked me to keep such matters confidential until he makes up his mind about us. Just take it as read that he represents a group of people with an enormous cash flow: cash that needs recycling in Western financial markets. We're in the frame. Thank you for taking him out, Eck. I don't suppose you can have done too much harm. If he's interested, he'll be in touch.'

Six

Charlie told me later, when we spent some time together, that after the first few weeks of his dog food business, the orders had started to dry up. This was not unexpected. There is only so much dog food dogs can eat, assuming a finite number of dogs within a given territory. So Charlie decided to prospect a little farther afield, venturing into Warwickshire and Oxfordshire. He would pile a few bags into the back of his pick-up, together with a handful of 'Yoruza' leaflets, and drive down the back lanes looking for signs that denoted a potential Yoruza customer. Children's toys in the garden often meant there might be a dog in the household. A kennel was another good sign. Two cars in the driveway was always promising. He avoided the few houses that looked as if they might still be occupied by people engaged in some agricultural calling; dwellings not yet swept up by the modernising tide and converted into second homes for bankers or advertising agents. Farmers and such like were grasping with their money and not inclined to indulge their dogs, which were often expected to work for a living. People like that bought their dog food at the cash-and-carry and might ask awkward questions about the formulation of Yoruza. When Charlie had completed his cold calls, he would round off a long morning's work with a pint of bitter and a pickled egg in some country public house. Then he would drive back to

Stanton St Mary for an afternoon nap at Piggery Farmhouse and an evening in front of the television, or else another pint or two at the Stanton Arms. This routine, enervating as it was, nevertheless produced a few orders and, as Charlie said to me the next time we met, 'Every order ought to become a repeat order in a few weeks' time.' Charlie had, however, begun to see the possible limitations of his new career, viewed as a way of life. The Yoruza business had not taken off quite as fast as he had once hoped.

On one of his excursions Charlie drove into Warwickshire, and found a well-cared-for cottage at the end of a long, single-track road. The properties that were looked after always represented his best prospects. Run-down farmhouses with plastic fertiliser bags blowing everywhere, and savage-looking collies tethered to a barn door with baler twine, rarely yielded potential customers. This particular dwelling was approached down a narrow road surrounded by fields of winter barley, the young plants just poking their heads above ground. As he drew up, Charlie could see no sign of a car and concluded that whoever lived there was out. But he thought he might as well have a look around, just in case, and perhaps leave a card. There was, as he had expected, no reply when he knocked on the door, but a small, angry-looking dog was racing around the garden, which was secured at all points by rabbit netting and entered via a stout wooden gate. When Charlie opened the gate, the small dog tried to bite his ankles, but luckily for him could not reach over the tops of his boots. It had another go at him as he walked down the path. Charlie was about to draw back his foot to give it a good kick, when a thought struck him.

He wasn't quite sure what make of dog this one was. He wondered whether it might be a chihuahua, but he wasn't sure. The important thing was this: here was a small dog, just the sort of animal that Mrs Bently might like. He picked it up gingerly; once he had done so, the animal gave up trying to bite him and instead started to emit a series of high-pitched yelps. Charlie carried it back to the truck and chucked it on the back seat; then he filled a dog bowl that he kept in the vehicle with a handful of Yoruza from the open sack he used for free samples. He chose not to leave his business card behind him this time.

The chihuahua, if that is what it was, sniffed at the bowl hesitantly, but then decided to eat the contents anyway. Charlie watched it eat and told it: 'There's no such thing as a free lunch, mate.' Then he drove them both back to Stanton St Mary. After eating the dog food, the little animal came and sat on the passenger seat next to Charlie, and by the time they arrived at the village, Charlie was beginning to feel quite fond of the mite: that is before it was sick over the car seat.

Back at his house he cleaned up the car and the dog as best he could. Then he rang Mrs Bently on his mobile, and asked whether he might drop in and see her that afternoon. She sounded surprised, but agreed to the proposal anyway.

When he arrived at Stanton House, Mrs Bently was waiting for him at her front door.

'So nice of you to look in, Mr Summers-Stanton,' she said. 'I hope you have time for a cup of tea? I mustn't be too long myself, because my daughter is coming to stay, and the house is in such a state I've decided I had better give it a spring clean.'

Then she heard a yap from inside Charlie's truck and in an instant her expression changed from one of guarded, perhaps minimal, welcome to something more eager.

'Oh my goodness,' she said. 'Whatever have you got in there?'

'Oh, just a little something,' Charlie replied carelessly. 'Or should I say: just a little someone?'

He walked back to the truck and opened the rear door of the cab, and the small dog scrambled out, looking around in confusion. It then lifted its leg against the rear wheel of Charlie's truck.

'Oh my *God*,' said Mrs Bently, 'what a heavenly little dog!'

'He's yours, if you like him,' said Charlie. His air of nonchalant generosity deeply impressed Mrs Bently.

'That is *so* kind,' she said, clasping her hands together as if in prayer. 'I just can't believe how kind. Such a darling: what is his name?'

This was not something Charlie had thought about, although he had, of course, checked to make sure that there was no name tag or other clue to the dog's previous ownership. All he could think of in that instant was his father's name.

'Ned,' he said. 'He's called Ned.'

'What a perfect name,' exclaimed Mrs Bently. 'It suits him exactly. Where on earth did you find him?'

'Oh, I have contacts in the dog world,' said Charlie vaguely. 'I said I'd keep an eye open for a suitable animal.'

'He must have cost you a lot of money,' Mrs Bently suggested. 'A beautiful little person like that: what do I owe you?'

For a moment Charlie was tempted to name an amount. Cash would have come in handy just then: but he reminded himself that there might be a longer game to play here.

'It's a present, Mrs Bently,' he said, 'please don't mention it again.'

*

The gift of Ned the chihuahua to Mrs Bently marked a change in her relationship with Charlie. He had earned her trust; he hoped he had also earned her generosity. For a few days she plied him with questions about her new dog, some of them quite challenging; for example: 'Did they give you his pedigree?' and 'Has he had all his injections yet?' Charlie dealt with these by responding, 'They said they would put it all in the post.'

In the end a story emerged: Ned's previous owners had had to go to Singapore in a hurry, and Charlie had done them a favour by arranging to find their dog a new home. It was perhaps too much to expect that the paperwork would follow quickly; if, indeed, it ever did.

These minor distractions did not detract from Charlie's growing sense that he was becoming Mrs Bently's new friend. He was asked for tea once or twice; then this progressed to 'looking in for a quick drink before dinner'. A week or two after Ned the chihuahua had become part of the Bently household, Charlie found himself clutching a substantial gin and tonic, sitting on Mrs Bently's sofa, and listening to her tell him, once again, how much pleasure she had gained from the dog's arrival.

'I can't imagine how his previous owners could bear to give him up,' she said. 'He's so sweet, a perfect little darling. Don't you think I ought to write to let them know how he is?'

Charlie scratched his chin.

'You know, I wonder if it wouldn't upset them to have to think about him living in someone else's house. Perhaps it would be best to leave well alone, just for now.'

'I hadn't thought about it like that,' said Mrs Bently. 'How wise you are, Charlie.'

It was on a subsequent evening that, as Charlie sipped his

gin and tonic, Mrs Bently explained that she needed to go upstairs for a moment. When she came down, after perhaps twenty minutes, she had changed out of her usual costume of slacks and a cardigan into what could only be described as a little black dress. She had a very trim figure for a woman in her fifties, Charlie thought. In fact, he hadn't quite appreciated before now how good a figure she had. It helped his appreciation of these matters that he had poured himself a second, very stiff, gin and tonic while she was upstairs.

'I thought I'd put a dress on, for a change,' she explained. 'One gets so bored of wearing the same clothes all day long. It's nice to make an effort, don't you think, Mr Summers-Stanton?'

Charlie stood up, took his blazer off, and hung it over a chair. Then he sat down again.

'Yes,' he agreed. 'Quite warm in here, isn't it? That dress suits you, Mrs Bently.'

She smiled complacently.

'I still have quite a good figure,' she said. 'Or haven't I? So vain of me to say so, isn't it?'

Charlie stood up once more.

'You have a wonderful figure, Mrs Bently,' he said, in a hoarse voice.

Mrs Bently went and stood in front of a long looking glass that hung near the door.

'When we were girls, we were always made to do exercises to keep ourselves in good shape.'

She started to flex her shoulders and arms in a way that emphasised her cleavage. Charlie watched in awe. As Mrs Bently performed these calisthenics she chanted: *'I must, I must increase my bust* – that's what we always used to say when we did our exercises, Mr Summers-Stanton.'

Charlie told me later that he had a theory about women; from a 'ladies' man', one would have expected no less.

'You see,' he explained to me, 'I've always felt that women want you to get on with it. They're so practical. A lot of chat just bores them to death. I know you've got to send them flowers, and remember their birthdays, and so on. But all of that comes later. That's a maintenance issue. At the critical moment, you've got to make a move. How bad can it be, after all? You might get a swift left hook. I've had a few of those in my time; one more isn't going to make much of a difference. Or, you might get what you wanted. The main thing is, not to muck about.'

I don't know whether this analysis, shrewd as it may have been, was before or after the fact. At any rate, he stood behind Mrs Bently as she pretended to admire herself in the mirror, and put his arms around her waist. She stiffened for a moment, then relaxed back into him.

'Oh, Charlie,' she said. 'You shouldn't. You really shouldn't do that.'

Later, when they were in bed, Charlie admitted that in the moments of ecstasy permitted to them, in between the small dog climbing about among the bedclothes and trying to get under the sheets with them, the most difficult thing was knowing what to call his new mistress.

'It was awfully hard not to call her Mrs Bently,' he said. 'As a matter of fact, on the first night, I think I did just that, at the critical moment.'

Charlie also recalled how Mrs Bently had looked at him, when the lovemaking was over, and they were sitting downstairs again, drinking white wine and smoking cigarettes. Charlie was half dressed in his shirt, which I am afraid, if it was like Charlie's other garments, would have had a greyish aspect, reminiscent of the 'before' look in television adverts for washing powder. He had on his trousers but no socks or shoes, and his bare feet, with their horny toenails, dug into the carpet.

Mrs Bently was dressed in a silk wrap over her nightgown. She looked over the rim of her glass at Charlie with a mixture of affection and sad reproach. Charlie knew the look. It was one he had seen on the faces of other women in his life, other participants in Charlie's dream of being what he called a 'ladies' man'.

'They all look at me that way,' he told me. 'Of course, they have a bit of fun romping in bed with me, or I like to think they have fun. No lack of enthusiasm on Mrs Bently's part, certainly. But afterwards it is always as if they were thinking: How on earth did someone like *you* talk your way into my bedroom? That's what gets me. You might be good enough for them between the sheets, but when you're back sitting in their front room with a glass of wine, they start to wonder whether you are what they really want, after all.'

This impression was reinforced by Charlie and Mrs Bently's first visit to the Stanton Arms a few nights later. In a small village, news of such romances travels fast. Charlie's liaison with Sylvia Bently was, if not a matter of common knowledge, certainly of common speculation. More informed observers, such as Kevin the butcher's boy, had predicted such a conjunction from the very beginning. As Charlie and Mrs Bently entered the Stanton Arms, she put her arm through his. He thought that this was very brave of her, and felt a sudden surge of affection for the poor thing. He squeezed her arm against his side as they came through the door. Then Mrs Bently stiffened in alarm, for she had noticed the vicar sitting in a corner. She withdrew her arm from

Charlie's. When they sat down, the vicar came over to greet them, and Mrs Bently said, 'Good evening, Simon. Did you know Mr Summers-Stanton has found me a dog?'

Charlie felt that she could have at least called him by his first name in front of the vicar. That much was owed to him. The vicar joined them for a drink. His stipend did not extend to buying rounds, but his keen sense of his parish duties made him feel bound to accept offers of refreshment from others. Mrs Bently left without Charlie. He knew that the spare key would be under the boot scraper beside the back door, and that he was expected later.

After half an hour he found himself at the bar, drinking a pint with Kevin and one or two other acquaintances from the village.

'So you'm be sweet on old Mother Bently?' Kevin asked him. When Charlie just looked into his beer, Kevin went on, 'I thought she might be a bit too stuck up for the likes of you, Charlie.'

Dave, the apprentice village undertaker, was encouraged by this licence on Kevin's part.

'It's Charlie what's doing the sticking up, ain't it, Kevin?'

There was some ribald laughter. Charlie raised his eyes to Kevin and Dave and said, in his iciest tone, 'Don't you speak like that about a lady. I know you've never met one, and never will, but show a bit of respect.'

He fixed them both with his blue eyes, and there was a glint in them that hinted of real trouble. Charlie was a long way from being a physical coward, and the other two sensed it. After an awkward moment Dave muttered, 'Din't mean nothing by it, Charlie.'

'Just having our bit of fun. Don't take it so seriously,' Kevin added.

'I do take it seriously,' said Charlie. 'She's a nice lady, and I won't hear anything said against her. Or me.'

When he left the pub a few minutes later, he felt a glow of pride. It would have been so easy to join in the laughter, but he felt protective towards Mrs Bently. Poor, vulnerable woman: right now she was cooking him some supper and later they would cuddle up in front of the television. Charlie knew she took some comfort in his presence. Who knew where the relationship might lead? He wondered whether he could ask her, later, to lend him twenty pounds, to cover a temporary shortage in cash flow.

Mrs Bently met Henry Newark the following Sunday, outside the village shop, as she was picking up her newspapers. Charlie was away that day: he had explained that he needed to go to Southampton to collect another shipment of 'Yoruza'. In fact he was moving his weighing and mixing equipment, and his stock, from his lock-up in Gloucester to another, following a disagreement with his landlord about the amount of rent owing.

'Good morning, Sylvia,' said Henry in a kindly way. They were old acquaintances, if not close friends; Henry had agreed to act as best man at the wedding of Mrs Bently's daughter a few years ago, in the absence of any suitable relation being available from the Bently family. Elizabeth's father, Mrs Bently's former husband, was tucked up somewhere outside St Tropez with a French girl half his age, and rarely, if ever, returned to England.

'Oh, good morning, Henry,' said Mrs Bently. Henry turned to go but then stopped, as a thought struck him.

'Do you happen to know if Charlie Summers is about today?'

Sylvia Bently blushed so deeply it spread right down to her collarbones. She tried to speak as nonchalantly as she knew how, hoping that Henry Newark would not notice the change in her colour: 'I'm afraid I couldn't say, Henry.'

Henry's voice took on a confidential tone. Of all the local inhabitants of Stanton St Mary, he and his wife Sarah were the only ones who had not yet heard that Sylvia Bently was walking out with Charlie Summers.

'Only they seem to be worrying about his bill back in there,' he said, jerking his head to indicate the shop behind him.

'Oh dear.'

'Another thing,' said Henry. 'They keep calling him Mr Summers-*Stanton*. It makes him sound as if he's some sort of relation of ours.'

Sylvia Bently looked at him. 'You mean he isn't? I thought that was his proper name.'

'Well, it may be,' said Henry, 'it may be. When I first met him he was just plain Charlie Summers. Of course, he may be a relation, going way back. One can never tell. But I must admit, it's the first I've heard of it. I wouldn't want people to get the wrong end of the stick and think he's my cousin.'

Seven

In November I accepted my annual invitation to visit the Newarks and shoot pheasants in the Stanton woods. I arrived at Stanton Hall the evening before the shoot, with a few other guests, a couple about the same age as the Newarks, and a single man, Freddie Meadowes, whom I knew slightly. Indeed, he was on my list as a possible future investor in one of our funds. Over dinner I became aware that Sarah was agitated about something. This did not escape the attention of Freddie Meadowes either.

'What's troubling Sarah?' he asked Henry before we went through to the dining room.

'Ask her about the Christmas Fair,' replied Henry. 'You'll get a fairly full answer.'

Of course there was no stopping Freddie after that, and he brought the subject up over dinner.

The Christmas Fair was an annual event, held by kind permission of the Newarks in the Great Hall at Stanton. This was a cavernous and chilly chamber that occupied the greater part of one wing of the house. An earlier Stanton, a Victorian property magnate, had caused it to be built, and perhaps as he decided upon its enormous dimensions, he was imagining the possibility of royal progresses stopping at Stanton Hall; or at the very least, the regular re-enactment of medieval banquets to the accompaniment of music from the minstrels' gallery. It was certainly not a room well suited to domestic use, and the Stantons of nowadays rarely opened it up: except for the annual Christmas Fair.

This fair was organised ostensibly for charitable purposes, and allowed ladies from around the county – occasionally followed around by their unfortunate husbands – to do their Christmas shopping as conveniently as possible. At the same time the fair gave them the chance to catch up on conversations with friends they might not have seen for as many as two or three days. Stalls were set out providing every sort of luxury one could imagine: children's clothes from France, jewellery from Sri Lanka, men's evening slippers with pointy toes from Turkey; quilted jackets and cashmere scarves and leather hats, in gorgeous colours, for ladies who wanted to bring a much-needed touch of glamour to a day's shooting. There were stalls selling home-made marmalade, fudge and carrot cake. There were stalls displaying stocking fillers of the sort unwrapped by men on Christmas morning and regarded with a look of bemusement: gold-plated clippers to remove nose hair; sachets of bath salts said to cure baldness or reduce flatulence; cufflinks ornamented by tiny, bejewelled pheasants; brightly coloured silk ties embroidered with flying pigs or leaping salmon. You might say that everything you never needed, but always wanted, could be bought at the Stanton Hall Christmas Fair.

Few of the goods on sale were cheap; some were undoubt-edly expensive, and a very few were priced so outrageously that one almost felt compelled to buy them, for the distinction of having been seen to spend so much money by one's friends and neighbours. Cash, therefore, did not often change hands, and the more modern stallholders had credit card machines so that each transaction was virtually pain free. It was very pleasant, and easy, to buy things at the Christmas Fair.

Everyone who was anyone was there, every Christmas, clutching huge carrier bags.

A committee of local ladies, which included Mrs Bently, helped arrange matters and allocate stalls and send out tickets, but Sarah Newark was, certainly in her own eyes, the presiding genius of the event; even if she did not involve herself in the details of its organisation. Sarah Newark ruled over it all, as the chatelaine of Stanton Hall should rule over such things. Henry was always obliged to do a tour of duty on the opening night, walking two paces behind his wife with his hands behind his back, rather in the manner of a royal consort, nodding to the stallholders he knew. Sarah would favour a few of them with a kind word. She never bought anything at the fair, but drove some sharp bargains afterwards while everyone was packing away their unsold goods.

On her tour of inspection on the opening night of that particular fair, not long before the Stanton shoot, she was walking among the stalls when she stopped so suddenly that Henry, who was not paying much attention to anything, walked straight into her.

'What is *that man* doing here?' she hissed at him.

'What man?' asked Henry, disentangling himself. 'Oh,' he said, as he saw what Sarah was looking at, 'well, that *is* a puzzle. You'd better ask Sylvia Bently.'

In between a stall selling different kinds of Iranian caviar, smoked salmon and quails' eggs, and another that sold champagnes and fine wines, was a very small stall piled high with bags of dog food. A large placard invited visitors to introduce themselves, or better still their dogs, to the new Japanese dog food Yoruza. Charlie was standing in the middle of the aisle handing out leaflets. He did not see Sarah and Henry approaching because a tall, grey-haired gentleman in a green tweed jacket and brown corduroys was busy quizzing him.

'I'm curious about this Yoruza dog food. I don't know it. I'm a breeder of show spaniels myself, and I'm always interested to find something new.'

'Oh yes?' Charlie replied. Henry thought that he seemed a little wary.

'People nowadays want to know what you are feeding the dogs, especially if they are about to buy one. I suppose that Yoruza complies with the new European Union Animal Feeding Stuffs Directive?'

'Oh yes,' said Charlie again. 'I'm sure that it does. Would you like to buy a bag?'

'For example,' the old gentleman said pleasantly, 'what percentage of this food is protein, and what percentage fibre?'

Henry longed to hear Charlie's answer, for he saw, or he imagined he saw, a look of fear and confusion cross his face, but Sarah dragged him away before Charlie could see them. Henry was unable to hear the rest of the interrogation, which may have been well worth listening to.

'The effrontery of the man, selling his ghastly dog food in this house right under my nose,' Sarah snorted, as she recounted this story while we sat at the dining-room table. 'Poor *Oogums* nearly died from eating that stuff. Why Henry bought some I shall never know.'

The next morning dawned cold and grey and windy. We had a very acceptable day's sport: the pheasants flew well, as the gusty wind got under their wings and made them go higher than usual. It was nearly dark by half past three when we came in to have tea in the hall. Then, one by one, the other guests left and Henry and I were on our own. We sat and talked for a while, first about the day's sport. Then Henry said: 'I've been thinking about what you said, you know.'

'Said about what?' I replied, my mind still on pheasants.

'About releasing some equity from the Stanton Hall estate and investing the cash in one of your funds. I thought I might go for it. After all, it's just sitting there doing nothing.'

'How much would you want to take out?'

'How much do you think?' asked Henry.

'Well, we don't normally start below a million. And you would need to bear in mind there's a five-year lock-up on Styx II. That's the private-client fund we'd put you into. You know we have a lock-up agreement with our private investors? Once you're in, you can't redeem your money for a while.'

'Oh, I understand,' said Henry wisely. I doubted that; no one ever really understood how we did what we did. I was not even sure that I understood myself.

'But the money is safer with you than with some of the bigger funds, isn't it?' Henry continued. 'I mean, you're a hedge fund. Doesn't that mean you always hedge your bets? And the returns look excellent. I don't see that I can go that far wrong.'

It was not my job to comment on such matters. Instead I said, 'I tell you what we should do. Come up to London and meet my boss Bilbo. He'll talk you through it all, and then we'll see.'

Before the conversation could progress any farther we were interrupted by Sarah. With an impressive and tireless disregard for what was appropriate to ourselves after a hard day's sport, she had arranged a children's tea party that afternoon for Simon, her eldest child. She announced that six children were about to arrive, and would we help organise some games for them? There was an unedifying exchange between Sarah and Henry, at the end of which it was agreed that after a token appearance at the tea party, we would go to the Stanton Arms for a drink, leaving Sarah and the nanny, Belinda, to get on with it.

As soon as we could get away, we drove to the village in Henry's old Land Rover. As we walked into the pub, the first person I saw was Charlie Summers, propping up the bar.

'Henry,' he said, as we walked in, 'let me buy you a drink – and you too, Eck. What a surprise to see you both in here. Quite like old times.'

Although it was only just past six o'clock, I had the feeling that Charlie was not sipping his first drink. Of course, Henry couldn't bring himself to be uncivil to Charlie Summers, even if having a drink with him was the last thing he wanted to do just then.

Charlie ordered the drinks, reached into his back pocket to pull out a battered leather wallet, searched inside it and then said to the landlord, 'Bob, I've come out without any cash for some reason – put these on my slate, would you?'

Bob looked as if he was restrained only by Henry's presence from making a distinctly chilly reply.

Henry rescued the situation by pulling out a twenty-pound note. 'No, Bob, these are on me.'

Charlie said, 'Oh well, I'll get the next ones in. The fact is I feel like having a few drinks tonight. It hasn't been the best of days. Shall we get a table?'

Henry raised a questioning eyebrow at me to see whether I was up to coping with Charlie's company. As a matter of fact, after the previous night's story, I was looking forward to hearing more about the dog food empire. 'I hear you had a stall at the Christmas Fair? How did you get on?' I asked as we sat down.

Charlie didn't answer at once. Instead he said, in an emotional tone: 'Eck, it's good to see you again; very good to see you.'

I began to think Charlie might not be entirely sober.

'Are you still in the Special Forces?' he asked. I reminded him that I had left the army some years earlier, but Charlie dismissed my explanation with a wave of his hand.

'Damned brave, you chaps. That's all I want to say. I know you don't like talking about it. Damned modest; unsung heroes. People like you do, and don't talk. People like me talk, and sell dog food.'

Henry was brightening up. He loved situations of this sort, provided they did not take place in his own home.

'So what's the news on the dog food front? Did you sell much the other night?' he asked. 'Our own dog was rather sick on the stuff, Charlie. I was going to mention it to you.'

'Some dogs take time to get used to that Japanese seaweed, Henry. Just keep feeding it to him. You'll see the benefits soon enough. That's the trouble, these days. Everyone expects everything to be instant. With dogs, you've got to have patience. All sorts of customers come and whinge to me about Yoruza. I don't mean that you are whinging, Henry: glad to have the feedback, actually. Anyway, I say to them, dogs aren't machines. Changing their diet isn't as simple as an oil change. Give it time, I say.'

There was a pause while Charlie stuck his nose into his pint glass and inhaled about half the contents.

'I'm sick of bloody dog food,' he continued, 'I'm sick of this village. I wouldn't stay here if it weren't for you, Henry.'

'Don't change your plans on my account, I beg you,' said Henry.

Charlie brooded on whatever was troubling him for

another moment, and then said: 'Let me tell you what happened to me this afternoon. I go up to Sylvia's – to Mrs
Bently's – and let myself in.' Charlie looked at me and said,
'Mrs Bently's my special friend, Eck. You'd like her.' He
went on: 'There's this tall fair-haired bitch standing in the
hall. "Who are you?" she says, as if I were a burglar. "Who
are you?" I reply. "I'm Elizabeth Gascoigne," she says, "Mrs
Bently's daughter," looking down her nose at me. "I suppose
you must be Mr Summers." "I suppose I must," I say, "and
call me Charlie." "Mr Summers will do for now," she says.'

Charlie's musical ear gave him a talent for mimicry and it
was easy to imagine Elizabeth Gascoigne's dismissive tones.

'It's only her bloody daughter,' said Charlie, 'trying to give
me my marching orders, as I soon found out. "Did you give
my mother that ghastly little dog?" she asks. "Are you trying
to get money from my mother?" There was a right to-do, I
can tell you. Then Mrs . . . then Sylvia comes downstairs and
her daughter sticks her nose in the air and marches off into
the drawing room. No way am I going to stand for that
nonsense. That's what I told Sylvia. "I'll be back when she's
gone," I told her. "Not before." '

Not all of this made sense at the time, although later it was
one of the pieces of the jigsaw puzzle that fell into place when,
on a separate occasion, Charlie told me more about his life.

Having gained some unexpected amusement from the
meeting with Charlie, Henry decided to drag me away
before we found ourselves lumbered with him as a guest for
dinner. Charlie was certainly hinting an invitation would not
be unwelcome: 'Do say hello to your lovely lady wife for
me, Henry. It's been too long since we last had a chinwag
together. Come and see me again soon. I'm in the old pub
about this time most nights. I'll give you both dinner. They

do a very good scampi and chips here, if she doesn't feel like slaving over the old chip pan herself. You too, Eck: very good to see you. Don't be a stranger . . .'

As Charlie mumbled these incantations, his head increasingly inclined itself back towards his beer glass.

'I don't know what you thought,' said Henry as we left the Stanton Arms to drive back to the house. 'Charlie seemed a bit under the weather to me.'

'Yes.'

'But it certainly sounded as if he was – well, carrying on – with our neighbour, Sylvia Bently. I would have thought her much too strait laced to take Charlie to her bosom. But that's exactly where he seems to have been taken.'

The long legal process of winding up my late Aunt Dorothy's affairs was slowly moving on, but I still did not have any idea of what my inheritance might be. Harriet wrote from France that she was doing all she could to speed things up. Mr Gilkes, the old family solicitor, was neither speedy at reading letters nor at writing them, preferring careful deliberation and avoiding anything as hasty as email altogether. Harriet, on the other hand, continued to answer my letters. Her replies were always affectionate and friendly, and when I wrote to apologise for upsetting her at lunch in Cirencester she wrote back:

Dear Eck,

Thanks for your last letter which has taken two weeks to get here for some reason, so I thought I should reply straight away. You didn't upset me at lunch. It was sweet of you to let me know you cared for me. It means a lot to me, although I am afraid that doesn't mean what you want it to . . . but you will soon grow bored of thinking about me, I expect, at least in that way. We are good friends and I hope we will always remain so.

Aunt Dorothy's will isn't very complicated but Mr Gilkes is taking his time over it even though he wrote it for her . . .

That was the best I could hope for, but it was less than satisfactory as a reply. Being told how sweet you are is something few men take much comfort in, should they be unfortunate enough to be described in those terms. My own feelings for Harriet had not changed one bit, but at least we kept in touch.

Sometimes I looked at myself in the mirror while I was shaving and wondered what the hell I was going to do with my life. I was well into my thirties, doing a job I found increasingly unsympathetic. My occasional forays with the opposite sex had been quite as unsatisfactory as my career: easy enough, perhaps, to start something, but absolute hell to disentangle oneself afterwards. My life seemed to be running away from me. Since meeting Harriet again that summer, I found I had no interest in other girls, and had become such a failure as a single man at dinner parties that I more or less stopped being asked.

A few days after the shoot, Henry came up to London. I met him in our reception area. It was strange to see Henry wearing a pinstriped suit: I was used to seeing him in tweeds, or shooting clothes, or jeans and an old pullover with holes in it. He seemed ill at ease, as if he did not belong in a town.

'How do you all manage to fit in here?' he asked me.

'We occupy the house next door as well. Bilbo wasn't keen on renting expensive office accommodation. He likes to keep the overheads low. He says he prefers to impress clients with our performance so he doesn't worry too much about smart offices.'

This seemed to cheer Henry. 'Quite right, quite right,' he said. 'You go into some of these stockbrokers' offices and all you can think is that they are doing themselves proud at your expense. We were at school with Bilbo Mountwilliam, weren't we?'

'Yes, he was a year or two above us.' This was not the first time Henry had asked the question but it seemed to reassure him. Bilbo's PA, Joan, came in and I introduced her to Henry.

'Mr Mountwilliam will see you now,' she said, and turned to lead Henry through the labyrinth of stairs and corridors to Bilbo's offices.

'I'll see you later,' I said.

'You're not coming?' asked Henry, looking alarmed.

'I will if you want me to,' I told him, 'but you don't need me in there. You're about to meet the real experts.'

Henry seemed a little dubious, but then he moved away and followed Joan.

An hour later Joan rang me to say that the meeting was over. I went down to reception and found Henry standing with that look I had seen before on the faces of new clients: dazed but happy. Whatever Bilbo's faults, he was a marvellous sales-man, streets ahead of me. The difference between us was that Bilbo was a true practitioner: he understood absolutely what he was doing. The decisions we took as a firm were sometimes based on the recommendations of traders such as Doug or Alan, but Bilbo's bets really drove the business. 'How did you get on?' I asked.

'Oh, very well, I think. We got a lot done in a short time. We've sorted everything out. They had all the information at their fingertips. Very efficient indeed.'

'Are you happy with the arrangements that were made?'

'Very happy,' said Henry. 'As a matter of fact Bilbo has arranged the release of two million of equity from my property. All that money locked up in land that does nothing more than provide grazing for a few lambs which are only worth twenty pounds a skull in today's market. The figures Bilbo showed me, the income that I'll get from investing in one of your funds will really make a difference to me.'

I had a queasy feeling in the pit of my stomach. Two million was a lot of money to pledge as collateral, even for Henry.

'The other man – I forget his name – was very convincing. He said that buying units in those funds would be a safe investment in good and bad markets. And the rate of return you chaps get is amazing.'

'Oh, yes,' I said, 'absolutely.'

'Just one thing,' said Henry. 'I haven't told Sarah yet.'

'I won't mention it, then,' I suggested.

'Quite so,' said Henry. 'Women never quite understand these things, and if I try to explain it all to her, I'll probably get it wrong anyway!'

We both laughed.

'Do you want some lunch?' I asked Henry. That was part of my job, too, to anaesthetise the clients with a couple of dry martinis and a bottle of good claret after they had sat for an hour listening to Bilbo's sales pitch. But Henry refused.

'I have to get back,' he said.

'Next time, then.'

'It will be on me,' said Henry. 'I owe you a decent lunch for making the introduction. Amazing chap, your boss.'

But Henry didn't owe me lunch: he was about to owe Mountwilliam Partners two million pounds.

Eight

Charlie's attempts to expand the market for Yoruza dog food had now led him as far afield as Northamptonshire, Herefordshire, Shropshire and Wiltshire. He was beginning to experience the phenomenon described by economists as 'the law of diminishing returns'. In the first place his working days had become unpleasantly long, as he left Piggery Farmhouse in Stanton St Mary at seven in the morning and sometimes did not return until seven at night. On some trips – more often than not in recent weeks – he did not manage to sell a single bag of Yoruza, so that the journey did not even cover the cost of diesel for his truck, let alone generate enough income to keep up with the rental charges. If it were not for the fact that Sylvia Bently was, to a considerable extent, subsidising the cost of his eating and drinking, Charlie's circumstances would have become intolerable. As it was, he had only just managed to meet the last rental payment on his truck, and had no idea how he would pay the next one. He was in considerable arrears on the rent for his new lock-up in Gloucester and his landlord was becoming impatient, threatening to change the padlocks if he did not receive what was owed him.

Nearer to home, matters were just as bad: the village shop in Stanton St Mary had declined to let him have a loaf of sliced white bread, six eggs and a carton of milk on the absurd grounds that he had run up bills of over two hundred pounds that remained outstanding. Charlie pointed out that he might be forced to take his custom elsewhere if they persisted with that sort of attitude, but they were adamant. Things were not much better at the Stanton Arms. Charlie looked in one evening after a particularly exhausting sales trip when he felt as if he had been driving all day and had sold only one bag of dog food. He was due to go on to Mrs Bently's for supper, where he knew he would be fed and given a glass of wine: even these comforts came with certain strings attached, however, and Charlie was feeling much too tired for that sort of activity. What he needed, above all else, was a pint of bitter. He pushed his way into the poorly lit bar. It was only half past six and, apart from one old man nursing an economical half of Guinness in a corner, there was no one else about. That suited Charlie. He sat down on a bar stool and called to Bob, who was polishing glasses with a filthy tea towel at the other end of the bar, 'Pint of bitter, please, Bob.'

Bob lifted the glass he had been smearing with the towel, breathed over it, and wiped the result around the rim of the glass. Bob was, if nothing else, a perfectionist. He moved down level with Charlie and pointed to a sign that hung above the bar. Charlie had not noticed it before. It said:

Do Not Ask For Credit – As A Refusal Often Offends

Charlie looked at the sign and gazed at Bob for a moment. Then he repeated his request for a pint of bitter.

'You've got me mistook for Oxfam, Charlie,' Bob said.
'How's that?' asked Charlie.
'You must think I'm a charity, that's what I'm saying.'
Charlie clenched his fists in frustration. Not another

penny-pinching, Scrooge-like, pot-watching, money-grabbing, mean-spirited . . . He checked his anger and said, as mildly as he could, 'To what might you be referring, Bob?'

'I'm referring to your slate, Mr Summers-*Stanton*,' said Bob. 'I'm referring to the hundred and fifty pounds that are owing to this establishment. Not another drop of beer do you get until that slate is paid.'

Charlie reached into his back pocket, and took out a small roll of notes. It was all the cash he had left in the world. He peeled off two twenty-pound notes and gave them to Bob. Charlie had learned to gauge to a penny how much tick he could extract, and how much cash to part with to oil the great wheels of the global credit system.

'That's on account,' he said. 'Now be quiet, and pull me that pint I asked for.'

Rather than sit at the bar and endure Bob's reproachful glances, he took his pint across to a table and nursed it there for a quarter of an hour.

What had gone so wrong? When he first thought of the Yoruza concept, he had felt he was on to an absolute winner. It had all the hallmarks of a really great scheme: low production costs, green credentials (apart from the unfortunate incident with the minced dolphin meat), and it probably did little lasting harm to the dogs that ate it. Was there some innate prejudice against things Japanese in this part of the world? He was sure this was not the case: you could buy sushi in Waitrose in Cirencester; everyone drove Japanese cars; he was renting a Toyota Hilux. Only one old man he had called on had actually expressed any anti-Japanese sentiment: 'Bloomin' Japanese,' he said. 'Won't allow them in the house. Me wife bought a Japanese telly once; I made her take it back. That's not what we fought the war for, I tells her.

And now you come along and try to get me bloomin' dog to eat bloomin' Japanese dog food!'

No, it wasn't anti-Japanese prejudice which was hindering the growth of the Yoruza brand; Charlie could see it clearly now. He jangled some pound coins in his pocket and realised he had enough change to buy a second pint without breaking into another note. Returning to his table, he sipped the froth from the top of his drink and tried to recapture his train of thought.

It was lack of capital, he concluded. What he needed to do, to launch Yoruza properly, was to build up a franchise. Lots of advertising in the trade press, selling the pet food whole-sale to retailers: it meant a smaller profit margin, maybe, but much bigger sales. To do that, he needed glossy brochures, better packaging, a fax, a computer, email: in fact, a proper office with a proper secretary in it. His thoughts were inter-rupted briefly by a vision of Dave the apprentice undertaker's sister Marie, who was seventeen and had long blonde hair and a nicely developing figure. She would be the ideal secret-ary. He dragged his mind back to the question now occupy-ing centre stage: capital, and where he could find it. There was at least one place he thought he could ask; it was a risk, but he was running out of choices.

Charlie sat nursing his beer for a while longer, and then caught sight of his watch. Draining the remains of his pint, he left in a hurry; he was late for supper at Stanton House.

He was very hungry by the time he reached Mrs Bently's front door. He had not even managed to eat a pickled egg at lunchtime, and had to make do with a cardboard cup of milky coffee and a packet of salt-and-vinegar crisps. That was all he had eaten or drunk all day until he arrived at the

Stanton Arms, as there had been nothing in the house for breakfast.

Sylvia Bently greeted him with a kiss. He noticed with dismay that she was only partially clothed, wearing her silk paisley wrap over a nightdress that was almost transparent.

'I've made you a lovely watercress-and-orange salad,' she said, after Charlie had managed to disengage himself from a rather clinging embrace. Charlie followed her through to the kitchen, where the salad was laid out and a bottle of white wine had been opened.

'Do you want a bath first?' asked Sylvia. 'You must be tired after such a long day.'

Charlie knew that it was just a short step from the bathroom to the bedroom, a step he would be expected to take. He sighed, but not too audibly, and allowed himself to be led upstairs. Mrs Bently took off her wrap while she ran the bath for Charlie.

'Do you like my new nightdress?' she asked. 'I bought it in Marks & Spencer's this morning. Don't you think it's pretty?'

'Marvellous,' said Charlie, as she pirouetted in front of him in the flimsy garment.

Later, as they lay in bed, Charlie felt that he was too tired even to eat the promised watercress-and-orange salad. What he needed was a bloody good drink.

'Darling,' said Sylvia. 'Do you mind if I say something?'

Charlie knew she would say it anyway, so he just grunted.

'Do you want to borrow my nail scissors for a moment? There are two red hairs, one growing out of each of your nostrils. They are becoming rather long. Quite like tusks,' said Sylvia, giggling.

Later on, over a glass of wine and the watercress-and-orange salad, Charlie unburdened himself to Sylvia.

'I know the Yoruza business has potential,' he said, 'I just need to take the next step, somehow. It's all about scale. It needs to be a bigger business.'

'Darling, I'm sure it will be, one day,' said Mrs Bently. 'You work so hard at it. Rome wasn't built in a day, you know. Give it time.'

Charlie could not easily explain to her that there *was* no more time: the demands of the credit card company, the van rental company, the owner of his lock-up and the landlord of his cottage were becoming more pressing by the day. It would not be long before he would, not for the first time in his life, be troubled by court orders, notices of repossession and other equally unpleasant documents tumbling through his letter box.

'It's capital,' he said, after a moment. 'What I need is capital.' He described to Sylvia his ideas on how to grow his business, omitting any reference to the role Marie the secretary might play. 'I'm just too small at the moment.'

'Go to the bank manager?' suggested Sylvia.

'Banks don't lend to you unless you've already got money,' explained Charlie. 'And I haven't.'

There was a silence.

'You don't mean you've got no money at all?' asked Sylvia. She seemed very surprised.

Charlie glanced around him. The room was warm and comfortable; well-polished furniture gleamed in the firelight and obscure but valuable-looking oil paintings decorated the walls.

'I had some bad luck a few years ago,' said Charlie. 'I won't go into it now – don't want to burden you with my troubles – but it's holding me back. A man can only do so much, but if he's restricted by a lack of capital, he may never succeed.'

'Poor Charlie,' said Sylvia.

The fire crackled and Charlie gazed into it then said idly, 'I suppose you've got a mortgage on this place, have you?'

'Oh, no,' said Sylvia, in a shocked tone of voice. 'I inherited this from my father. It's the one thing I can call my own.'

Charlie stood up, found the wine bottle and refilled both their glasses.

'I suppose you could raise ten or twenty thousand against this property without even noticing it,' he said, in a philosophical tone. 'I mean, it must be worth the best part of three-quarters of a million in today's market; probably quite a lot more.'

'I wouldn't know. I've no intention of selling it.'

Charlie sipped his wine.

'Of course not: it's a lovely home. I just meant that if I went to the bank manager and asked him for a ten-thousand-pound loan, or, let's say, twenty thousand pounds, which is a more realistic figure for what the business needs, the first thing he'd ask me is what security I could offer. Security? Don't make me laugh. I risked my life for ten years in Her Majesty's armed forces, and now I can't even raise the scratch to borrow twenty grand from the bank.'

Whenever Charlie had referred to his mythical past as a soldier before, Sylvia Bently had exhibited signs of admiration. She did not do so on this occasion. Instead, she sat and waited for Charlie to finish what he was saying. He felt a little disconcerted, but realised he had to press on to a conclusion.

'Whereas,' said Charlie. He liked the sound of the word, so repeated it: 'Whereas if you went to the bank manager, for argument's sake, and asked for a loan of twenty thousand pounds, and offered this house as security, he'd take your hand off. Give you a cheque on the spot.'

'But why would I borrow twenty thousand pounds?' asked Sylvia. 'I don't need it. Elizabeth is off my hands, married, and quite independent from me. I have enough money to live on, what with Daddy's share portfolio and my alimony, pitiful though it is. It even just about stretches to two, Charlie, and I don't begrudge a penny I spend on feeding you, darling, it does me good to see you eat so well. But I've never been in debt, and never intend to be. My parents never had an overdraft, and I don't see why I should want one either.'

Charlie was not beaten yet.

'But if you borrowed twenty thousand pounds from the bank, the house would have increased in value by that amount before the ink was even dry on the cheque. So you wouldn't be taking any sort of risk. Then you could lend me the money, and I would invest it in Yoruza. I'd pay you back, and more, before twelve months had gone by.'

There was a long silence.

'I'm sorry, Charlie,' Sylvia Bently said, 'I don't borrow money, and I don't lend it. Debts prevent you from sleeping and loans lose you friends. It would come between us. This house is all I've got. Don't ask me to risk it; please don't ask me again.'

There was another long silence, broken only by the crackling of the fire. At last, Charlie stood up.

'Well,' he said, 'I've got another early start tomorrow. I'd better be getting home. If I can't do it the easy way, then I'll do it the hard way. Goodnight, Sylvia. Thank you for the watercress salad.'

'Oh, Charlie,' said Sylvia. 'Don't go so soon. Couldn't we

just cuddle up by the fire for a bit? I hate talking about money. It always upsets me. I'm not upset with *you*, Charlie. Don't go just yet.'

But Charlie would not be dissuaded. He felt a dignified withdrawal was the best choice open to him at that moment. As he walked across the gravel to his truck he thought: Silly old cow, it would mean nothing to her and could be the making of my business. He wondered whether he would bother to see her again. He felt she had used him for comfort, and then when he had asked her for the smallest bit of help, she had refused it. Then his irritation subsided: she had, after all, taken him into her bed, and fed and watered him for some weeks now. He really was quite fond of her and would hate to have to leave her. Leave her he must, however, if his business prospects did not improve soon.

It must have been around the time Charlie's credit crisis began to loom that my aunt's will was at last probated. Harriet and I arranged to meet again in Cirencester. She came over from France and stayed with her mother the night before. We arranged to meet at eleven o'clock the next morning, a Friday, at the offices of Mr Gilkes. I obtained leave of absence from Bilbo and drove down from London. I managed to find a parking space outside the solicitor's office just as Harriet arrived in a taxi. My first thought as she turned to me after paying the taxi fare was how pretty she looked. She smiled at me, as I pressed the automatic locking button on my car key and all the lights of the Audi flashed obediently.

'My God,' she said, 'you are doing well, Eck. I had no idea!'

I muttered something about 'boy's toys' and leaned across

to kiss her on the cheek. She smelled warm and fresh. We walked into the reception of Mr Gilkes' establishment, a modest area with a threadbare carpet and a few well-thumbed copies of *Country Life* from the previous century scattered on a low table. An oil painting of Gilkes senior hung on the wall, the sitter presumably long since dead and buried. Young Gilkes, his son and present incumbent of the office, must have been about seventy. He came downstairs after a moment and ushered us back up to his office, a room dominated by a large partner's desk, two upright chairs and a bookcase displaying a few rows of leather-bound volumes.

Mr Gilkes poured us some weak coffee and helped himself to a pinch of snuff, which he placed between forefinger and thumb, then inhaled. He sneezed for minutes on end into a handkerchief stained brown from previous expectorations.

'It's helped me to give up smoking,' he said to me, apologetically. 'Do have some yourself.'

I declined and caught Harriet's eye. She was trying to suppress a laughing fit, and was not entirely successful. Mr Gilkes poked around among the file of papers on his desk.

'Ah, yes: the late Miss Branwen's will. I think it's best if I read out to you the relevant clauses. Quite a lot of what we lawyers call boilerplate, I'm afraid. I'll skip over all of that and concentrate on the essentials.'

He picked up a document and began to read it to us. It did not take long. Apart from some minor bequests to a former housekeeper, and to a charity for distressed gentlefolk, the bulk of the estate was left in equal shares to Harriet and me. There was a share portfolio, copies of which were handed to us. To my eye it looked safe and conservative: not a single stock in it would have been touched by Mountwilliam Partners, who would have sold the lot and reinvested in much racier and more exciting opportunities. The sum of money, when divided, took each of us just into six figures: a very welcome addition to one's worldly well-being, without offering any immediate prospect of spending the rest of one's life on a sun-kissed beach, sipping margueritas. Apart from the share portfolio, there was a deposit account at the bank with a few thousand pounds in it. The only other item was Aunt Dorothy's house and all its contents: The Laurels, on the outskirts of Cirencester, where Aunt Dorothy had lived for nearly all of her life.

'I expect you're familiar with the property?' asked Mr Gilkes. I shook my head. Aunt Dorothy had visited my parents' home when I was a child; but we had never visited her.

'I used to go and stay there sometimes when I was little,' Harriet said.

Mr Gilkes replied, 'A well-respected lady, Miss Branwen, and a long-standing client, but I don't believe she ever had many visitors. I have had valuations prepared of the house and its contents, but I suggest it would make more sense if you took them with you and examined everything *in situ*. Of course, I would be more than happy to accompany you. I have the house keys here, and Mrs Graham, the housekeeper, has drawn all the curtains and turned on the heating so that you will be comfortable while you look over the place.'

We declined Mr Gilkes' offer to accompany us, and instead took directions from him, the valuations and the set of house keys. After thanking him, we went downstairs and got into my car.

'I think you take the second left,' said Harriet, 'then straight on for a mile. I so nearly got the giggles in there.'

'I've never heard anyone sneeze so much,' I added. 'It must be terribly good for you.'

'Please don't let me ever catch you taking snuff,' Harriet warned.

We drove on, and after a few minutes entered a very gloomy road of late Victorian and early Edwardian villas, all detached, and surrounded by gardens thick with mournful growths of laurel and rhododendron. At the end of this cul-de-sac, the road became even more potholed and the pavements were cracked and uneven. In harmony with this air of neglect, a pair of wooden gates that had once been painted green marked the entrance to Aunt Dorothy's property. One of the gates had been dragged open slightly and was lodged in the gravel. I parked the car in the road, and we walked up the short path to the house. The grass in the garden had recently been strimmed, but the vegetation, mostly shrubbery of one sort or another, looked dank and overgrown. It seemed that Aunt Dorothy had not, at least in her later years, shown much interest in her garden.

The house itself was of a sooty red brick, with two bays on either side of the entrance and sash windows. It was not large. A path wound around the side of the house to some sheds at the back. The keys had been thoughtfully labelled by someone, so I had no difficulties opening the front door. Inside was a small, dark hallway, with a side table as the only furnishing. Someone – presumably the cleaner – had removed a pile of post from the doormat and placed it on the table. I flipped through one or two envelopes: most of it looked like junk mail.

'You know the place,' I said to Harriet, 'you conduct the tour, and I'll follow.'

Harriet looked doubtful and said, 'It's years since I was last here. But how hard can it be? We aren't likely to get lost.'

Together we inspected the ground floor: a dining room, filled with a mahogany table and chairs, and a vast brown sideboard on which were propped a few family photographs. I noticed among them a picture of my parents, taken on a day's racing. Although the house was warm, the dining room had the chill of somewhere rarely visited or used. Harriet shut the door, and we inspected the drawing room: two armchairs and a sofa, with a few faded watercolours hanging on the wall. There was also a glass-fronted bookcase. I inspected the contents: a row of *Reader's Digest* potted novels, and not much else. We moved on.

The kitchen was more cheerful. A wooden table with a well-scrubbed top occupied the centre of the room and an electric oven, a kettle, a toaster and an ancient fridge completed the scene. Everything looked as if it had been bought circa 1950, and probably had been. The floor was lino, in a pattern that might once have been a tartan. This was indeed the house of someone who had been careful to live within their means.

'God,' said Harriet. 'This doesn't look as if it's been touched for fifty years.'

Opposite the kitchen was a small sitting room. This was where Aunt Dorothy must have spent most of her time, as it showed more signs of occupation. An old armchair with all its springs gone was where she must have sat; a small television set with an aerial on top stood across the room on a table. There was a gas fire, a small glass display cabinet with a few items of china in it, and some knitting laid on a stool in front of the armchair, never to be picked up again. We gazed at it all in silence. Harriet looked less cheerful than when we had arrived, and I too was feeling rather oppressed by these surroundings. The house radiated a sense of loneliness, as if that one aspect of Aunt Dorothy's character had survived even when the rest of her personality had been disaggregated by death.

'Let's go upstairs,' I said. We went up and opened doors: a bathroom, a linen press, and then a spacious bedroom looking out over the garden. There was a large bed, two mahogany wardrobes and a dressing table. The bed was covered in a dustsheet.

'She died here,' said Harriet, 'quite on her own.'

She walked across to the bay window, but the view was uninspiring.

'I suppose she was happy enough,' I said, 'otherwise, why would she have stayed here?'

'I don't think she knew what else to do,' said Harriet. 'Something happened to her a long time ago. I don't know what it was – a man, probably – but whatever it was, she withdrew from the world. The older she got, the less anyone saw of her.'

'Perhaps it was a broken engagement, like Miss Haversham's,' I suggested.

'Quite possibly,' said Harriet. Something in her voice made me look at her. She was standing sideways on, still looking out of the window, and had turned quite pale. A tear trickled down the side of her cheek. I turned away, pretending not to have noticed.

'She was eighty when she died,' said Harriet. 'She spent almost fifty years entirely on her own.'

I thought of Harriet, living in self-imposed exile in her rented house in France; of myself, shuttling between a bleak little flat in West Hampstead and a farmhouse in Teesdale that stood empty for weeks on end.

'Our family seem to have a talent for shutting themselves away,' I said, without thinking. Harriet turned and looked at me. She bit her lip.

'Oh, Eck, what a cruel thing to say.'

Then she burst into tears. I didn't know what to do, so I stepped forward and put my arms around her, and she stood and sobbed into my shoulder for a moment.

'I'm so sorry, Harriet,' I said. 'I didn't mean to be hurtful. I simply wasn't thinking.'

She lifted her head from my shoulder and said, 'You just said what was in your head, didn't you? And it's perfectly true.'

She went and sat at Aunt Dorothy's dressing table, dabbing at her face with her handkerchief as she brought herself back under control. Then she stood up and said, 'Come on, let's finish our tour of inspection.'

She took my hand and we went and inspected the next room, a spare bedroom. This was south-facing, and a gleam of sunlight lit the room as we stood in the doorway. The bed had a faded yellow bedspread, and there were cheerful watercolours that looked like Beatrix Potter reproductions on the wall.

'This is where I used to sleep, when I came to stay with Aunt Dorothy,' said Harriet. 'I don't believe it's changed a bit since then.'

She sat on the edge of the bed and gazed up at me. Her eyes were still shiny from the tears she had shed, and had a bruised look about them. Her lips were parted, as if she were catching her breath. She patted the bed beside her, inviting me to sit next to her.

'Come on, Eck,' she said. 'This is what you want, isn't it?'
For a moment I had difficulty in grasping her meaning.

'What do I want?' I asked foolishly, but even if I could not quite believe what was happening, at last I began to understand. Harriet swung her legs off the floor, kicking off her shoes. She lay back on the bed and regarded me, not smiling, but waiting for me to say, or do, something. I must have stood there with my mouth open for a while. Harriet raised herself slightly on the bed and unbuttoned her skirt, pushing it on to the floor. Then she began to unbutton her blouse.

'I'm what you want,' said Harriet, 'and now you can have me.'

My mobile phone began to ring.

Nine

When I attempt to recapture the amazing moments in that bedroom in Aunt Dorothy's house, it is all a confusion of memories. I try to turn off the mobile phone. Instead I hit a button that switches on the loudspeaker and broadcasts Bilbo's voicemail message, squawking at me from the landing where I have thrown the handset in frustration. The phone then rings despondently at intervals as it lies unanswered. I can see Harriet's calm expression, as she draws me down towards her on the bed, the only words she has spoken burning in my consciousness: 'I'm what you want – and now you can have me'. I remember my own desperate fumbling, carried along on a sudden torrent of emotions quite unknown to me. Raising my eyes for a moment from Harriet's face, her eyes closed, I see that a picture of Peter Rabbit hangs above the bed, and is looking down at me in encouragement.

I remember reading somewhere that the shortest unit of measurable time is called a nanosecond, and that is how long it took from the beginning to the end of our lovemaking. I had waited too many days and months and years for this union, often dreamed of, but always dismissed as so wildly improbable that I had tried to suppress the idea from my imagination, only to find it resurfacing as thoughts of Harriet came unbidden to my mind. Now it was real, it *was* happening – and then it had happened, almost before I knew what was going on. Afterwards we lay beside each other, and I held Harriet as close to me as I could.

'Lovely but quick,' she said into my chest. I felt her smile, rather than saw it.

'The best thing that's happened in this room for some time, all the same,' I said.

'The best thing that's happened in this house,' said Harriet. 'Poor Aunt Dorothy.'

We were silent for a few minutes. Then I asked, 'Why, Harriet? Why me, and why now?'

'Because you wanted me, Eck, and because I've begun to realise how important it is to be wanted. I'm not going to end up like Dorothy.'

Harriet sat up and looked at me as she said this. Her face, heart shaped and naturally pale, was now tinted with a faint flush. Her eyes were more grey than blue. She seemed beautiful and unknowable. I could not believe what had just happened. After a few moments, and without saying anything more, we dressed again on opposite sides of the bed. Then Harriet straightened out the bedspread. The idea of continuing with our inspection of Aunt Dorothy's belongings was unappealing.

'I've got to go and see my mother this evening,' said Harriet.

'And I have to go back to London to meet my wretched boss tonight,' I said, having retrieved my mobile and listened to Bilbo's urgent summons to his house in Kensington Gate. 'But you're not going to vanish back to France,' I added anxiously. 'I am going to see you again, aren't I?'

'I am returning to France, Eck, but we *will* see each other again. I'm not making any promises, but I won't disappear for ever. Call me, or write to me. I won't come back to England just yet: I need more time. I'm not ready to make any big decisions yet.'

It seemed to me that she had just made some kind of decision, but for once my tact overcame my instinct to tell her so. We talked for a little longer, but that was the nearest to a commitment I could persuade her to give me; I realised that, for now at least, it would have to do. After we had locked up The Laurels, I drove her to the village where her mother lived and, declining an invitation to go in, I dropped her off outside the house. Before she got out of the car I reached across and kissed her and, although she resisted for the briefest of moments, she then yielded and returned the embrace.

'Goodbye, Harriet – don't be away for too long.'

'Goodbye, darling Eck – don't be too impatient with me.'

Then she let herself into the house.

As I drove back along the M4 all these images crowded everything else from my mind: the last image – that of Harriet disappearing into her mother's house, one minute framed in the light from the hallway, the next second gone behind the closed door – stayed with me the longest. I wondered, despite her reassurances, whether I would ever see her again, or whether she would retreat once more into her self-imposed exile.

By the time I arrived in London the traffic was relatively light. I parked close to Bilbo's new home – purchased the previous year, the most recent and compelling testament to Bilbo's stellar accumulation of wealth – walked to the front door and rang the bell. After a few moments the door was opened by a butler wearing a black coat and striped trousers. I was shown up to the drawing room on the first floor, where

Bilbo awaited me, dressed in plum-coloured corduroy trousers over which he wore a green velvet smoking jacket and a cream silk shirt open at the neck. He looked like the national flag of some former Soviet republic.

'Eck, dear boy,' he said, as I came into the room. 'Have a glass of something? There's some champagne open.'

'Whisky and soda, if you have it,' I said. Drinks were dispensed by the butler, who then withdrew. We went and stood with our backs to an elaborate imitation of a roaring log fire. Bilbo gestured across the room to an enormous oil painting, a violently coloured pointillist composition of red and black. It was difficult to say at first glance what it was intended to represent.

'Do you like my new Horowitz?' he asked me.

'Impressive,' I replied. 'Bilbo, it's Friday night, and if you remember I took the day off for personal reasons, yet here I am, at some inconvenience to myself.'

Bilbo examined his champagne for a moment and then looked up at me.

'I paid nine and a half million for this house a few months ago. Do you think that sort of money just falls into your lap?'

'I don't know, Bilbo,' I said. 'I expect you're going to tell me.'

'Five years ago,' Bilbo continued proudly, 'I could hardly afford the rent on a three-bedroomed flat in Ladbroke Grove. Now I find myself, and my family, in more comfortable surroundings. Some of my good luck has been the result of hard work. What is more important, in our industry, is knowing how to stay one step ahead. It's spotting the "alpha"; knowing something the other man doesn't; having the balls to put your money on the table when other people are trying to take theirs off.'

'What game are we playing now, Bilbo?' I asked, wishing he would get to the point.

'The game of buying what other people are selling; and selling what other people are buying. Right now, no one wants to know about sub-prime loans, for example. The investment community is beginning to treat them like toxic waste. You can buy sub-prime debt from US banks for twenty cents in the dollar and that's in a falling market. But what I know,' said Bilbo, tapping the side of his nose, 'is that sooner or later the central banks will have to step in and support the market, before the whole banking system goes into default. So, Mountwilliam Partners is buying up mortgage debt at low, low prices. We're buying equity positions in US mortgage corporations and German banks that we think might be affected, where we can leverage our position and effect break-ups. A lot of these banks will soon be trading below asset value. If you've got steady nerves, and don't blink, there is a lot of cheap debt and banking stock out there.'

I had heard Bilbo philosophising like this before. Last year it had been underpriced oil stocks, and he had been right about that. There was no doubt he had a nose for making money, but most of what he said went over my head. It wasn't really my job to understand the arcane investment strategies of Mountwilliam Partners, although I did need to know enough about them to communicate the broad ideas. My real value to Bilbo was my ability, so far, to provide a steady flow of private clients, of whom Henry was a recent example.

'That's very interesting,' I said.

'You ought to be interested, Eck. We pay you a very good salary for a little light lunching and your attendance at a few cocktail parties and roadshows. You ought to be interested in how we earn you your salary,' Bilbo said, snappishly. I had noticed him becoming a little more stressed of late. He was certainly more abrupt with me. The silky charm that had been on display when he recruited me seemed, for the time being at least, to have disappeared.

There was a silence. I decided that, if I could manage to keep my mouth shut, I would get away from there sooner rather than later. Having made his point, Bilbo regarded the champagne bottle standing on a silver tray on a side table a few feet away, and decided he could get there and back on his own without ringing for the butler.

'The problem is our capital base,' he said, while topping up his drink. 'To take full advantage of the opportunities we are now seeing, we need more funding of our own. The banks who act as our prime brokers have agreed we can go to thirty times margin and that will help, of course.'

I blinked. Thirty pounds invested for every pound we actually owned was racy stuff. I wondered how Bilbo had persuaded the men in grey suits to give us this additional facility. Five times margin was conservative. Ten times was still reasonable. Last time I looked, we were trading at twenty times. Now we appeared to be entering the stratosphere.

'But that's not the answer, not in the long term,' continued Bilbo. 'We need a larger capital base to be able to play in the same league as the major funds. That's why we need people like Aseeb.'

I had wondered why Bilbo was so keen on doing business with an Afghan of uncertain provenance living in Dubai.

'I'm going to tell you something in absolute confidence,' said Bilbo. He stared at me as if to reassure himself that I was going to be a good soldier, and follow orders. 'We've had an indicative offer from him,' he told me. 'We like Aseeb. My partners and I think that he would be a useful addition to the business. Money used to flow from west to east. It's going in the other direction now. People like Aseeb have very large cash flows, but they want to invest in businesses in which they can have a measure of inside information and control.'

'Where does the cash come from?' I asked.

'Where does the cash come from? Who knows? Who cares?' replied Bilbo. He drank some champagne and shrugged. 'Where do any of these people get their cash? There are petrodollars being recycled by the Gulf families, squeezed from our pockets by OPEC. Huge funds coming out of China, no doubt earned from the sweat of labourers paid forty dollars a month. God knows where the Russian investors are getting their dollars. Of course,' said Bilbo, 'we are doing our due diligence on Aseeb. But cash is cash, and Aseeb has mountains of the stuff. He probably got it through trading activities of various sorts. The Gulf is a great entrepôt, nowadays.'

Vanessa, Bilbo's wife, came into the room, dressed in a glittering dark blue evening dress covered in sequins.

'Darling, are you ready yet? Oh, hello, Mr Talbot. I didn't realise Bilbo had visitors. You mustn't keep him long. He never seems to get away from the office, does he? We are already late for dinner.'

She left the room. Bilbo looked at his watch and sighed.

'I have to go now,' he said. 'Aseeb is waiting for you at the Berkeley. Give him dinner, same as last time. Answer his questions, if you can. He might have something for you.'

'Such as what?' I asked.

'He might want to return that memory stick you gave him;

if he does give you something, bring it to me here tomorrow morning, but not before ten o'clock.'

'Couldn't all this be done by email?' I asked.

'Silly boy,' said Bilbo. 'You never know who is looking at emails.'

The evening with Aseeb passed much like the previous one, except that this time he did not ask me any more questions about Mountwilliam Partners. I had already told him everything I knew. Instead, he asked me about myself. We were eating mezze in a small Lebanese restaurant in Mayfair. He approved of my choice. Our meeting appeared to be a purely social occasion.

For a while the conversation was inconsequential: Aseeb helped me with the unfamiliar menu, and told me about *Mourgh* and *Chelonachodo* and other Afghan dishes. He was friendlier this time, but there was still that uncomfortable quality in his gaze.

'You met Mr Bilbo in the army, I think?' he asked me.

'No. We were at the same school, although he is older than me.'

'But you were also a soldier for a long time, no?'

'Yes.'

'You served in Iraq as well as Afghanistan?'

'Briefly,' I said.

'You are discreet.' Aseeb nodded approvingly. 'That is good. I will ask no more questions about your soldier's life. So: why are you working for a man like Mr Bilbo in an investment fund? It is very different to what you did before.'

'Because there's no money in sheep farming; which is what I would be doing now if Bilbo hadn't rung me up.'

'Ah, yes,' said Aseeb. 'Farmers have a hard life everywhere.

Afghanistan was once a country of farmers, before the Russians came. Now it is more difficult. You like what you do now?'

'It's well paid,' I said. 'I'm lucky to have a job at all.'

Aseeb's saturnine face creased in the briefest of smiles.

Then I asked, 'And what do you do, exactly, Mr Aseeb?'

The smile vanished.

'I represent various families and business interests in the Middle East. I myself am a trader, and a banker.' He made a pushing-away gesture with his hands, to indicate the subject was closed.

'I wish to give you something for Mr Bilbo. Only he has the password to open it. Please take care of it. No doubt we will meet again.'

Aseeb made it clear by his attitude that the flow of information would be strictly one way. I was there to answer his questions; he was not there to answer mine. He reached into a pocket and then pushed a small silver memory stick across the table towards me. It might have been the same one I had given him a few weeks ago. They all looked the same.

Little more was said: Aseeb relapsed into his watchful silence, and made no objection when I offered to escort him back to the Berkeley. He didn't suggest that any further entertainment would be required: no nightclubs, no last glass of whisky, no dancing girls. Aseeb was strictly business.

After dropping him off at his hotel, I drove back slowly to my flat in West Hampstead. It was late, and I was tired out by the day's events. Images of Harriet kept flashing into my brain, like fireworks that were too bright and too noisy. Yet I wanted to concentrate on something that had been worrying me for a while. Two principals in a deal who never seemed to meet; documents too sensitive to be sent by email; a 'trader and a banker' from the Middle East doing a deal with Bilbo, who was burning through unimaginable quantities of cash.

When I got to the flat and let myself in to the gloomy hallway, these random incongruences had begun to knit themselves together into a longer thread. I went into the sitting room and poured myself a whisky, only my second drink of the evening, and thought for a while longer. More questions were beginning to form in my mind. Why did Bilbo never have time to meet Aseeb, if the deal they were discussing was so important? What was the problem with using emails and telephone calls, or even dropping a letter in the post? Which particular eavesdroppers were Bilbo and Aseeb so concerned about? And why did they use me as an errand boy – because that was what I was? All the questions about Mountwilliam Partners that Aseeb had asked me had been a waste of his time, and mine too. Everything I could tell him he could have learned by taking the *Financial Times* for a week. Our conversations on both evenings had been stilted and unreal. With hindsight I now realised Aseeb had not been the least bit interested in what I had to say.

He already knew it all.

I sighed, and tried to push the subject from my mind. The world of hedge funds was still quite new to me; who knew what tricks some companies might use to get ahead? The information on the memory stick was no doubt commercially sensitive and electronic espionage was not out of the question. If Bilbo felt more secure using me as a go-between, I couldn't complain, as long as it was legal. Of course it was legal: Bilbo was trying to build a reputation as well as growing his business. Of course it was. I finished my whisky and went to bed, dreaming of Harriet.

The following week, on a gloomy Monday morning in December, Bilbo sent me down to Stanton St Mary to obtain Henry's signature on some paperwork. It was our practice to be with clients when they signed important documents, to answer any questions they might have, and of course to make sure they did not change their mind.

The meeting with Henry was even more clandestine than my meeting with Aseeb. Henry still hadn't told Sarah what he was doing, so I had to arrive at a time of day when he knew she would be out, hang around for a few minutes while Henry signed the documents, and then leave again as quickly as possible. It all seemed a bit cloak-and-dagger to me, but if that was how Henry wanted to conduct his affairs, then that was how we would do it.

When I arrived, it had started to drizzle. Henry barely smiled when he opened the door to let me in and, mumbling an apology over his shoulder, led me straight to the estate office at the far end of the house.

'I'm sorry, did you want coffee?' he asked. It was clear coffee was not a good idea, so I shook my head. Henry just wanted to get the whole business over with. I handed him the papers, and waited patiently for him to look through them. Henry was suffering from a bad case of nerves. Suppose he decided to put off signing? In that case, it would be my job to talk him round. Bilbo would skin me alive – or reach for a tent peg – if I failed to close a deal with one of my oldest friends. But Henry did not bother to read the documents. He looked at me as he sat at his desk and asked, 'I suppose it will be all right, won't it?'

What a question. He meant: would we lose his money? He

meant: would Sarah find out he had mortgaged Stanton Hall almost to the hilt? But we had already gone beyond all that.

'Of course it will be all right, Henry,' I said reassuringly. 'There has never been a better time to invest. What I'm here for today is to make sure that you are completely happy that you understand the documents I'm asking you to sign.'

Henry said nothing. His complexion was paler than usual, almost grey. I went on, because that was my job: 'You are investing two million pounds in our Styx II fund. You are not entitled to redeem your money for a period of five years from the date of signature. You see here – and here – where you agree to pay our management fees and administrative charges?'

I paused. Henry was still silent and chewed the top of the pen he had taken from the inside pocket of his jacket.

'You are assigning to Mountwilliam Partners collateral in the estate of Stanton Hall to the extent of two million pounds sterling. You need to sign here,' I pointed to the box on the form, 'to confirm it is yours absolutely and unencumbered to assign to us. Mountwilliam has the right to assign this debt to a specialist third-party mortgage lender. Mount-william Partners undertakes that you will receive two million pounds, less commission of one per cent.'

My patter was not unlike that of a surgeon just before you are taken into the operating theatre: 'Just sign the consent form here, and here. We may have to cut off a leg or two if we find something suspect, but we won't be able to wake you then to ask for your consent. Ha ha. So it's better if you sign now, please.'

'Yes,' said Henry. 'I know all that. Where do I start signing?'

'Hold on a moment,' I said. 'You agree that you will not

actually receive the cash but that it will be invested on your behalf by Mountwilliam Partners to buy units in their Styx fund to the same amount. The price of each unit at market closing last night is the number shown *here*.'

Again I stabbed my finger on the page. But for Henry, and for me too, the exchange was becoming too painful. Never do business with friends, someone once told me. You'll find it easier to look them in the eye if you don't. But that was all I did in those days: business with friends.

'Yes, yes,' said Henry. 'Don't let's worry about all that. Don't make it sound so technical, Eck. I've made up my mind it's a good thing, and once I've made up my mind, you know quite well I don't like to change it. Where do I sign?'

It was clear to me that, for Henry, the deal was already done, the money invested, with the dividends about to roll back in. Perhaps he was already spending the money in his imagination. Perhaps – I hoped to God not – he had already started spending it. It was none of my business what Henry did, or whether he listened to what I was telling him or not, but I had a feeling that if I asked him in five minutes' time to tell me what I had just said, he wouldn't have had a clue. He was closing his mind to the details of the transaction, and all its implications, in the way a man walking along the edge of a cliff closes his eyes to the drop below, thinking only about the next step he has to take.

The documents were flagged with yellow and red stickers in the numerous places where Henry had to sign his name, or where I had to countersign on behalf of Mountwilliam Partners. I showed him where to sign, and Henry called for his secretary, Mrs Vane, to come in from next door and witness his signature. The whole procedure took ten minutes, and then Henry pushed the documents back to me and said, 'That bloody man.'

For a moment I thought he must mean Bilbo, but then he added: 'Charlie bloody Summers.'

'What's wrong now?' I asked. 'Has he finally poisoned your dog?'

'No, but he's got debts running all over the place, and everyone in the village seems to think he's something to do with me.'

'Maybe you should have a talk with him,' I suggested.

I put the documents back in my briefcase and Henry stood up.

'Anyway, Sarah might be back soon. You'd better go. Sorry to chuck you out like this.'

'I'll see you soon, Henry,' I said.

'Yes, and don't forget: I'm going to buy you lunch in London one of these days.'

'Somewhere nice, I hope?'

'Somewhere there's a good wine list and they know how to feed a man properly.'

I said goodbye to Henry and drove off. On the main road out of Stanton St Mary, I saw a figure trudging along in the sleety rain that had now succeeded the drizzle; a damp-looking man in a shabby wax jacket and flat cap walking at the side of the road, weighed down by a heavy canvas bag he carried in one hand. Some instinct made me slow down: then I saw that it was Charlie Summers. For a moment my foot hovered between the brake and the accelerator.

I should have ignored him. What was Charlie Summers to me? He was a minor con man, living off borrowed time and the misplaced goodwill of strangers. But I found I couldn't drive past him, or pretend I hadn't seen him. Was it because he looked so much like me that it could have been me there by the roadside, breathing in exhaust fumes and dripping in the rain? Was there something like enchantment in Charlie's ability to weave a fantasy around him? I couldn't simply ignore him. I decided I had better give him a lift and make sure I got him away from the village before he was lynched, or made any further trouble for poor Henry. As I passed he stuck out his thumb and waggled it. When he saw my car slow down, he lurched towards it with the eagerness of a practised hitch-hiker.

'Are you going anywhere near Cirencester?' asked Charlie, his face, covered in raindrops, beaming through the nearside window. Then he said: 'Oh, good heavens, Eck, it's you. I say – what a frightfully lucky coincidence!'

'Hop in, Charlie,' I told him. 'I can take you as far as Cirencester.'

Ten

For the first mile, Charlie simply sat next to me and dripped all over the interior of the car. He was wetter than I had thought and I had to turn on the demister to compensate for the sharp increase in humidity. The car smelled of stale, damp clothes. I couldn't think of a word to say to him. I was already regretting the charitable impulse that had made me stop.

'Funny you driving past like that,' Charlie said after a time.

'I've just been looking in on Henry.'

'Ah,' said Charlie. 'Nice chap, Henry. Jolly decent chap, in fact: very kind to me during my time at Stanton St Mary.'

I drove on without replying to this unexceptionable observation. Then I asked, 'Where do you want me to drop you off in Cirencester?'

'Oh, anywhere; it doesn't really matter,' said Charlie. He pulled a grubby handkerchief out of his pocket and blew his nose.

'I thought you might be off somewhere with that bag. Do you want the railway station, or the bus station?' I suggested. Charlie didn't answer for a while. Then he said, 'Fact is, Eck, I may as well tell you: I'm doing a runner.'

'Doing a runner, Charlie?'

'I'm leaving behind a few unpaid bills in the village. I don't know if Henry mentioned it. I wouldn't have wanted him to be inconvenienced in any way: a decent chap like that. People are so impatient these days. There's no trust any more. Everyone knows it takes time to get a new business off the ground. Money doesn't grow on trees, does it? I mean, I'll pay everybody every shilling I owe as soon as things look up a bit.'

He lapsed into silence again. I made no comment as nothing seemed more improbable to me than Charlie clearing his debts in Stanton St Mary. Road signs indicated that we were approaching Cirencester.

'You didn't say where you wanted me to drop you off,' I said to Charlie.

He was slumped in his seat: a picture of despondency.

'It doesn't really matter, Eck. Anywhere you happen to be going past.'

'But what are your plans?'

Charlie replied, 'I don't really have any plans.'

He reached into his pocket and took out his battered black leather wallet. There was a thin sheaf of notes, which he counted.

'Fifty pounds I've got,' he said, 'and then that's it. I believe I might have a couple of pound coins about me. There's no point in blowing what's left on a train ticket, or even a bus ticket. I don't *want* to ask you for money, Eck, but the fact is I'm broke: absolutely down to my last few pounds in the world. When that's spent I'll be dossing down on the streets of Cirencester.'

Charlie's words came home to me. Few of us know what it is really, truly like to be poor. When we say we are hard up we mean perhaps buying a cheap bottle of wine from the Pays d'Oc when we would have liked a bottle of Burgundy; taking our fortnight's holiday in Cumbria instead of Tuscany. When we say we are broke, we mean negotiating an increase in our overdraft, or raising a loan against the house, or simply ringing up and getting a better credit limit on our card. There might have been a time when I was, in my own way, fairly hard up. Now every post bore offers of further credit, loans at zero per cent, and my emails were full of special offers. I had not the least conception of what Charlie must be feeling. If he really was down to his last fifty pounds, that was so close to the edge of the precipice that I could hardly bear to think about it.

I turned off the main road that led to the city centre.

'Where are we going?' asked Charlie. 'I'm probably better off in the middle of the town, Eck, if it's all the same to you. I thought I'd find a café somewhere, have a cup of tea and dry off. Gather my thoughts, that sort of thing.'

'I have a better idea,' I said. I couldn't leave Charlie alone and dripping on a chilly December day. I wasn't sure that I liked Charlie. I felt that I had summed him up correctly the first time I saw him: a middle-aged drifter who left a trail of debts and damaged hopes wherever he went. But I couldn't find it in me just to abandon him.

We drove down the street at the end of which stood The Laurels. I still had the keys with me and had been meaning to drop them off with Mr Gilkes on the way back to London. Instead, as I switched off the ignition, I turned to Charlie and said, 'Come on, bring your bag. This house belongs to me and my cousin, and it's empty at the moment. You can stay here for a few days.'

Charlie looked at me, his mouth open, displaying teeth in need of a visit to the dentist.

'Are you serious, old boy?'

I didn't answer and climbed out of the car. Charlie did the same. The rain had eased off and a squally wind was rattling the leaves of the laurels and rhododendrons. A small dark woman in a brown coat was walking down the path from the house, carrying a plastic carrier bag. I decided it must be Mrs Graham, the cleaning lady, and greeted her.

'Thank you for looking after the house,' I said. 'Is everything all right?'

'Oh, yes, sir. Are you the gentleman Mr Gilkes was telling me about?'

'I'm Eck Chetwode-Talbot,' I said, 'and the house belongs to me and my cousin Harriet, now that Miss Branwen has passed away.'

'And is this your brother, sir?' asked Mrs Graham, looking cautiously at Charlie. Charlie flashed his Norman Wisdom grin at her, which did not reassure Mrs Graham in any way.

'This is Mr Summers,' I explained. 'He'll be staying in the house for a day or two. I'll leave him my keys. I was wondering, if you have the time, whether you could make up the bed for him in Miss Branwen's room?'

Mrs Graham obliged, and a ten-pound note changed hands. While she was upstairs, I showed Charlie around the house.

'Don't use the back bedroom,' I told him. Seeing the place where Harriet and I had made love suddenly gave me the most tremendous pang, and I had to turn away from Charlie in case some treacherous emotion showed on my face. The thought of Charlie lying on that bed would have been too much to bear.

We went back downstairs, where Mrs Graham was waiting for us in the hall.

'There's nothing to eat in the house,' she reported, 'but everything works, except the television. The telephone is still connected. Mr Gilkes is paying all the bills until the house is sold, he told me.'

'That's all right, Mrs Graham,' I replied. 'Thank you.'

'I'll be back same time next week. Unless your brother – the other gentleman, I mean – wants me to come in and do some ironing?'

I didn't want Charlie to feel he could take up permanent residence at The Laurels, so I noted down Mrs Graham's phone number and told her I would call if we needed her. When she left, Charlie and I stood and stared at each other.

'Well, this is tremendously kind of you, old chap,' he said.

'It's only for a day or two,' I told him. 'We'll be putting the house on the market soon, so we'll need you to be out of here.' This wasn't strictly true, but I felt Charlie was quite capable of settling in for the next few months, if nothing better turned up. I was at a loss what to do next, and had a sudden irrational desire to jump into my car and drive off to London, leaving Charlie to fend for himself. Once again, some inner monitor prevailed and I remembered that there was no food in the house.

'I suppose we'd better go to the nearest supermarket and get some supplies in. We can't have you starving to death here,' I said.

Charlie followed me meekly back to the car and we drove around the ring road until we came to a supermarket where I bought some basic supplies. As an afterthought I added a couple of bottles of cheap wine and a litre bottle of whisky to the haul. Charlie kept thanking me every time I put a tube of toothpaste or a roll of loo paper in the trolley until at last I told him to shut up. Then we drove back to the house.

By the time we had unloaded the car, the day was getting on. I looked at my watch. I wouldn't be back in London now before the middle of the afternoon, and Bilbo was away this week in New York. The fact was, there was nothing much to do at the office except file expense claims and write up a few notes on my meeting with Henry Newark. These activities would take about a quarter of an hour, and then I would have to sit in front of my computer, pretending to be busy, until half past six – the earliest feasible time to leave the office without attracting contemptuous glances from my colleagues, for whom long hours were a badge of merit. There wasn't any point in going back to London just now, I thought, and I wouldn't be missed.

I took a jar of Nescafé and a pint of milk from the carrier bag that lay on the table, and found a couple of mugs.

'Come on, Charlie, let's have a cup of coffee to warm ourselves up. Then I want you to tell me everything that's been going on in Stanton St Mary.'

Over the next couple of hours I heard a great deal about Yoruza, and the intransigent nature of the British dog lover and his (or her) reluctance to accept progress in the field of dog nutrition. Once he had started to talk, Charlie began to take me into his confidence. I heard about his relationship with Mrs Bently.

'I was so fond of that woman,' he said, becoming sentimental for a moment. 'I would have done anything for her. I thought she would have done anything for me too, but I was wrong. When push came to shove and I asked her, just once, to put her hand in her pocket for a perfectly marvellous little investment opportunity, she wasn't there for me.'

This intrigued me, and I began to feel I wanted to hear more of Charlie's story. But listening makes you hungry and it had been a long enough day already without eating anything. I looked in the telephone directory and found a Chinese takeaway not too far way from The Laurels that did deliveries.

To kill time while we waited for the food to arrive, I poured us both a tumbler of whisky and water. For a while Charlie was silent, staring moodily at the gas fire I had lit to keep out the chill of the December evening. I too was absorbed in my own thoughts. My mind kept going back to that morning's meeting with Henry. I believed that investing in Mountwilliam Partners was the right thing for him to do. Bilbo's track record as a hedge fund manager was beyond doubt. Still, what if something went wrong? What then? But that was not how the City worked, I reassured myself. These days, nothing went wrong: there might be a few ups and downs along the way, but it would come out right for Henry, and all our other investors, in the long run. The doorbell rang; the Chinese food had arrived. While I paid for it, Charlie disappeared with the silver-foil packets into the kitchen. I heard him singing to himself a moment later, in that sweet, clear voice I remembered from the first time he had sung for Henry and me in a little Provençal village. It was not Handel this time, however:

'There was heggs, heggs, walking round on legs
In the stores, in the stores
There was heggs, heggs, walking round on legs
In the Quartermaster's stores
My eyes are dim, I cannot see, I have not brought my specs
     with me . . .'

A moment later he appeared with two plates laden with sweet-and-sour pork, chilli prawns and egg fried rice.

'What did you do before?' I asked Charlie, as we forked the food into our mouths. 'I mean, before we met you in the South of France?'

'Before I was in the dog food business, you mean?' asked Charlie. 'I did various things. My experience is broad rather than deep.'

I wasn't going to let him get away with such a general answer.

'Give me an example,' I pressed him.

'Well, for instance, I was a travel executive for a while,' said Charlie. 'I enjoyed the work. We went to all sorts of interesting places. We did coach tours, and outings for elderly people. My job was to chat to them over the PA system in the bus, point out places of interest and stop them falling asleep. I did karaoke for them as well. They liked to hear me sing. The clients were not always our sort of people, Eck, but they were good people at heart.'

'Why did you give up the job?' I asked.

'My style was not compatible with the management's. I value my independence, as you probably realise. I don't much like being ordered around.'

'Come on, Charlie, what was the bust-up about?'

Charlie had no objection to telling me more about his career. He was, I realised, a not uncommon type: so absorbed in himself that he found it almost impossible to engage with the real world.

'We had to organise a knees-up for a group of pensioners. We arranged an outing to a pub outside Birmingham: scampi and chips for dinner, one free glass of white wine and then a cash bar and a karaoke session. They loved to hear me singing to them. Some of the old dears used to dance around their handbags. Sometimes they'd get so carried away you'd worry they'd do themselves a mischief, give themselves a heart attack or something. But they had fun and that was the important thing. We reserved a room at the pub for the party and drove them there in a coach. At the karaoke, I sang the songs I knew they liked. You know: 'Twenty-four Hours to Tulsa'; 'Edelweiss'; 'Puppet on a String', all the classics. The old girls were happy as could be, but our driver was an odd lad. He hated it when I was the centre of attention. Said he didn't like my singing. He insisted on going to the jukebox and playing 'YMCA' by the Village People, over and over again. It wasn't the clients' sort of music. I told him to stop but I think he'd had a few by then. He was goose-stepping up and down the room doing Nazi salutes, and singing completely out of tune.'

'So what happened?' I asked.

'I knocked the driver down. Put him on his arse. But then he wasn't fit to drive. I don't think he was anyway. There was a fuss. The old people were upset. When we eventually got everyone back I was sacked; rather unfairly, I thought.'

'And then you moved on to dog food?'

'Well, there were quite a few other things in between. I've had an interesting life, Eck, although at times things have been difficult for me: very difficult.'

There was a silence. I had a feeling I had learned enough about Charlie's career. He seemed to long for my approval, and the approval of the world in general, yet each action he took removed him further from the possibility of ever being accepted, of ever having a proper job – no doubt by now he was quite incapable of anything so mundane – and of ever achieving the respectability and wealth he so desperately wanted.

What is it about people like Charlie? I know now that he was a good man, or a man capable of goodness, which is perhaps not the same thing. From what outer margins of the world he came I do not know; but he remained stranded there, and nothing anyone could do would ever change that.

We both sat wrapped in our thoughts: Charlie, no doubt, reflecting on the mutability of Fate; I, on the room upstairs with the yellow bedspread, thinking of how Harriet had lain down upon it and said, '*I'm what you want – and now you can have me.*'

I looked at my watch. It was almost eight o'clock. By now I'd drunk too much whisky and water to consider driving. The best plan would be to stay in the spare bedroom tonight and leave first thing in the morning – perhaps earlier than that – and drive back to my flat in London. Then I could change and get into the office at a reasonable hour. Charlie had a disruptive effect on people's lives, I decided, even when it was not intended. There was something about him: he got under your skin. He was the last man in the world I would have chosen to spend an evening with and yet here I was, listening to him talk. I realised I had started to feel sorry for him. It had gone beyond the passing guilty impulse that had made me offer him the shelter of Aunt Dorothy's house.

'People are so ungrateful,' said Charlie suddenly. 'You do your best for them and, when things don't quite work out, they don't even try to understand. They never say, "Oh, bad luck Charlie, let's write it off to experience and start again." No; they just shout at me for money. I don't have any money. I've never had any money. I don't understand how you get money if you don't have it in the first place. I mean, I know how to obtain credit. The means might not always be strictly kosher, but you can always get credit, and once you have a little, you can stretch it. But what I've found,' said Charlie, 'is that it's like an elastic band. After you've stretched it a bit, and a bit farther, something snaps, and then you're in trouble.'

I poured us both another drink.

'I mean you, for example,' said Charlie, as he accepted the top-up, 'you were born with a silver spoon in your mouth.'

'No I wasn't,' I protested.

'Yes you were, Eck. You may not think so. You may not have thought it was silver, but silver it was, compared to the way I started out in life. I've always been on thin ice, Eck. That's where you have to walk when you don't have any money of your own, when your mother has pushed off and your father is half crazy, and you haven't got any qualifications. God knows, I've tried hard enough to make ends meet.'

'Life's tough,' I said. Then I thought Charlie might think I was being flippant at his expense.

He took the comment as if it were intended seriously, though, and replied, 'Isn't it? I wish I'd done what you did, Eck. Joined the army and served with the Special Forces. Now that would have been a life to be proud of; that would have been something to tell my children. Not that I'm likely to have any. Telling children and grandchildren stories about your time in dog food or pensioners' coach tours doesn't quite match up to serving behind enemy lines, risking your life every minute of the day. *If* you could tell them, of course: national security and all that. I do understand you've got to be careful what you say.'

'I work in the City now,' I told Eck, 'and I was never in the Special Forces, as you call them. I've been out of the army for a long while.'

'Oh, I know you've got to say that,' said Charlie. 'Mum's the word. You can trust me to keep a secret. I just want to say I really admire people like you, people who do their bit for the country and keep quiet about it. What about another whisky?'

Later that night, I lay on the bedspread in the spare bedroom trying to sleep. I had thrown a blanket over me, and was comfortable enough, but I kept remembering the last time I had been in that room, and imagining I could still capture the faint scent of Harriet. I tried to change the track of my thoughts by recalling fragments of my earlier conversations with Charlie.

At one point in the evening, Charlie and I had wandered into Aunt Dorothy's drawing room. There, on a bureau, were some old photographs and what I had failed to spot before: a picture of Harriet, standing next to Bob Matthews and looking radiant.

'What a pretty girl,' said Charlie, picking up the photo and looking at it closely. I resisted the urge to snatch it from his hands.

'She's my cousin,' I said as neutrally as I could.

'Sounds like you have a soft spot for her,' said Charlie, winking at me. He put the photograph back down on the bureau and stared at it some more.

'*I'd* have a soft spot for a girl who looked like that,' he added. 'Is that her intended?'

'He was killed a couple of years ago in Iraq,' I replied.

'I'd have a crack at her, then,' said Charlie, 'cousin or no cousin. You ought to have a go, Eck.'

I had tried to get him off the subject by wandering back to Dorothy's sitting room.

'The trouble with my life,' said Charlie, following me, 'is that all the girls I really fancy don't want to know a bloke like me.' He sat down and hummed another fragment of a sentimental song by George Formby. When Charlie sang, no matter how banal or obscure the words of the song, he managed to invest in them a haunting quality that was all his own.

'Trouble is,' Charlie repeated, 'the certain little lady never has come by, in my case. Not unless you count Mrs Bently. But that would never have worked. The daughter would have been at me until I slung my hook.'

I noticed how Charlie's way of speaking seemed to loosen up the more he drank.

'I mean . . .' said Charlie. He took a gulp from his glass.

'I thought you said you were fond of her?' I commented.

'She was a real lady, Mrs Bently,' he said. 'I'll say that. I haven't known many of those. She was very good to me.'

Suddenly, and to my intense surprise and embarrassment, he had burst into tears. After a moment he recovered, and blew his nose loudly into his handkerchief.

'She'll be wondering about me,' said Charlie. 'She'll be worrying about where I've got to and what I'm doing. She will, you know. She cares for me. It was just too complicated for me to stay: too many debts and no money. It always comes down to that, doesn't it?'

Later, when I had yawned and said I was off to bed, Charlie had stopped me.

'Before you go, I want to show you something.'

He had gone out into the hallway and rummaged around in his canvas bag. After a moment he came back with a very old leather document case. From it he took out a much-fingered and worn set of papers. Some of them were type-written, appended to what seemed to be an immense family tree, drawn with great precision by someone who was no slouch at penmanship. Charlie handed it to me.

'Have a look at that.'

It was difficult to concentrate by that stage of the evening, but after a few moments I managed to grasp what I was looking at.

'Who is Ned Summers?' I asked.

'My father,' replied Charlie.

'So you're related to the Royal Family?' I asked.

'That's what it says there,' agreed Charlie. 'Wrong side of the blanket at one stage but that's what my father believed. I've never told anyone about this: not even Mrs Bently . . . Sylvia, I mean. I suppose I wanted her to respect me for who I am, not because of any grand connections I might have.'

'You're a relation of this Grand Duke Ernst, the brother of Prince Albert and the brother-in-law of Queen Victoria. Is that it?'

'Not the Grand Duke as such: a member of his family. It comes to the same thing, though.'

'Congratulations,' I said. 'I had no idea.'

'Come on,' said Charlie, 'I know what you're thinking. There's no "congratulations" about it. It hasn't done me any good, has it? I mean, no one's ever rung up from Buckingham Palace to ask if I'm a bit short, or whether a couple of grand would be of any use, have they?'

'Haven't they?' I said stupidly.

'My dad was obsessed with the whole thing,' said Charlie. 'Obsessed isn't a strong enough word. Ever since I was a boy he was always off to public libraries and county archives, even trips to the British Library. He spent all his spare time and money doing research. Imagine being brought up by a dad like that. "Can we go and play football in the park, Dad?" I'd ask. "Not today, Charles, I'm tying up some loose ends with regards to our ancestor the grand Duke Ernst." It was the Saxe-Coburgs he thought were the link, through their pastry cook's wife.'

'Goodness,' I said. 'Do you think it's true?'

'I don't know,' said Charlie. 'He's put it all down there in black and white. Some of it must be right. Otherwise he spent about forty years living in a fantasy world, didn't he? My mum thought so. She left him when I was about twelve. So there you are: I was brought up by a man who thought he was the great-great-great-grandson of the wife of the pastry cook of a German duke and the bastard descendant of the same family as the kings and queens of England.'

The thought of Charlie's royal descent finished me off. 'Charlie,' I said suddenly, 'I'm going to bed.'

Charlie ignored this.

'It was awful,' he said. 'Everyone at school knew about my dad's hobby. He managed to persuade the teachers to invite him to give a lecture to the History Society about it. I couldn't stop him. Nothing I said made any difference. He thought everyone was bound to be as interested in our royal connections as he was: even an audience of fourteen-year-old boys from one of the roughest housing estates in the country. He told them that we were descended from a "pastry cook". I was a little lad in those days. They called me "Biscuit Boy" at school after that. And that was the nicest nickname I was given. My father didn't mind, or he didn't notice. He had a job then, working for the council, in the accounting department. He was always daydreaming. They sacked him, in the end. I don't know if it was for daydreaming as such, but one way or the other they managed to get rid of him. By the time I was sixteen we didn't even have a home.'

I didn't know what to say and simply shrugged.

'Goodnight,' I said. 'I'll be gone in the morning. You'll be

fine here for the rest of the week. I'd better come back next
weekend and then we'll make a plan. I'll leave my mobile
number on the kitchen table before I go, in case you need to
speak to me.'

'Thank you for everything, Eck, you've been a real pal,'
said Charlie, as I turned to go. Then I stopped: curiosity
made me ask one more question.

'Is your father still alive?'

'No,' said Charlie. 'He died when I was still quite young.
The Royal Family, or the people that work for them, wouldn't
acknowledge him. He wrote lots of letters, and they stopped
replying after a while. He wasn't after money, just recogni-
tion. It broke his heart. Family connections meant a lot to
him, you see.'

Eleven

The next morning dawn never seemed to break and rain spattered the windscreen from time to time as I drove back to London. I felt light headed and apprehensive. Charlie had that effect on people, of dislocating them from their own reality. My mind was cluttered with disjointed thoughts: Harriet somewhere in the South of France, thinking, or not thinking, about me; Henry signing a two-million-pound loan package; Charlie and Mrs Bently; Charlie presenting himself as a remote member of the House of Windsor. Why had I taken pity on him? For pity is what I had felt, pity and guilt, when I saw him trudging along the side of the road. But why should I feel pity for Charlie, still less guilt? He lacked the basic competence to be called a con man. He was a pedlar of his own half-baked dreams, and yet people fell for them, even though they knew he was fantasising – one might as well say lying. I had fallen for Charlie's line of talk too. There he was, living in Aunt Dorothy's house. God knows what he might do there unsupervised. I began to feel more and more nervous with every mile I put between us, almost to the point that I wanted to do a U-turn and return to Cirencester to evict him.

All the same, I was not immune to Charlie's charm. His absolute poverty, his total unsuitability for survival in this world, so that he almost seemed an evolutionary anomaly, were carried by a quality one could almost describe as courage. He refused to recognise that he was beaten; that he had been beaten from the day he was born. Perhaps if life had turned out differently, he could have been an artist of some sort, a good, even a great, singer. But that was not how the cards were dealt. And it was not the hand he drew.

In any case, I could not turn back. I had to show up for the morning strategy meeting at the office. I had a text message on my phone from Bilbo, saying he was back from New York. All the partners and most of the associates would be there. I was an 'associate'; my business card said 'Director – Client Relations', but back at the office I was just one grade higher than the tea lady would have been, if we'd had a tea lady.

As I approached London the sky grew blacker. It infected my mood. The last few hours with Charlie had unsettled me to the point where, not for the first time, I wondered what on earth I was doing working for Mountwilliam Partners. If Charlie was selling downmarket dreams, was I not simply peddling the same at the upper end of the market? Was I going to spend the next twenty years commuting between a decrepit farmhouse in the Pennine Dales, which I could not afford to do up, and a grim little flat in West Hampstead? No doubt one day, as my salary and bonuses increased, I would be able to afford a grim little flat off Sloane Street instead of West Hampstead. I might even be able to do up the farm-house and convert it into a mansion. But to what purpose? It would be wasted on just me. And what miracle was required to bring Harriet back to England? Wouldn't a real human being have abandoned his job and gone to France in pursuit of her?

'The US mortgage market is going through some stress at the moment,' said Bilbo. We were sitting in the one conference room in the building, a cramped space into which the dozen or so people attending the briefing could barely fit. Bilbo sat at the head of the table, a porcelain cup beside him in which fresh coffee steamed. The rest of us clutched disposable plastic cups of a hot liquid dispensed by the vending machine, and perched wherever we could find a space. Attendance at Bilbo's briefings after his trips was always a three-line whip.

'The thinking over there is that there might be as much as twenty billion dollars of write-downs that US banks will have to take as a hit to their balance sheets.'

'Will it happen over here in Europe?' asked Doug Williams, one of the senior traders.

'We don't believe so, no,' said Bilbo. 'We are viewing this purely as an American problem at the moment. It is a financial problem, but more of a blip than a crisis. The US economy remains strong. Our own economy is in tremendous shape. There is a temporary weakness in some US bank shares, particularly those that have been active in the mortgage market, but we think this may be a buying opportunity for our new Styx II fund.'

A flash of lightning flickered across the window and there was a huge crash of thunder outside. Someone giggled nervously.

'However,' said Bilbo, 'we must be mindful of the fact that lack of confidence among the US banks can spill over into the credit markets, to the extent that it might affect funds like our own for a short period. As a precaution we are talking to representatives of a large sovereign wealth fund who might be future investors in the firm.'

I wasn't aware that Aseeb represented any particular country, but if Bilbo chose to present him in this favourable way, it was not my job to contradict him.

'This information is highly confidential at the moment,' Bilbo continued. 'I don't want to start a guessing game about which sovereign fund it might be. Any speculation or leaking of this matter would be something I and my partners would have to take very seriously indeed.'

Bilbo looked around the room. His expression made it clear that indiscretion of any sort would be a hanging matter.

'This particular fund sees an investment in Mountwilliam Partners as a way of buying a ringside seat. They are willing to inject significant liquidity – I mean hundreds of millions of dollars – into our balance sheet, to enable us to take advantage of future buying opportunities in bank debt. They benefit from our expertise and we benefit from their cash flow, which I might add is very strong.'

There was a mutter of comment at this news. Bilbo held up his hand.

'To sum up, then: the house view is that we are buyers of distressed US bank debt at the moment and will continue to be so until further notice. The global economy is robust and we expect US banks and mortgage lenders to make a sharp recovery. This is a period in the markets when aggressive, confident trading is required. I will want to discuss details of our current strategy with each of you over the next few days.'

The meeting broke up. As I left the room, Bilbo signalled to me that I was to wait behind. As soon as we were alone, he said: 'Not a word to anyone about our conversations with Aseeb, Eck. This is a very sensitive transaction.'

I nodded.

'I mean, not one word, not to *anyone*. Did you get Henry Newark signed up?'

'Yes, the paperwork's in the system.'

'Good. We need more private clients for the Styx fund. Let me have your ideas as soon as possible. I want a target list.'

I was beginning to feel guilty about Henry, and worried, too. I had thought his investment would be in the things we used to buy into: gold shares; German commercial property; soft commodities. We didn't often buy shares in these businesses, but contracts for difference, options to buy or sell at a future date, swaps: complex derivative instruments that I didn't really understand. I hoped somebody at Mountwilliam Partners did. Now we appeared to be putting all Henry's money into a fund buying up the risk in low-grade mortgages owed by people trying to migrate from trailer parks to backstreets in mid-town USA. I must have looked concerned, because Bilbo asked, 'Is something bothering you?'

'I didn't realise the Styx fund was so high-risk,' I said. 'That's not the impression I gave to Henry Newark.'

'Oh God,' said Bilbo. 'Come and sit on my knee and I'll give you a lesson in investment strategies.'

I ignored the invitation and waited for him to say something more helpful.

'We make money by taking risks,' explained Bilbo. 'If Henry wanted a risk-free investment he could have raised two million on his estate and put it in the post office. He invested in us because he likes the story we gave him when he came here. We create higher returns from our funds than anything else he's ever heard of. He doesn't want to be left out. He understands what we do here: leverage, take risks, make money, and move on.'

'And are we always right? Do you believe all that stuff you just told us?'

'It doesn't matter what I believe any more. The partners believe in me. The market believes in me. If I take a position, the market follows me and wants to take positions in the same things. The price goes up, and we sell and move on to the next thing. It's a self-fulfilling prophecy. It really is quite hard to go wrong, Eck.'

'It sounds like easy money,' I said, intending irony. Bilbo ignored my tone.

'It is easy money for people like me, Eck: impossible for people like you, who think too much. You've got to have nerve. You've got to have scale. If you're big enough, nobody's going to let you go bust. That's why the deal with Aseeb is important to us. We go up into the Premier League on the back of his money.'

And who did Aseeb get his money from? I wondered.

'What happens if the Styx fund gets into trouble?' I asked Bilbo.

'It won't get into trouble,' he replied. 'When have any of our funds got "into trouble"?' He looked annoyed. 'Haven't you got any work to do? What about that target list?'

I left the room and went back to my desk. Bilbo's emphasis on confidentiality made me feel uneasy. If the deal with Aseeb was that good, why was it a secret even to the inner circles of the firm? Everything about Mountwilliam Partners was making me anxious. We were betting the house every time we made a trade. Meanwhile, out in the world, the storm that had just passed seemed like an outrider to the bigger storm that was coming. We heard its mutterings every day now, as it grew closer. The markets were nervous – whatever Bilbo said. A few weeks ago the interbank market, on which we, along with a lot of other people, relied, had dried up and we had had to draw on an emergency credit line from a Japanese bank to keep us going until we were able to liquidate some positions. Bilbo had not mentioned this in any of his briefings but it was common knowledge throughout the firm.

That evening, as I left the office and walked towards the tube station, somebody tapped me on the shoulder. I turned, startled, to see Nick Davies. I hadn't met him since I came back from Colombia and gave up my temporary job with the private security outfit he worked for. We had parted on reasonable terms, as far as I could remember. He looked unchanged, taller than I was and very thin, with receding black hair, a pale face, dark stubble on his chin, a thin mouth and a firm jawline. He was wearing a dark blue overcoat over a dark suit.

'Hello, Eck,' he said.

'Nick, my God! Where did you spring from? How are you?'

'I'm well,' said Nick. 'And you haven't changed, from the look of you. Have you five minutes for a cup of coffee?'

We went to the café down the street and sat and talked for a while. Nick was friendlier than I remembered. Although we had worked together we had never been close: he was a reserved, private man, and very ambitious. Someone had told me he had gone into the security services after leaving the private security contractor we had both worked for and it wouldn't have surprised me. He was very vague about his career, when I asked him, which made me think the rumour must be true.

'Oh, I'm in some government agency you've never heard of,' he said. 'Liaison with the police: all I do is go to meetings all day long. But what are you up to? I heard you went into the world of money?'

'Yes, I'm a City boy now,' I admitted.

Nick laughed. 'So who are you with? Would I know the name? Some grand bank, no doubt?'

I explained about Mountwilliam Partners, and Nick laughed again.

'Funny, that,' he said. 'If someone had told me you would end up working for a hedge fund, I'd have bet a lot of money against it. But you must be enjoying it?'

'It has its days,' I said.

'Well, I might give you a ring for some advice,' said Nick. He looked at his watch. 'I must get back to the office; I'm late for an after-hours meeting.'

We agreed, with that absolute insincerity that attends such encounters, that we must meet again, and then Nick stood up and flagged down a taxi.

As I resumed my interrupted journey, I wondered why I hadn't been more pleased to see Nick. We might not have been great friends but when you work together, as the two of us had, there is usually some basis for warmth: shared memories, and old jokes. The encounter with Nick had an odd sort of quality that I could not pin down. What was he doing in that street? I wondered. There were few shops, and he had needed to take a taxi to get back to his own place of work.

I soon forgot about Nick Davies, however; my new worry was Charlie Summers.

The thought of what he might be doing at – or to – The Laurels was becoming a serious concern. I had called Charlie once or twice on Aunt Dorothy's number but he had not picked up the phone. Was he still there? Had he left, leaving the house in disarray? Had he fallen asleep with a cigarette in his mouth and burned the place down? He had not rung me from his mobile and when I tried that number, it failed to connect. It was impossible to tell what Charlie was up to, and the lack of information made me increasingly worried. In the end I decided I would have to drive down to Cirencester that Friday afternoon, to see what was going on.

We had arranged that if Charlie was out he would leave the house keys under the hedgehog-shaped boot scraper beside the front door. When I arrived at The Laurels, to my surprise, the keys were in exactly the place I had specified. I went into the house and switched on the lights. Everything seemed to be the same as when I had left except for a faint stale smell that had not been there before. The house was tidy, with no other trace of recent occupation. In the kitchen I found a note on the table:

Dear Eck,
Not being one to trespass on other people's hospitality, I am off now. Eck, I will never forget yr kindness to me when I was down and nearly out. There's not many that would have done what you did for me. I shall not forget it in a hurry. If the day comes when I can repay you in any way C. Summers Esq. is yr man.

I hope all in the house is shipshape and as I found it. Something has come up, a great opportunity, a real bonanza of an idea, from someone I have got to know in Holland. You will be surprised when I tell you, but for now it has to be a secret.

You will be proud of me, Eck, one day. We will meet again I am sure.

Yrs in haste
Charlie

I could not imagine what had lured Charlie away from the comfort of The Laurels. Perhaps the gloom of the house had finally got to him. Perhaps he really had uncovered 'a bonanza of an idea'. At any rate, he was gone – off my conscience and off my hands. I don't know what I would have done if Charlie had still been there. I suppose I would have had to give him some sort of deadline, but that was no longer necessary. I didn't think I needed to worry about bumping into him any time soon. In fact, I doubted that I would ever see, or hear from, him again.

I sat at the kitchen table wondering what to do with myself. Most weekends I spent at my real home, at Pikes Garth Hall. I wondered whether I should drive up north, or go back to London. I hated being in town on Saturday and Sunday as there was never anything to do. All my friends who still lived there were married by now, and were either away in the country most weekends, or else busy with their families. I didn't feel like looking up Henry and Sarah. I wasn't sure I could see Henry again at the moment without somehow giving the game away. What a way to feel about one's oldest friend. Sarah was very sharp. If she saw the two of us together, she would know something was up, and would nag away until she discovered that I had talked Henry into borrowing two million pounds by mortgaging the house they lived in, so that he could invest it in one of our funds. The more I thought about it, the more uncomfortable I felt about what I had drawn Henry into. And what about all the other people I had persuaded to invest in one of Bilbo's funds? I needed to get away from these thoughts, which were beginning to wreathe themselves about me like black smoke.

I could drive up to the North of England. I could go back to London and spend the weekend watching television. I took out my mobile phone, which had a web browser among its many other features. After fiddling with this for a quarter of an hour I managed to establish that there was a flight leaving Gatwick for Nice at six the following morning.

After a few more minutes, I had managed to book myself a return flight to the South of France. Then I got back into the car and drove to my flat in London, to pick up my passport and some clean clothes.

I wondered whether I should ring or text Harriet to tell her I was coming or just turn up. I thought that if I did the former she'd find some reason to put me off, so decided that I would take my chances. The worst outcome would be that she would be away, and I would spend Saturday and Sunday watching French television in a French hotel bedroom. No doubt it was raining as hard there as it was here. I could probably do better than that. If she wasn't there, I decided, and she probably wouldn't be, I would go and have the most expensive dinner money could buy, somewhere in Nice. If she was there, then whatever would happen would happen.

It was a long time since I had done anything truly spontaneous. It was a long time since I had taken a step without any thought or premeditation, without calculation, where I was absolutely blind to the future. That was what was in my mind the next morning, as the plane carrying me south reached the cloud base and plunged into the soft, wet vapour: would we emerge into darker, stormier landscapes or a brilliant blue sky?

Twelve

No further memory remains of that flight, or which car I hired, or how I found my way to the small town in Provence, near to where Harriet lived. I remember very clearly arriving in Fayence and parking the car with the vague idea of buying a present: a bottle of wine, a bunch of flowers, some sort of peace offering to make up for my sudden, and perhaps unwelcome, arrival. A number of images had flashed through my mind on the journey here: Harriet sitting drinking a glass of wine with a muscle-bound Frenchman and saying, 'Oh, hello, Eck . . . perhaps you don't know my old friend François . . .'

Other, more dreadful versions on the same theme ran through my brain as I drove: walking into her house and finding Harriet sharing, not a glass of wine, but a bed, with François. After all, what right did I have to assume there would be no such rival? What promises had she made to me: none, except that she had given herself to me.

In the end our meeting was much more prosaic than these caffeine-fuelled phantasms that chased through my brain. I got out of the car, locked the doors, and turned around to look for the exit to the car park nearest the shops: and saw Harriet. It was so unlikely that, for a few moments, everything that followed had an almost cinematic quality. She was walking slowly past a row of cars, carrying a plastic carrier bag. She didn't see me at first as her head was slightly bent.

I called her name, not too loud, and she turned in my direction. My memory says that she dropped her carrier bag when she saw me, that there was a splintering sound as a bottle smashed. I believe that all that really happened was that she put the carrier bag down, and a bottle fell sideways, perhaps breaking something.

'Eck,' said Harriet. Then, more coherently: 'Eck? What are you doing here? Are you on holiday?'

Harriet says now that she did not say anything quite so stupid but I am sure those were the words she spoke. I walked across the car park to her, drew her to me and embraced her.

'I had to come and see you,' I said. It was not much of an explanation.

'Why?' she asked, but she was smiling.

'Can we go to your house and I'll explain myself there?'

A short while later we were sitting in her house, a lime-washed dwelling west of the town. You could not see the Mediterranean from Harriet's villa, but somehow it was there, in the distant haze. From its hillside, the house looked down over a fertile plain that was covered by a patchwork of small vineyards and farms, and the occasional stand of poplars. The house itself was small and single-storey. There was a kitchen, a utility room, a small sitting room, a bath-room and two bedrooms inside. Outside, an area of rough grass contained by a terraced wall formed a sort of garden in which sat two wrought-iron chairs and a round wrought-iron table.

I had done my best to describe what had moved me to make this journey, trying not to apologise too much, and after a while Harriet simply took my hands, folded them in hers for a moment and said, 'Don't worry, Eck: there's no need to explain, although your idea of patience isn't mine. It's no more than a couple of weeks since we last saw each other.'

I must have looked crestfallen because she added, 'I'm glad you're here, all the same.'

A pale sun shone down through a pearly sky. It was chilly, but I did not feel cold. A great sense of calm had spread through me, as if I had taken some drug and could hardly move a limb. After a while Harriet collected up the coffee pot and cups from the table and started being practical.

'Now I'll have to go all the way back to town and do some more shopping. I suppose you haven't eaten yet. Are you staying somewhere?'

'I've made no plans beyond booking the plane seat,' I told her. 'I'm not presuming on staying here, or having you cook for me. I'll check into a hotel and we can go out to lunch. I'll do whatever suits you best.'

'We'll have lunch here,' said Harriet. 'It's nearly one o'clock now. I'll just go back into town and buy a few extra things – no, don't come, I'll be much quicker without you. Then we can see what to do with you.'

When she was gone, I stood up, stretched, and walked about the little house. It was immaculately tidy and clean. There was a small desk in one corner of the sitting room with a laptop on it, and a pile of folders full of letters and documents. There was also a photograph of Bob Matthews and Harriet standing beside each other. He was in uniform. I was not sure, but I thought it might be a copy of the picture that stood in Aunt Dorothy's house. I resisted the temptation to peer into Harriet's bedroom. Having finished my tour I went back into the garden and sat there: the sun was stronger now. This was not someone's home, I thought, but a place to live and eat and sleep in. There was no sense that it belonged to anyone in particular. Harriet had reduced herself to a condition of perfect anonymity.

Later on, after a lunch of *salade niçoise* and a couple of glasses of white wine, Harriet said: 'I suppose you had better stay here. I can make up the bed in the spare room.'

'Haven't you anything planned?' I asked. 'Don't worry about me if you have – I don't expect you to drop everything just because I turn up out of the blue.'

Harriet laughed.

'There's nothing to drop. I don't have much of a social life here. I was a bit of a recluse when I first came to France, and it's been hard to change the habit. People give up asking you out after a while.'

'No François, then?'

'Who's François?'

I explained about the muscle-bound Frenchman.

'You do have a vivid imagination! No, there is no François at the moment. I'm sorry to be so boring.'

'I'm not really that disappointed,' I said.

Harriet gathered up the plates, and I got up to help her. In the small kitchen she stood with her back to me, loading the dishwasher; her fair hair was cropped so that the nape of her neck showed when she bent her head. I kissed the exposed part of her neck and she shivered.

'Don't, Eck, you nearly made me drop a plate.'

She finished loading the dishwasher and turned to face me. We stared at each other for a moment.

'No mobile phone ringing this time?' she asked.

'It's turned off.'

'You'd better come into my bedroom, then.'

Making love to Harriet this time was infinitely less strange and more joyous than it had been in the spare bedroom of Aunt Dorothy's house. Perhaps the South of France is more conducive to lovemaking, particularly more so than The Laurels, a house steeped in the loneliness of its former occupant. I also think it had something to do with the fact that we were now in Harriet's home: anonymous enough, it was nevertheless where she existed, and lived her life.

'I never used to think it was worthwhile getting involved with girls,' I told Harriet later, as we caught the last of the afternoon sunshine. It was getting quite cold, but the peace and beauty of the afternoon light had drawn us outside.

'Why was that?' asked Harriet.

'It was all the talking one had to get through before going to bed. A quick bonk and a large gin and tonic used to be my motto. Unfortunately as one gets older the bonking gets quicker and the drinks – whisky, nowadays, I'm afraid – get larger. That's been my system until now. I admit that it hasn't often worked.'

'Don't feel you have to talk to me if you don't want to,' said Harriet. 'I'm quite used to silence. Anyway, I'm not in the least fooled by you. You present yourself as a simple soldier, but you're not at all simple. I think you are a rather complicated person.'

'But I like talking to you, Harriet,' I told her. 'That's the point. I'm here because I need to be with you. And when I go back tomorrow night, which I must, I don't quite know how I will manage without you.'

Harriet stopped smiling.

'You know I can't promise you anything. I'm very happy you came out here – but I don't quite know what it all means. Let's not rush things.'

I frowned.

'But when I go back, to a job I don't much enjoy, I'll spend the whole time wishing you were with me. Won't you ever think about coming back to England?'

'That's exactly what I mean, Eck. You're trying to rush me into decisions I don't feel I have to take just now. When I came out here I was so distraught because of Bob's death, I could hardly get from the beginning of the day to the end of it. For a long time it was like a wound that wouldn't heal. But I've got over Bob's death now and I know he'd have been the last person to want me to throw away my life. All the same, I've found a sort of peacefulness that I enjoy. I know it's selfish, but I've got a life here now. I don't want to give it up without being more certain about what would happen next.'

Harriet paused for a moment, and then changed the subject in rather a determined way.

'Anyway, why don't you enjoy your job? I thought you'd become hugely successful in the City?'

'I'm just a glorified salesman,' I said, 'and half the time I don't understand what I am selling. It's beginning to bother me.'

For a while we talked about Bilbo and my job.

Then Harriet said, 'It's getting too cold to sit out here any longer.'

The sky was darkening and red and purple streaks crept up from the horizon. Lights had come on in the farms dotted about the plain below.

'I'm going to take you out to dinner tonight,' I said to Harriet as we went inside. 'Tell me where we should go.'

Later that evening, over dinner in a small café in the centre of Fayence, Harriet asked me why I had left the army.

'You could have gone on, couldn't you? You can't have been more than thirty when you left.'

'I could have gone on, but then something happened that made me sick of the whole thing.'

'What?' asked Harriet.

'I don't really want to tell you about it,' I replied.

'Oh, I think you have to tell me now you've said that,' said Harriet. 'No secrets if you want to stay friends with me.'

So I found myself telling her – something I had told no other person except Bilbo since leaving the army – what had happened seven years previously at dawn in the valley above Gholam Khot.

On Sunday afternoon, I said goodbye to Harriet. She stood at the door of her small white house as I kissed her.

'When will I see you again, Harriet?' I said.

'I don't know,' she answered. 'It was a lovely surprise to see you. Let's just take it as it comes. Don't ask for any more promises right now.'

I felt an ache as I left her. I don't know what she was feeling. She turned away quickly as I drove off. She may have been hiding tears or she may have been keen to catch up on the ironing. I knew that Harriet felt affection for me. She had taken me into her bed twice now, if not yet to her heart. One day Harriet would, I had no doubt, learn to live a normal life in a normal way, stop being a recluse, marry, have children, and join a book club. A girl like that deserved a happy life. The question was: with whom would she spend it? I wished I could be sure that it would be me.

I tried to stop thinking about her on the plane back to London. Instead I read the Sunday papers from cover to cover, without really taking much in. One small article caught my attention, however:

> Bright Star Mortgage Inc. filed for Chapter 11 today, in another sign of stress in the sub-prime mortgage sector in the US. Analyst Dave Stratton at Capital Trust noted that sub-prime lending was not typical of the UK mortgage market and events in the United States were unlikely to impact on the UK debt markets.

Bright Star Mortgage: the name rang a bell. The Styx fund had just bought a chunk of its stock, and in an internal email Bilbo had trumpeted 'another successful trade in oversold financial sector stocks that will come good for our investors'. Maybe not this one, I thought.

The next few weeks were increasingly difficult for me. Christmas came and went with no sign to mark it other than a dull little office party. I went north and took off for a few days in the Yorkshire dales. January passed, and then February. Ever since my visit to Harriet in France I had been consumed by restlessness. The simple part of that, the part I also understood, was a desire to be with her. But I also understood very clearly that she did not want to commit herself just yet. Harriet had made one big commitment in her life so far, and that had been destroyed when Bob Matthews had been shot in Iraq – or possibly in Iran, the gossips said, a place where British soldiers should not have been. The death of the man Harriet had been expecting to marry was compounded by the murky, even sinister, circumstances surrounding the event. I had fallen for a girl who had become frightened of commitment: getting her to come towards me felt, at times, as if I were trying to talk a jumper off a ledge. It was a task that needed tact, sensitivity and patience: none of them qualities I possessed to any great degree.

We talked occasionally on the phone, but the conversations led nowhere. Harriet was always friendly, even affectionate, and seemed to like me calling her. But at the same time she sounded remote, as if she were speaking to me from another planet.

At work, too, the sense of restlessness assailed me. I did my day job, and I had two more meetings with Aseeb at Bilbo's request. I was becoming used to acting as Bilbo's go-between, but still found it very odd.

'Why don't you meet him?' I asked Bilbo each time he asked me to collect or dispatch yet another memory stick, or more likely the same one.

'Aseeb trusts you,' Bilbo told me. 'With these people, it's a relationship thing. He has faith in you because you were a soldier. He likes the fact that you don't talk too much, I'm sure. I will meet Aseeb one day soon, but at the moment we're at a stage in the negotiations where I might risk giving away some of our position if I were to sit down at the same table as him. The moment he sees me in the flesh, he'll know I'm ready to sign a deal, and he'll use that to squeeze more from me. A few extra points on the equity, no doubt.'

Aseeb and I no longer dined together; instead we had the briefest of meetings over cups of coffee. He seemed to be in London intermittently, and then only for fleeting visits. He had stopped staying at the Berkeley or, at least, I never met him there any more. The most recent meeting had been in a coffee bar at Heathrow, where the memory stick was handed back to me with the words, 'Mr Eck, tell Mr Bilbo this has gone on long enough. We will deal on the terms we have stated in the files I have given you. No other terms. Not one word different. Please make Mr Bilbo understand that we have no more time for discussions.'

I relayed this message, which did not seem to bring Bilbo any great sense of satisfaction.

'Bastards,' he muttered, chewing his lip. Bilbo was definitely not in good form at the moment.

Nor was I. I was beginning to feel like a travelling salesman who suddenly realises that he is peddling snake oil. I felt guilt now, rather than any sense of achievement, when I chatted up friends and acquaintances, trying to sign them up for a ride on Bilbo's magic roundabout. Some of them had begun to ask questions I couldn't answer, about the jitters we read about in the financial press, about the relative safety of our investments.

'Seems to me I'd be better off in property,' said Freddie Meadowes. 'Shares can go up or down, and even you hedge fund types can't beat the market all of the time. Property just goes up. It's the one reliable place to put your money.'

Freddie and I were fishing together on the Tweed near Kelso. It was late March but there was an unseasonable warmth in the sun, as if summer had arrived early. No doubt the following week it would be snowing. It was a good beat, and very expensive, exactly the sort of place our investors liked to be taken to. The river flowed around wide stately bends, over a gravel bottom on which it was easy to wade. Behind us were low wooded hills; on the other bank, fields of winter wheat. Every year Mountwilliam Partners took a few days' fishing early in the season to entertain its present, and future, customers who liked the sport. As I was the only person at Mountwilliam Partners – apart, possibly, from Bilbo – who could tell the difference between a golf club and a fishing rod I was usually in charge of this expedition.

We stayed in a comfortable hotel with its own golf course, and if we got as far as the river there was a ghillie, if we needed him, to point out where the fish would have been if the river hadn't been so low. There were long, alcoholic lunches on the riverbank, when the fishing became hopeless, followed by long, alcoholic evenings at the bar. On this particular day, two of our party were on the golf course; Freddie and I had decided to give the river a try, and had dispensed with the ghillie's services for the day. I didn't want anyone hanging around while I tried to talk Freddie into taking an interest in our Styx fund.

Freddie Meadowes had been on my target list for a while, and I had been pleased when he accepted the invitation to come fishing. Freddie didn't much care for fishing, or shooting, or racing or anything else that I knew of, for that matter; but he liked the idea of being asked to the best places, and this was one of them. Freddie was much richer than Henry. He had inherited a *quinta* in Portugal from an aunt, a brewery in Staffordshire from his father, and a large house with a farm attached in Oxfordshire from his mother. That was just for starters: Freddie had hopes of further inheritance from at least three more aunts who had yet to drop off the perch. Meanwhile, he had popped the brewery for a few million, and there were signs that the money was burning a hole in his pocket. I thought I might have a chance of persuading him to invest in one of our funds.

Freddie had waded a yard or two into the river while I stood on the bank. Now he executed a particularly dangerous cast; the line flew back and sideways and I felt the fly embed itself in my cap.

'Just a minute, if you don't mind, Freddie,' I said. We recovered my cap, which had flown into the river on the end of Freddie's line, and disentangled the fly. Freddie decided to come and sit on the bank with me. It was obvious even to the most optimistic fisherman that there was about as much chance of catching a fish that day as of winning the lottery. The spring sun had got out and beat steadily down on us, and the river seemed to be getting even lower as we watched it.

'I'm thinking of making a few buy-to-let investments,' said Freddie. 'That's the place to be.'

I reached behind me into the drinks cooler and extracted a bottle of white wine and a couple of glasses. It was only eleven o'clock, but Freddie would say good morning to any alcoholic drink almost as soon as the Rice Krispies in his cereal bowl had stopped crackling. I poured us both a glass and handed one to Freddie.

'We might know of a better bet, if it's property you're after,' I said. 'Have you heard of sub-prime?'

'Haven't I read about that in the papers somewhere?' asked Freddie. At the time, it would have been difficult to avoid the subject if you ever opened the newspapers, for they had finally woken up to the growing debt crisis in the United States. Freddie's attention span was, however, limited at the best of times.

'You may well have done,' I said. 'The subject *has* been in the news a bit.'

I explained Bilbo's theory about buying up distressed sub-prime debt and waiting for the market to turn.

'I like the sound of that,' said Freddie. 'I mean, people are always going to want houses, aren't they?'

'That's right, Freddie,' I agreed.

'I mean, they aren't making land any more, are they?'

'Absolutely, Freddie, they aren't.'

'Quite a clever wheeze of your chaps – you buy up

mortgages at half-price and wait for the market to turn, is that it?'

'Got it in one,' I told him.

Freddie looked at the river, considering.

'I might put fifty large ones into this little scheme of yours, Eck. Perhaps even more.'

'We normally start at a million, Freddie,' I told him.

'Oh, well, that's OK too,' said Freddie quickly, not wanting to appear mean or short of cash, 'Much better to have one or two biggish investments than lots of little jobs you can't keep your eye on.'

'You're quite right, Freddie.'

'Do you think there's any more vino in that bottle?'

Freddie was interested, but in these nervous times it was becoming more difficult to get people to commit: the really bright investors were staying out of the market, or buying very old-fashioned things like gilts. The easy-money boys were beginning to run for cover. Only Freddie and a few like him hadn't yet noticed what was going on. Once I might have found one or two new investors for our funds each month; now people with Freddie's wealth and impetuous nature were increasingly hard to unearth. Bilbo called me into his office one day, and asked me why I thought he should continue to pay my salary.

'People are very edgy at the moment, Bilbo,' I told him. 'They're sitting on their hands.'

'Then your job is to calm them down,' he replied. 'Get them to put their hands in their pockets instead. We need to book at least ten million pounds of private-client funds every quarter to keep the momentum going. This quarter you've billed only two million. I'm not joking, Eck. At that rate you're not covering your overhead. You're not even paying for the share of rent taken up by your desk.'

'But there are stories in the press. What about Bright Star? They've gone bust. Everyone knows we were in there. The press got hold of it.'

'Not from me,' said Bilbo. 'And we invested through nominee accounts, so how did the press find out? Someone's leaking, or spreading rumours about us. I don't suppose you know anything about that?'

As he spoke, Bilbo got up from behind his desk. He could look quite intimidating if he wanted to. Today he wanted to, and in a foolish moment I wondered whether he was thinking of striking me to the ground as punishment for my failure to meet sales targets. But all he did was walk across the room and straighten a crooked picture.

'You know,' he said, 'I hired you because I thought you might be hungry for money, and be keen to have something to occupy yourself with. Now, all you seem to do is reel off excuses. I hope you haven't been talking to anyone about our work here?'

'Of course not, Bilbo, only when you pay me to.'

'Well, someone is talking about us in the market,' said Bilbo. 'If I find out who it is I'll make life very uncomfortable for them; very uncomfortable.'

The interview was over, and I went downstairs in a troubled state of mind. There was a general paranoia beginning to develop at Mountwilliam Partners. It wasn't only us. Other people we talked to were becoming jumpy. Rumours spread in the marketplace: banks running out of capital, and not just in America; big corporations having difficulty refinancing. I knew how bad things were when I rang Freddie a week or so after we came back from the Tweed, to persuade him to come and meet Bilbo in the office. That usually clinched it, but Freddie didn't want to know.

'Frightfully kind of you to take me fishing, Eck,' he said, when I rang. 'Sorry about the bread-and-butter letter not arriving yet – I'm a bit slow to put pen to paper sometimes.'

'No need to write, Freddie,' I said. 'The pleasure was all mine. Have you thought any more about investing in our Styx fund?'

Then Freddie dropped his bombshell.

'I met a chap in the bar at my club the other night who said he'd heard another fellow say he'd heard a story that your outfit was about to go tits up.'

'Freddie, that's absolute nonsense,' I said. 'You know that. I'm ringing you from the office now. We're all still here. Everything's fine. They're even still paying me.'

But Freddie wouldn't be persuaded.

'All the same, I'd rather not just at the moment, Eck. The fact is, I was thinking of buying a smallish sort of yacht, and if I put a million in with you boys it would seriously cramp my style. I'd end up having to make do with a rowing boat.'

We both laughed, but not heartily. Freddie wasn't going to change his mind.

After that phone call, I lost my appetite for ringing people. I just didn't know that I wanted to do any more networking at that precise moment. I decided to leave the office, although it was only three in the afternoon, and go for a walk. Outside, the early spring sunshine was strong. The brightness of the day made me think with longing of my home in Teesdale.

I went and bought a cup of coffee at the café down the road. A moment after I rose to my feet, a man in a wax jacket and corduroys paid his bill, stood up and began to saunter down the street behind me. There you are, I told myself: paranoia. It's catching. The other night there had been a blue Ford Transit van outside my flat, with a dim light on somewhere in the back, and I had almost convinced myself there was a surveillance team inside it. It was gone the next morning. Now there was this perfectly innocent man walking down the street behind me. I turned once or twice to check that he was still there, and he was; on the third occasion I saw that he had hailed a cab. Maybe I was just nervous because I disliked my job so much.

But could I afford to give it up? I knew now that I wanted to. I had inherited a sum of money from Aunt Dorothy, and the sale of the house outside Cirencester would yield a decent amount of money even after tax. Apart from my inheritance, I had my investments in Mountwilliam Partners funds. I had even taken a sum via equity release on my flat in West Hampstead to add to those investments, as Bilbo strongly encouraged partners and employees to do.

'It's called putting your money where your mouth is. If you can tell the punters that you have invested in the firm, it helps build their confidence.'

When I added it all up, I could probably survive living at home in Teesdale. If I left Bilbo's employment, there was no point in trying to get another job in London. No one else would pay me the salary I earned at Mountwilliam Partners. I was getting past my sell-by date anyway: perhaps that was the message Bilbo was beginning to transmit in my direction. There were only so many people I could chat to as potential investors and I was beginning to exhaust the seams of friendship and acquaintanceship. Once I had used up all the people I knew, I was really no better than one of those telephone salesmen who ring you from remote-sounding places, offering investments in some obscure company. In fact, I'm not sure that I had ever been that much different to the cold callers.

Living in Teesdale on my own was one thing; living there with Harriet another. The latter prospect I could look forward to, could endure any amount of financial hardship to realise. The former was less inviting. I wasn't sure I could do it. I would probably drink myself to death after a year or two through sheer boredom.

My thoughts jumped out of this track and settled into another. Who was spreading rumours about Mountwilliam Partners? And was it true, or was it just Bilbo's paranoia? If someone was spreading gossip, we were in trouble: firms like Bilbo's depended on confidence, on the belief that they could do no wrong; that funds were without limit, credit was always available, and investments would always increase in value. Up until now that had always been the case. But supposing that things were about to change?

There was a sense of fragility in the air these days, a feeling of walking on thin ice. I remembered Charlie Summers telling me he had always walked on thin ice, and now that was how I felt too. It was cracking underfoot; far away, great bergs were being calved, and floating out blindly into the shipping lanes. Stories, rumours, counter-rumours were flying around the industry: most of them not yet in the press or in the public domain. Was the miracle of endless growth about to come to an end? For ten years we had been told that the cycle of boom and bust had been broken. Fortified by this belief we had gone out and borrowed: borrowed money on the back of our house prices going up; borrowed money on the strength of our future income; borrowed money, because money was cheap, and could be invested in almost anything without risk. Risk was dead; it had been abolished.

Feeling as I did now, how could I go back to my desk and summon the confidence to make another phone call, to Simon or to Mark or to anyone else on my list? How could I have the nerve to ask them how they were, how things were going, knowing that the conversation would end with an invitation to meet Simon or Mark for drinks somewhere, or for them to join me at Mountwilliam Partners' next roadshow (more cocktails and canapés in the smartest hotels in Bristol, Birmingham, Leeds, Manchester or Newcastle)? How could I tell them that Mountwilliam Partners was launching another fund, Styx II, and that – if they wanted – there might just be a chance I could get them in on the ground floor, while units could still be bought cheaply?

And if I didn't go back to my desk and make those phone calls, and reel in the punters, then Bilbo would take my desk and my phone away and put me back out on the street. Then what would I do with my life?

I felt the sun's warmth on my face, and a bead of perspiration trickled down my back. I came to a pedestrian crossing. Forward, or back?

I stood still for a while. Decisions had to be made, and I didn't feel capable of making any of them.

Thirteen

It was in this state of indecision that I watched the spring pass by, and the summer begin. London was heating up, becoming stuffy and oppressive. In the air-conditioned offices of Mountwilliam Partners, the trading floor buzzed with activity. The new and adventurous strategy of trading at thirty times margin allowed us to take positions that we would never have dreamed about a few years ago. Global banks and corporations shuddered if they thought we were in their shareholder register. Mountwilliam Partners had become a colossus among other colossi, with pension funds and more staid investment funds than our own piling in behind the private investors, looking for the magical rates of return that only we, and a charmed few like us, could produce.

Bilbo was in his element. He was positively godlike. His internal emails had the force of Old Testament pronouncements: 'Wheat futures will go up to one hundred and forty pounds a tonne,' the emails would say, and wheat obediently went up to one hundred and forty a tonne, the Mountwilliam Commodity Fund piling in with all the others. The world is going to run out of wheat, press stories would scream. We knew – or thought we knew – that Bilbo and others like him fed stories to financial journalists morning, noon and night. Gold and oil: the same dynamic, the same stories. We rarely saw Bilbo these days. He had bought a timeshare in a

Gulfstream and used it to fly to hedge fund conferences in Cannes, Rome, San Francisco, Bali. There, more rumours were swapped and more deals were done.

'UK property prices will show double-digit growth in the medium term,' said another email proposing the establishment of a fund to buy repossessed properties at auction. Medium term was a phrase that we used a lot: it was longer than short term, and shorter than long term, and no one quite knew how near or far away those horizons actually were. In response to Bilbo's email, it seemed, UK house prices obediently jumped by ten, twelve, fourteen per cent.

And yet, and yet. While tens, then hundreds, then billions of pounds and dollars flowed ceaselessly through Mountwilliam Partners, darker currents were swirling beneath the surface of the markets we dealt in. There were too many rumours to ignore; too much volatility. One week the share price of a major bank fell by forty per cent as short sellers spread rumours of default in the marketplace, then cashed in as the share price fell. An enormous bank on Wall Street tried, and failed, to organise a refinancing package. Things did not feel right; they felt very far from being right.

I saw Bilbo now and again for more pep talks. My performance was dismal. I knew he would have got rid of me before now, if it hadn't been for the fact that my departure might unsettle some of the investors I had lured into Styx I and Styx II.

At our last meeting he was almost avuncular, at least to begin with.

'My dear Eck,' he said, showing me the monthly sheet recording the investments I had booked, 'if I weren't so very, very fond of you, I would sack you on the spot.'

'Bilbo, people just aren't feeling that brave at the moment, at least not the people I talk to,' I explained, not for the first time.

'Perhaps you are talking to the wrong people? Perhaps you are talking to the wrong people *and* talking to them in the wrong way?'

There was a silence while I waited for Bilbo to say something further. He was wearing another new suit. Bilbo always wore dark blue suits, cream silk shirts with heavy gold cufflinks adorned with his cat crest, and dark blue ties from Charvet. Nowadays it seemed as if he wore a new suit every week: he always looked so immaculate, the creases in his trousers so knife-edged, the linen so pristine, that everything down to his shiny shoes looked as if it had just come out of a box and been put on for the first time.

'Would you be happier back in Teesdale, rounding up sheep on a quad bike?' Bilbo asked tenderly. 'I do sometimes feel that dealing with a dozen old ewes might be more suited to your temperament than trying to sell our funds to high-net-worth individuals.'

'I've been asking myself the very same question,' I admitted. There seemed no point in dissimulation. I simply didn't have the energy to pretend I enjoyed my job any more.

Bilbo picked up a gold paperknife from his desk. I wondered for a moment what he was thinking about as he turned it to catch the light.

'Why don't you take some time off?' he said, putting it down. 'Try and get a bit of perspective on things. Go home now and come in again next Monday. Then you can tell me whether you still want this job, and are prepared to put in the effort as the rest of us do, or whether you would prefer the kind of life where you can be tucked up in bed with your cocoa at half past eight. Cocoa's about all you will be able to afford if you leave us. No one else in the City will want you.'

'I'm sorry, Bilbo,' I said. 'You're right. I do need to make up my mind.'

'Being sorry pays no rent,' said Bilbo, as I got up. He always liked to have the last word.

I left the office about midday and, as I had absolutely nothing to do and no plans, I decided to stop at a wine bar and have a glass of white wine. My nerves were jangling after the conversation with Bilbo. I couldn't tell whether I was furious or relieved that the subject of my dismissal was now out in the open. It didn't help matters when Nick Davies sat down at my table, just as the waitress arrived with my glass of St Véran.

'Bring a bottle of whatever he's drinking, and another glass,' he told her. Then he turned back to me.

'Good morning, Eck. Drinking in the middle of the day, now? Have you been fired?'

'Christ, Nick,' I said, as soon as my heart had stopped hammering. 'You gave me a shock. How did you know I was here?'

Nick said, as if it was the most natural thing in the world, 'Oh, I thought you might have spotted it by now. We've been taking an interest in you, and the company you work for, for quite some time.'

The waitress arrived and Nick smiled encouragingly at her while she opened the bottle, and poured some wine for him to taste. It gave me time to regain some of my composure.

'Why?' I asked. 'Why are you taking an interest? And what do you mean by "we"?'

Nick raised his glass in a mock toast.

'Death to all money launderers,' he said. 'I have been seconded to the Serious Organised Crimes Agency. Didn't I mention that the last time we spoke? Tell me more about Mr Aseeb.'

Once again I felt as if I had been poked sharply in the solar plexus.

'Aseeb?' I said stupidly. 'What do you know about Aseeb?'

'Quite a lot,' replied Nick. He wasn't smiling any more. 'It's what *you* know that interests me. He's been in our sights for a while now. Imagine my surprise when I saw a surveillance tape with your cheerful face in the middle of it. And that's happened more than once. The obvious conclusion is that he must be quite a friend of yours.'

For a moment I struggled between my fast-fading loyalty to Bilbo and the conviction, which now seemed to me to have the weight of an established fact, that there was something wrong about Aseeb, and something even more wrong about the way Bilbo and Aseeb had used me to ferry encrypted memory sticks between them. It began to dawn on me that there might be a very good reason why Bilbo hadn't wanted to meet Aseeb himself. Perhaps he suspected, or even knew, that Aseeb might be watched. If I was the one who met Aseeb, then it would be my name, not Bilbo's, in the frame if Aseeb was up to no good.

If my relationship with Bilbo had been a little warmer, or had lasted a little longer, I might have prevaricated, and tried to buy a little time so that he could explain to me what this was all about. But Bilbo was so obviously ready to discard me that I felt I owed him nothing. My first duty was to myself.

I gave Nick a brief account of my meetings with Aseeb.

'That's all I know,' I said. 'He's an investor representing various trading interests in the Middle East who want to acquire a stake in Mountwilliam Partners. Bilbo sees him as a way of strengthening our balance sheet.'

'Well, the trading interests Aseeb represents are also known as the Taleban,' Nick told me. He sipped his wine, then pushed the glass away from him and leaned forward with his elbows on the table, gazing intently at me. His words shocked me, yet at the same time they were not all that surprising.

'Eck, what I'm telling you must go no farther.'

I nodded.

'Bilbo met Aseeb when he was in Afghanistan, a few years before you got there. At that time our policy was to finance, arm and train the Taleban so that they could kill Russians more effectively and keep the Soviet army tied down. It worked very well. The collapse of the Soviet military effort in Afghanistan was the beginning of the end for the Soviet empire. Bilbo worked side by side with the same sort of people you were sent to kill a few years later. That's the way it is with our foreign policy. Everyone gets their turn to be shot at.'

Nick topped up my glass. I took a long sip from it to steady my nerves.

'Aseeb is a money launderer,' Nick told me. 'The drugs trade out of Afghanistan is one of the biggest businesses in the world. The opium is harvested in Afghanistan and then processed into morphine base in factories in the disputed border regions. The morphine base is distributed through various networks and refined into heroin either in northern Pakistan, or in Europe. The biggest customer is an organisation based in Calabria in southern Italy that is now bigger than the Mafia. Aseeb spends a lot of time in Calabria and Sicily. He has a home in Palermo. The money the Taleban raise from their pharmaceuticals business is used to keep themselves armed and well equipped. It's also used to fund some of the al-Qaeda networks in Iraq and in Europe, as a way of making sure Western intelligence services are permanently overstretched.'

'But why would Bilbo have anything to do with that?' I asked. Bilbo had never struck me as a nice man, and probably not a good man, but helping to fund terrorist networks seemed a bit extreme, even for him.

'Bilbo doesn't care,' Nick told me. 'Bilbo is doing exactly what you said he was doing: propping up the balance sheet at Mountwilliam Partners. And from what we hear, it needs propping up. He gets the cash to rebuild his company and stop it going bust. Aseeb will no doubt earn a big dividend on his equity investment. It's a money-laundering operation as far as Aseeb is concerned. And the fact that Bilbo's talking to someone like him says to me that Bilbo has his back against the wall.'

I thought about Bilbo's behaviour over the past few months. It was true: behind his smug exterior, the anxiety was increasingly visible. He lost his temper much more easily: I wasn't the only one who had received a tongue-lashing in recent days.

Nick said, 'Where that money ends up is of no concern to Bilbo, although he has a damned good idea, I'm sure. He knows what Aseeb is.'

There was a silence. I no longer felt like drinking my wine. Outside it was a sunny day, but I felt cold and shaken. I wondered why Nick was telling me all this, but it became obvious with his next question.

'Have they done the deal yet? Would you know?'

'Bilbo has mentioned it to the team,' I said, 'so it must be very close. But he would have told us if it had actually been signed on the dotted line.'

Nick leaned back in his chair.

'Well, you'd better be careful not to give yourself away. You were never much good at hiding your feelings, Eck.'

'Give myself away? You're not going to ask me to wear a wire or something, are you?'

Nick laughed.

'God, no.' He reached into his pocket and pulled out a card with his name and mobile number on it, and gave it to me. 'Get in touch on this number if anything happens. Meanwhile, I'll give you some advice, instead.'

'What?' I asked, although I thought I knew what it might be before he spoke.

'Get a new job.'

For the last couple of months I had been talking to Harriet about what we should do with the house in Cirencester. A valuer had been instructed and we were ready to put the property on the market. We both agreed that we needed one more look at the house and its contents before it was sold.

My communications with Harriet were warm enough: she sounded happy and friendly on the phone, and pleased to hear from me. But my instincts told me not to press her to come back to England just yet; if I didn't know what to do with my life, I wouldn't be very convincing trying to tell her what to do with hers. I missed her terribly; I could not tell, from her voice or her messages, whether she missed me as much; or whether she missed me at all.

After leaving Nick, I rang Harriet and told her I had been given a few days off, and asked whether she would come over and meet me in Cirencester. I knew Harriet's professional instincts meant that she hated having an empty house just sitting there, producing no income. We agreed she would come over in the next couple of days. I would collect her from Heathrow and then we would drive down together to meet the estate agent and Mr Gilkes, and get things moving.

I met Harriet at the arrivals gate of Terminal 2. She smiled at me and gave me a sisterly kiss as we greeted each other.

'You look well,' I told her as we walked towards the short-term car park.

'I am well, very well.'

She spoke in a bright, cheerful but distant way, as if nothing had ever happened between us. On the drive down to Cirencester she didn't tell me how she felt about seeing me again, and I didn't tell her how I felt either. It was a great social success.

As we turned into the road at the end of which The Laurels stood, and I started to weave the car around the potholes, Harriet said, 'What's that white van doing there?'

I took my eyes from the road. There was a large white van, of the kind preferred by low-budget rental companies, parked next to the entrance. As we drew closer I could see two large men in boiler suits. One was at the front door, obviously ringing the bell, while another was peering through a ground-floor window, as if contemplating other means of access to the house. We pulled up in the Audi, and both climbed out. I said to the nearer of the two men, who had turned to face me, 'Can I help you?'

'Morning, mate,' he said. He was unshaven and pasty faced, and looked cross. 'Glad you turned up at last. Don't seem to be very good at answering letters, do you?'

He held up a piece of paper.

'You might want to look at this, Mr Summers.'

'I'm not Mr Summers,' I told him. An awful realisation was dawning on me: I was beginning to think I knew what this was all about.

'This is a court order, Mr Summers,' said the man. 'I'm a bailiff and I'm authorised by the court to . . . what did you just say?'

'I'm not Mr Summers,' I repeated.

'Who are you, then?' asked the man. 'Was you expecting to find him in? Do you know when he'll be back?'

'I'm not expecting him back at all,' I said. 'This is our house, not his.'

Harriet was looking confused.

'Who is Mr Summers?' she asked.

It took a while to sort things out. Endless pieces of paper were produced by the first bailiff, while the second lurked in the background looking as if he might welcome some physical recreation in the form of a punch-up. At last, an explanation emerged. Charlie had used this address in an application form for a credit card. He had then, it seemed, used the card to go straight to his credit limit. The credit card company had received no response to the bills it had sent to this address, and had sold the debt to a credit recovery company.

Once I knew what had happened, I had to get the first bailiff to speak on the phone to Mr Gilkes, before I could convince him not to decamp with all the furniture from the house in the back of his van. After the call he gave up.

'Here's something for your trouble anyway,' I said, giving him a twenty-pound note. It seemed better to part on good terms.

The bailiffs gone, I unlocked the front door and we went in.

'Now you must tell me what on earth that was about,' said Harriet. '*Who* is Charlie Summers? What was he doing here?'

But a further surprise awaited us. In the kitchen, a large cardboard box sat on the table and next to it was a note from Mrs Graham dated the day before saying, 'This was delivered for you today. I thought it best to leave it here for you to collect.'

Harriet and I looked at the box. On one face, 'This Way Up' was stencilled along with wineglass symbols indicating the fragility of the contents. On another was an elaborate coat of arms in gold and blue hinting at connections with nobility, if not royalty. Above this were the words:

Chateau kloof
Vin de Pays de zeeland
Appellation controlee
Prix d'or Dusseldorf weinfest 2006
(RUNNER-UP)

'Someone's sent us a box of wine,' said Harriet.

'Dutch wine,' I said, feeling that I might know who the sender was. I opened the top of the box. Inside was a leaflet, made to look like faded parchment, as if it were a fragment of the Magna Carta. On this was written:

A unique opportunity to invest in one of the few Dutch vineyards producing premier cru quality wine

Chateau Kloof is, at present, known only to a small number of connoisseurs of fine wines. Although its output comes from only a few hectares, it produces several thousand bottles a year of an intense beetroot-coloured wine, with an unusual and distinctive aroma that has reminded many who have tried it of a great St Emilion.

In order to make it available to a wider public, it has been decided to offer the future output of the wine to investors. Units can be purchased at £1,000 each, and each unit entitles the investor to . . .

I didn't bother to read any more; I felt I had the general idea. I looked down at the bottom of the parchment, which was signed off by Charles Edward Gilbert Summers, Master of Wine. Beneath this was a handwritten scrawl in black felt tip, distinctly out of place with the elegant calligraphy on the rest of the document:

Dear Eck
This is my new business – what do you think? The wine's on me, drink my health and hope we meet again one day.
 Your Friend Charlie S.

I showed the note to Harriet, and pulled out a bottle to look at it.

'Who is Charlie Summers?' she asked again.

'Let's go round and agree what has to be sold, and then we'll open a bottle of Charlie's wine and I'll tell you about him.'

We did our tour of the house, pausing only for the briefest of moments outside the bedroom with the yellow bedspread. Harriet looked inside it as if she were seeing it for the first time in her life. There was nothing worth keeping. In any case, there was no room for more furniture at Pike's Garth Hall, nor in my London flat.

After half an hour we had achieved what we came for. We

sat at the kitchen table and agreed to go with the valuer's recommendations on price, then I rang the estate agent on my mobile and told them to put the house on the market. The sooner it was sold now, the better. The unwanted contents could go off to auction or to the scrapyard and that would be the end of it.

'Let's try this Chateau Whatsit,' I suggested. 'Perhaps there's a corkscrew somewhere.'

'You stayed here with Charlie Summers? How did that happen?'

'If you want to know about him, Harriet,' I told her, 'I have to begin at the beginning.'

I found one of those combination tin-opener, bottle opener and corkscrew gadgets that are designed to perform several different tasks, each in an unsatisfactory way. Then I began to tell Harriet how Henry, Charlie and I had all met in a restaurant the night after she had been to dinner with us, in the South of France. At this point the story was interrupted as I struggled to extract the cork from the bottle. It was plastic, and came out reluctantly. I poured two glasses of wine as I told Harriet about Charlie singing Panis Angelicus as the sun sank over the hills of the Var.

'That's an interesting colour,' said Harriet, looking at her glass of wine. It was: a red richer than rubies; the liquid looked more like a Bloody Mary gone wrong than the Queen of Clarets, as it was described in Charlie's marketing literature.

'Let's allow it to breathe for a while,' I said cautiously.

I sniffed the glass: it did not smell of much, except for a faint vegetable aroma, familiar but difficult to place. I continued with Charlie's story, piecing together events as best as I could from what Henry and Charlie had told me at different times, going on to Charlie's arrival at Stanton St Mary, and describing the Yoruza saga. We had just come to the place in Charlie's story relating to Mrs Bently when, feeling a little parched from so much talking, I decided to sip the wine.

I have never before sprayed the contents of a glass over a table and I hope I never will again. It can't be an attractive sight.

'Christ,' I spluttered.

'I'll get you some water,' said Harriet. She found a clean glass, went to the sink and ran the tap for a few moments, then brought back the water for me to drink. I gargled and spat into the sink for a few moments, then drank two more glasses of water to try to take away the taste of Charlie's wine.

'Don't touch your glass,' I warned Harriet, between gargles.

'I think I've got the message,' she replied. When I turned around to face her, she was laughing. 'Your face,' she said. 'I wish I'd had a camera.'

'I've never tasted anything like it,' I said, 'never.'

We abandoned the idea of further wine tasting. I told Harriet that I would leave the case as a house-warming present for whoever bought The Laurels. There was nothing more for us to do there.

'Now what?' I asked Harriet.

'Could you drop me off at my mother's house?' she said. 'She's not been very well again. I'm going to stay with her for a couple of days.'

'And then?'

'Back to France – it's my busiest time of year. I've got more clients than ever.'

I stood for a moment, thinking about this clear statement that I had no place in her future plans.

'Harriet,' I said, 'you know perfectly well how I feel about you.'

Her face screwed up immediately, as if she had toothache.

'You have to listen to me for a moment. I deserve that much,' I told her, 'and then I'll take you to your mother's.'

Her expression changed to contrition.

'Of course Eck, only—'

'Only you don't like me talking about it. I know that by now. But I'm giving up my job in London.'

There was a decision, right there, that I had not known I was going to make before I spoke. 'I'm going to move back North and try to scrape a living at home. God knows what I will do. But I can't go on selling dodgy investments to people any longer. It seemed like the answer at the time. Now I know it's not. I want you to come and live with me at Pike's Garth Hall.'

Harriet raised her eyebrows.

'I know it's not the South of France. But I'm sure you could get a job in our part of the world. Between us we could scrape a living, and be very happy. I'd be happy, at any rate.'

Harriet listened to this speech intently, but said nothing in reply. There was an awkward silence, which I felt compelled to break.

'It's not a proposal of marriage,' I said, 'at least, not yet. We could live together in sin if you prefer it, for a while. But I do want to marry you.'

'Eck,' said Harriet.

'You wouldn't even have to change your name if we got married,' I blundered on. 'Have you thought how convenient and economical it is that we both share the same surname already? Think of the expense most married couples have to go to, changing their writing paper and the initials on their handkerchiefs?'

'Eck, you're babbling,' said Harriet. She took both my hands and kissed me briefly, as if to command my silence.

'Is that a "yes"?' I asked her.

'I don't know. If there were to be anyone in my life again, it would be you. That's the most I can tell you.'

'Will you think about what I've said? Will you come and live with me?'

'I don't know,' said Harriet. At last I felt some sympathy for what she might be feeling. My irritation faded and was replaced by compassion. I took her right hand in mine and pressed it. I understood her: this girl really could not make up her mind. She would be a nightmare to go shopping with.

'I don't know,' repeated Harriet. She sounded in pain as she spoke.

In every relationship there comes a moment when someone asks a question that perhaps should not have been asked: about sex, or money, or commitment. Sometimes that question becomes the rock on which the relationship founders. I wondered whether that was what I had just done: asked Harriet a question that she didn't want to answer, a question that might force a reply I didn't want to hear.

Fourteen

Maybe it wasn't Armageddon. Only the historians will be able to say when things become really bad. But that autumn, we knew that the world was about to change: and not for the better.

A stream of financial crises made the front-page news here and in Europe, and in the United States. But it wasn't the front-page headlines which scared those of us who worked in the markets. It was the gossip between the traders, the rumours of potential defaults, including some of the biggest names in the banking and insurance world, the unwillingness to do deals, the closing down of credit lines. Cash was becoming scarce; credit scarcer.

In the midst of all this speculation, which seemed almost feverish in its intensity, Bilbo gave a dinner at his house in Kensington Gate for associates of the firm. I had returned to work but it was still a surprise to me that I had been included. I realised it would be unsettling for everyone else if I had been omitted from the guest list as I was still officially employed by Mountwilliam Partners. I had not yet given my notice in, as I was waiting for the right moment; or, as I admitted to myself in more candid moments, was still trying to summon up the nerve. Bilbo would lose his temper if I sacked him, so to speak, before he sacked me.

Most of the crowd from the Bloomsbury office were there:

Doug Williams, Alan McNisbet, and several others. Twenty-four of us, including Bilbo and his wife, sat down to dinner that night. I was placed somewhere in the middle, not deserving a place of honour close to Bilbo or his wife.

The dining room was a splendid scene. Silver pheasants, wild boar and other fauna decorated the table. There were five crystal glasses in front of each place setting and innumerable knives and forks, all silver and engraved with Bilbo's crest with the heraldic cat licking its heraldic paws. A gold plate had been set at each place setting as we sat down, and was whisked away by a waiter after we had had only a moment to admire it. It was replaced by plates from a service of Sèvres porcelain.

'We bought these plates at Christie's,' I heard Vanessa Mountwilliam say. 'I've been dying for an opportunity to use them. Don't you think they're attractive?'

Billy O'Brien, a mathematics graduate from Cambridge to whom the remark was addressed, said, 'Yes. That daffodil design is charming.'

He had graduated only five years ago and, until recently, had furnished his flat entirely from Ikea.

'They are fleur-de-lis, as it happens,' said Vanessa coldly, turning to her other neighbour.

Now that everyone was sitting down, I could do a proper tally of who was there. None of the more junior staff had been asked. What intrigued me more was that there were no unfamiliar faces.

'Where are Bilbo's partners?' I asked Doug Williams. 'I thought we might see one or two of them here tonight.'

Doug Williams had been employed by Bilbo longer than I had. I thought he might have been introduced to them.

'I've never met anyone apart from Bilbo, Eck. But if there

are such people they'll be rushing around trying to cover their positions, instead of sitting here. That's what we should be doing. Weren't you in the office this afternoon?'

I was thinking about Aseeb and wondering whether the deal had been done. Then I realised what Doug had just said.

'No, I wasn't in. What do you mean? What happened this afternoon?'

'Bilbo took calls today from two prime brokers and half a dozen repo officers from the various banks we deal with.'

Prime brokers were the people who lent us our funds on margin, on the basis of which we were able to take those huge leveraged positions in the market. The repo officers worked for the credit departments and it was their job, if necessary, to ask for the money back.

'What did they want?' I asked.

'What did they *want*?' repeated Doug, looking at me as if I were mentally deficient. 'They want their money back.'

'How do you know that?'

If what Doug said was true, Mountwilliam Partners was in for a bumpy ride. We might have to close positions when we did not want to, and that could mean taking some big losses. Doug shuffled slightly in his seat to allow a waiter to fill his glass with champagne, and I did the same.

'I know because I've heard the rumours in the market. There's a lot of talk flying around, not just about us. People are saying some of our subordinated debt trades have tanked. Bilbo bet the firm big time on the US housing market.'

'He might be right in the long run,' I suggested.

'Sure, he might be right in the long run. But you know what they say: we might all be dead in the long run, including Bilbo. At the moment, it doesn't look like he made a very clever bet.'

'What on earth's going to happen?'

Subordinated debt, sub-prime, was what the Styx II fund was invested in; and so of course was Henry Newark's money.

'I just heard the headlines. You'll have to ask Alan McNisbet. That's his desk.'

I glanced across at Alan. He looked pale and strained.

We were interrupted by Bilbo rising to his feet at the far end of the table.

'Gentlemen,' he said, tapping a wineglass with a silver knife to command our attention. There was immediate silence. Bilbo was wearing his green velvet smoking jacket, and tartan – presumably the Mountwilliam tartan – trews. His large, pale face glistened in the light from the enormous chandelier that hung overhead.

'*Ladies* and gentlemen,' Bilbo corrected himself. 'I propose a toast. To the continued success and prosperity of Mountwilliam Partners. Ladies and gentlemen: to ourselves.'

We all stood and sipped from our glasses.

'The champagne is Bollinger 1996, by the way,' said Bilbo, and sat down with a satisfied smile on his lips. The buzz of conversation resumed. Waiters came round with plates of potted shrimp and lobster tails.

'Bilbo's doing all right,' I said to Doug.

He smiled without mirth. 'If I wasn't worried before,' he replied, 'I am now. This feels like dinner in the Berlin bunker, with the Red Army about five minutes up the road.'

I laughed. I would miss Doug when I left. He would be the only one, though.

'Well, let's tuck in while the going's good,' I said.

The dinner was everything you would expect from Bilbo. Five more courses came and went: sorbet; fillet of beef and sauce Béarnaise; pudding; a savoury; cheese. With these came wines to match: white, then red burgundies of fabulous vintages; Sauternes. While Doug was talking to his other neighbour, I attempted conversation with the man on my left, whose name I did not know, but who had joined us as a trader in mining stocks. I asked him how things were going on his desk.

'OK,' he said, and buried his nose in what he was eating. I tried again, once or twice, and managed with some effort to extract three or four more syllables from him. After that I gave up and concentrated on enjoying the food and wine. I had a feeling this was going to be the last dinner I would be treated to by Bilbo. If so, it was a very good one. We were all feeling quite full when Bilbo rose to his feet again.

'Ladies and gentlemen,' he repeated. 'If I can ask for your patience a few moments longer, I would like to say a few additional words. Mountwilliam Partners was set up on a wing and a prayer about six years ago. The office consisted of me and Alan over there, and we had no money and no clients on the day we started. Now we are one of the biggest and most respected funds of our kind in Europe. We have an excellent team [*prolonged applause and thumping of the tabletop*] and a track record second to none. It is that track record that will allow us to grow further and compete with anyone in London or New York.

'Some of you may have heard rumours that the market is going through a period of uncertainty. That's what markets do, from time to time. If it was easy to make money, nobody would pay us to make it for them. We don't bury our heads in the sand at times like this: periods of turbulence are often periods of opportunity, as we all know. When confidence ebbs, pricing errors are made: that's when we must be at our busiest.'

Bilbo paused and looked around, smiling. In that dining room, the table laden with silver and crystal, oil paintings of earlier Mountwilliams staring gloomily down at us from the walls, it was difficult to imagine what could ever go wrong. We waited to hear what Bilbo would say next.

'I thought this little dinner would be a good idea for three reasons,' continued Bilbo. 'Firstly, to celebrate our own success over the last six years; secondly, to say to you that in times like these competitors, financial journalists and others will feed the rumour mill whenever they can. You will even hear stories about Mountwilliam Partners. Ignore them. These people will do anything to get attention and they are not worth bothering about. Mountwilliam Partners is as solid as – I was going to say the Bank of England, but maybe that's not the right comparison at the moment [*laughter and more applause*] – as solid as it can be. There was a third reason for bringing you here tonight: to thank you all for your hard work.'

Bilbo raised his glass and said: 'Thank you!'

There was more applause. Everyone had drunk quite a lot by this stage. Someone tried to start up a chant of 'Six More Years', which ran around the table like a Mexican wave for a brief interval. Bilbo was still standing, beaming at us, resplendent in his green velvet smoking jacket and the immaculate silk of his evening shirt and beautifully knotted bow tie. Then an odd thing happened: everyone at the table fell silent. People looked sideways at each other. There was a chill in my own heart as if someone had walked over my grave. For a moment everything in the room was thin and cold as if all of us, dressed in our finery, surrounded by the remains of an epicurean feast, were in reality crouching around a pile of bones and scraps by the mouth of a cave. Even Bilbo, as he stood there, looked at a loss for a few seconds. Then he clapped his hands to gain our attention, and the moment passed.

'And now,' he said, 'drinks next door in the drawing room: port, brandy, whisky, champagne. Help yourselves to whatever you want. Enjoy yourselves!'

Everyone broke into groups. The drawing room was full of noisy people, laughing and joking, on the outer edge, if not yet over it, of sobriety. Vanessa Mountwilliam was showing a small cluster of acolytes the new Horowitz painting and telling them how much Bilbo had paid for it. I decided that I would help myself to a glass of port and then, as soon as I thought I would not be missed, I would vanish into the night. As I poured myself a glass from a decanter a hand fell on my shoulder and the smell of a good cigar enveloped me. It was Bilbo.

'Cockburns '63,' he said. 'Hope you like it. Come over here and sit with me for a moment, Eck. I wanted to have a word with you tonight.'

There was nothing I could do but follow him to a couple of unoccupied armchairs in one corner of the enormous room. Even Bilbo would not fire me at his own dinner party, I told myself. But then there was no knowing what Bilbo would or would not do.

'Splendid dinner, Bilbo,' I told him as we seated ourselves.

'Yes, very jolly,' he agreed. 'I'm so glad you liked it. I gather you've been talking to Nick Davies, at the Serious Organised Crime Agency. That's very naughty, Eck. I'm really quite annoyed with you.'

For a moment I was speechless. I could feel the blood draining from my face, then rushing back so that my skin must have glowed like a bonfire. Where or how had he found out about Nick? Bilbo smiled at me, pleased at the effect of his words.

'You look quite shaken, dear boy. Can I get you a glass of water? No? It doesn't go with port, does it? Yes, you have your old army friends, and so do I. You've been talking to them, and some of them have been talking to me. All these government agencies leak like sieves. The days when people kept secrets are long gone. I knew that there was a rat talking to the authorities and I thought it was you; now I know it's you.'

A young analyst, whose name I could not remember, came towards us. He looked quite drunk.

'Super party, Bilbo,' he said. Bilbo did not even turn his head.

'Go away,' he said coldly. The young analyst jerked as if he had been slapped in the face, and then walked off. Bilbo leaned forward and tapped me on the knee.

'So your friend at SOCA talked to someone at MI5, and one of my mates at MI5 talked to me. But the damage is done. Someone malicious has been spreading rumours that we are going down, that we can't get new funding from our banks. All complete nonsense, of course, but that kind of gossip can be very damaging. We think – my partners and I think – that same someone is deliberately trying to destabilise us. We don't like it.'

Bilbo paused to draw on his cigar then exhaled a cloud of fragrant smoke.

'These Hoyos really are the business,' he said. 'You don't smoke, do you? Sure you won't try one? What was I saying . . . oh, yes, they nearly nabbed Aseeb at Heathrow. They missed him by about five minutes and he's now lying low, as they say – I won't tell you where, if you don't mind. I hope you're not offended by my total lack of trust. And so he can't do any more business just at the moment.'

'I thought it was drug money,' I said slowly and thickly. 'I thought he was laundering cash for the Taleban.'

'That's what Mr Davies told you, is it?' asked Bilbo. 'Well, where the money comes from is none of your business. It's money. That's all that matters. We could have done great things with the firepower from Aseeb's cash. That is not to be, thanks to you.'

Bilbo paused, as if waiting for something.

'Aren't you going to say you're sorry?' he asked.

'Bilbo, I'm not sorry. If it's dirty money – and it is, isn't it? – then I'm not sorry, whatever happens.'

'Oh, I think you will be,' said Bilbo. 'I think you will be *very* sorry. One good stab in the back deserves another, that's what I always say. If you are fussy about where our money comes from, or where indeed it goes, you shouldn't be working for us. You shouldn't be in the business. That reminds me: don't come back to the office. Your P45 is in the post. Meanwhile, you ought to know that I've been talking to people about you too.'

'Talking to which people?' I asked. I knew he wouldn't tell me.

'Well, I mustn't monopolise you,' said Bilbo, rising to his feet. 'It's been marvellous to have this little chat, but I must look after my other guests. Goodbye, old boy. I don't think we will meet again.'

He turned away and, seeing Alan McNisbet, threw an affectionate arm around his shoulders and said, 'Now then, Alan, what about a proper drink? I've got a thirty-year-old Macallan over there that I want your opinion on.'

It was after midnight when I left the house in Kensington Gate. The streets were deserted and damp, with a fine drizzle forming haloes around the street lamps. Outside Bilbo's house were half a dozen pre-booked taxis and a minibus, the drivers smoking and chatting in a small group on the pavement. I had not had the forethought to make any such arrangement. As I walked homewards, searching for a cab, a feeling of profound unease crept over me. I found myself listening to the echo of my footsteps in the deserted streets as I walked. Once or twice I turned sharply, in case someone was following me. It was just nerves: Bilbo had certainly achieved his intended effect with his last few words. Who had he been talking to? Would he try anything more substantial in the way of retribution? I didn't think so: he would have his hands full trying to rescue Mountwilliam Partners, if the rumour mill really was working against us now. Us? It wasn't us any longer.

No, I decided, Bilbo had his own problems. From the sound of it, he was at risk of being taken in for questioning by SOCA, for example. And he'd already sacked me from Mountwilliam Partners. All the same, I felt a sense of relief when at last I saw a taxi with its yellow light on coming towards me.

It was two o'clock in the morning by the time I went to bed. I felt cold and tired and rather depressed. The fact that I had just lost an extremely well-paid job was beginning to sink in. I reminded myself, as I brushed my teeth, that I had become more and more unhappy in my work and had been planning to give it up. Unhappiness was one thing; an income another. I climbed into bed and switched off the lamp. At least it meant that I could go home to Pikes Garth Hall.

Tomorrow I would ring Harriet and tell her I was leaving London for good. Then she would have to make up her mind. Clutching that thought, like a child clutching a teddy bear, I let sleep overtake me.

The following morning the alarm went at its usual time of six o'clock and I started to climb out of bed until it dawned on me that I didn't have a job to go to. I could lie in bed the whole day if I chose. But I was awake, so I showered, shaved, dressed, and went to brew up some coffee in the kitchen. As I sat and sipped my coffee, I tried to think what on earth to do next.

When the post arrived an hour or two later there was, as promised, a letter for me franked with the Mountwilliam Partners stamp. When I opened it I found my P45, and a short letter signed by Bilbo saying that the partners intended to sue me for breach of trust, and that their solicitors would shortly be in touch.

Great. I could imagine what sort of claim I would face. Bilbo would try to wipe me out financially if he could. I wondered whether Nick Davies would help me. I decided I ought to ring him anyway; tell him I was no longer at Mount-william Partners, and report on my last conversation with Bilbo.

Reaching Nick by telephone was not easy. I left several messages for him, but it was early evening before he called back.

'Hi,' he said. 'Got your message. Thanks for the update. I told you you'd need a new job soon, didn't I? And I have some news for you, too.'

He didn't sound too concerned by the fact that I'd lost my job, or that Bilbo knew of his agency's interest in Aseeb.

'Oh? What's that?'

'One of my colleagues has the tedious job of monitoring various jihadi websites. Last night about six of them lit up with your name. I thought you'd want to know.'

He might have used the same tone of voice if my name had appeared in the Births, Marriages and Deaths page of the newspaper.

'Oh,' I said again. 'What do they say about me?'

'The ones we've seen so far are either calling for your head – not necessarily the rest of you – or demanding that you be put on trial in a people's court in Afghanistan. Someone's told them about your involvement in that incident near Gholam Khot.'

I noticed that Nick said 'your involvement'. His own name hadn't been mentioned.

'That will be Bilbo's doing,' I said.

'That's what we think, too. It's more evidence that Aseeb is connected through his Taleban friends to some of the al-Qaeda networks.'

'What am I supposed to do?' I asked. I didn't like the feeling that my name was being broadcast around the Internet, and being discussed by God knows who.

'Well, I suppose you ought to take some notice of it. I mean, most of these websites carry all sorts of rubbish and usually it means little or nothing: just disaffected youngsters trying to make a noise. But one can't be sure.'

'So do I sit here and wait for the doorbell to ring?' I asked Nick. He wasn't being very helpful.

'Well, that's an option. You could tough it out. No doubt it will blow over soon enough, although don't be surprised if it gets into the newspapers. I suppose there is just a slight chance that someone will decide to take the matter seriously and pay you a visit.'

'Is that all you can tell me?' I asked Nick.

'What else can I say? We haven't got the budget to look after you. As far as my boss is concerned, you're just someone who acted as a go-between for one of the Taleban's money-men. Of course, *I* know that Bilbo set you up, but from the outside it doesn't look too good. Still, what can you do? Let's hope no one takes much notice. It's an old story, after all.'

That made me feel a whole lot better.

Fifteen

Charlie told me later that on the day I left The Laurels to drive back to London he had woken about ten in the morning.

'I had a bit of a head after all that whisky we drank,' he said. 'Still, it was jolly nice yarning away; very good to catch up on things. Hope I wasn't a terrible bore. I think I must have told you all that stuff about my being connected to the Royal Family. I hope you didn't take it too seriously. I'm not holding my breath for a knighthood, or anything like that.'

After a satisfactory breakfast of scrambled eggs and bacon and finding himself with absolutely nothing to do, Charlie decided to go and get the newspapers to kill some time before the next meal. He knew he could not stay at The Laurels for ever, and that sooner or later I would ask him to leave, but he was enjoying, for the moment, the absence of any compelling need to sell dog food.

It took him a while to find the nearest newsagent's, but by the time he had walked there and back, Charlie's headache was gone. A strange sense of optimism filled him, as it had done in the past after other business ventures had gone astray. There was a feeling of liberation: that the world, once again, was his oyster, provided he had a reasonably effective knife.

Having returned to the house with the papers, he made himself a cup of coffee and sat down to read them.

There was not much in the news: the usual stuff about house prices going up at the fastest rate ever; an article about the fifty wealthiest towns in Britain; another about the big jump in that month's unemployment figures. None of it interested Charlie too much. His thoughts strayed to Sylvia Bently. Had he been wrong to leave her without a word? He knew she had been good to him; if only she had been a little less demanding. Charlie was quite keen on a bit of nooky from time to time, but this woman knew no restraint. Then again, by her own account, she'd been on short rations for quite a while. If only her daughter hadn't looked down her nose at him in quite the way she had. Charlie thought he would send Sylvia a postcard one day, just to keep her sweet: you never knew, did you, how things might turn out in the end?

It was while he was turning through the pages at the back of one of the newspapers that he made his discovery. He'd read the sports pages, and the cartoons, and tried and failed to do the Sudoku, so now he was flicking through the classified ads. One caught his eye:

Want to make six figures a year without leaving your armchair? Interested in fine wines? Want to become rich AND have fun while you're doing it? Then call me, Hans van der Kloof, at this number . . .

There were several aspects of this proposition that appealed to Charlie. There was no mention of sending in a CV, or providing evidence of a first-class degree from a major university, or having one's own car, or having to prove one-self beyond reproach in any other way. This advertisement was aimed, Charlie knew, at people whose CVs would not take up much space, whose means might be limited, and whose lives might very well be subject to reproach in a number of different ways: in other words, people like himself.

He also knew from the way in which the advertisement was worded that, whatever the chances of a six-figure income in some distant future might be, the first thing that would happen would be that he would be asked for money up front. Even if he could find the sum in question, the second thing that would happen would be that he would never see that money again. That might not matter. If the scheme was compelling enough, then the people who ultimately never saw their money again might be the people down the line from Charlie. He would be asked to sell something, and if he could find buyers, the risk moved on down the line and some decent commission might stick to his fingers. It had to be worth a phone call to find out more, especially as the phone call from this house would cost him nothing.

With an ingenuity I can only admire, Charlie spent the rest of his day negotiating new lines of credit, taking advantage of his temporary residence at a respectable address. He managed to find enough bits of paper – old utility bills, a driving licence Aunt Dorothy had possessed but not used in recent years, a savings book – in drawers and in an old file in the kitchen to provide enough documentation to obtain credit cards. I do not know the detail of how this was achieved, but people like Charlie are past masters at it. Over the next few days he obtained two credit cards: one in his own name, and one in the name of Mr D. Branwen. Once he had done this, he was able to extract a few hundred pounds in cash from a high street bank in Cirencester. With the cash he opened a bank account in another bank a street or two away, and with that he managed to negotiate an overdraft facility. From a state of absolute poverty, Charlie had achieved modest affluence within the space of two or three days. It would be a week or two, perhaps even a month, before the credit card companies and banks shut down his credit and asked for their money back.

These were the last of the days of wine and roses, when credit was limitless and the optimism of bankers and their faith in their customers was a thing of beauty to behold.

He rang the number in the classified ad and, after one or two failed attempts, managed to speak to Mynheer Hans van der Kloof somewhere in Holland. This gentleman had a rich, confident voice that somehow reminded Charlie of thick-cut marmalade; he greeted Charlie with pleasure and within a few moments the two of them were on first-name terms.

'You are interested in fine wines?' Hans asked Charlie.

'Rather a hobby of mine,' said Charlie. 'Don't get as much time to explore it as I'd like, and I don't pretend to be especially knowledgeable. But I'm semi-retired now; I've just liquidated various investments, and I'm looking for something to keep me busy.'

'Ah yes,' said Hans van der Kloof. 'You are the typical English businessman; you don't know how to stop working. You are in the habit of making money, I think. Well, Kloof Wines might be the answer for you.'

Charlie admitted modestly that the cut and thrust of business life was hard to give up, but his medical advisers had suggested stepping back to two or three days a week.

'Then what we are offering is ideal for you. As we say in Holland, it is a pigeon flying into your mouth,' said Hans. 'It is not so necessary to have much knowledge of wine. You must learn something of our very special production methods at Chateau Kloof. You must love the wine to sell it.'

They agreed to meet and Charlie said that he would come

over to Holland in the next few days. Just before the conversation came to an end, Mynheer Kloof added casually, 'One small thing: our minimum investment for distributors is ten thousand euros. Cash only, of course.'

This sparked off a brief discussion after which it was agreed that, if Charlie liked what he saw on his visit, he could take away one hundred cases for five thousand euros. The minimum recommended retail price was two hundred euros a case.

Charlie left The Laurels a couple of days later, and got himself to Kemble station and from there to London. In the city, he used his new credit cards to buy himself a dark grey suit and a pair of shiny black shoes. Sylvia Bently might not have recognised him, he looked so neat and tidy. Next he found a budget van rental company, hired a large white van, and drove it to Harwich. There he took a ferry to the Hook of Holland and, on disembarkation, drove south through sheets of rain, following the directions given by Hans van der Kloof.

At this stage of any new business venture, Charlie would normally have been in a state approaching elation. As I had begun to realise the last time I met Charlie, what kept him going was his ability to delude himself. He was the perfect example of hope triumphing over experience. Experience told him that any new business he became involved in was probably doomed to failure: either because it was an enterprise no one else would consider undertaking or because it was an enterprise that a very great number of people had already undertaken – people who were far better equipped to succeed, both financially and intellectually, than Charlie. Hope, on the other hand, usually reigned supreme in Charlie's plans, at least in these early stages.

On the ferry, Charlie went to the bar and ordered himself a celebratory glass of champagne. He fell into conversation with a man in a fur-lined suede coat who bred schnauzers and was off to Germany to purchase a new breeding bitch from a very particular bloodline. For a while they talked dogs, and dog food, and Charlie only just managed to stop himself from selling the man some Yoruza. That was finished, he told himself. The man asked Charlie what he did and Charlie replied, 'Oh, I'm in the wine trade, myself.' He was satisfied to see that this information was greeted with respect by the dog breeder.

'Rhine wines, is it?' asked the man. 'Hocks? Moselle?'

Charlie shook his head.

'Well, you won't find much wine in Holland,' said the man, laughing. 'Germany or France is where you'll be heading, that's my guess.'

These words echoed in Charlie's mind as he drove south, through flat countryside dotted with charming small farms and criss-crossed by drainage ditches. Contented-looking cows, which Charlie thought must be of the cheese-producing variety, grazed in lush meadows. Pigs rooted about in muddier enclosures, and ducks and geese floated on sheets of water or paddled along silty banks. Cyclists pedalled slowly along roads that ran flat and straight to the horizon. This rural landscape was interrupted from time to time by the occasional modernistic structure; metal pipework and tanks that indicated the location of a factory or sewage treatment plant. Of vineyards, however, there was none.

This expedition may have been the beginning of the tenth, or perhaps even the thirtieth, of Charlie's business ventures.

He had lost count. Each time one of his schemes failed, it took a little longer for him to get over the disappointment. Each time he started out, he had to dig a little deeper to find the well of optimism that kept him going, as disaster after disaster proved beyond reasonable doubt his absolute unfitness for any form of business. As Charlie drove, these feelings arose in him once more and he experienced, not for the first time, the state of accidie: familiar to medieval monks and once known as the eighth deadly sin, this numbness of the heart, this loss of faith and belief, this weariness of the world and all its ways, was now invading Charlie's soul.

He knew, even as he drove south entertaining visions of himself as the host of wine tastings in great houses up and down England, that selling Chateau Kloof probably wouldn't work. He told himself that the wine trade was the most respectable, profitable and interesting business that he had attempted; deep inside he knew that after a few days, or weeks, at best months, failure would be knocking on his door once again. He knew that he had to impress Mynheer Kloof with a show of enthusiasm, combined with that innate integrity and charm that in Charlie's mind were the defining characteristics of the English upper classes. He knew he had to convey, above all, confidence: the confidence of a man with the Midas touch, a man who could get rich in his sleep, a man to whom bankers would fall over themselves to lend money.

He didn't think he could do it any more.

As he drove on, what he most wanted to do was to stop the van, climb out and lie down in one of the muddy ditches that ran alongside the road. For a long time he had presented a brave front to the world. I don't think it had ever occurred to him just to go and get a job working in a pub or a shop, or any of the countless unskilled jobs that he was qualified to do. Perhaps it was the result of an upbringing during which he had been taught to believe – among other fantasies – that he was a distant member of the Royal Family. I think, more likely, it was some fatal disconnection with the real world which led him to want the things he did not have, and yet could have had if only he had applied his brains and courage to more conventional lines of employment.

Over the last twenty years or so, Charlie had lived by deception, mostly of a minor nature, but even there he had failed to make his mark. He was not on the Ten Most Wanted list; he had barely registered on the fraud radar of banks and credit card companies. His crimes were regular, but small. Nevertheless, they were using up his stock of courage. Courage to go on; courage even just to exist: it is a finite commodity in most of us and so it was with Charlie.

At length he came to a crossroads which he thought he recognised from the directions he had been given. He took a right turn and, as promised, found the two white-painted posts by the side of the road exactly one and a half kilometres from the crossroads. Rain continued to sweep across the flat landscape under low clouds. In every direction were fields of vegetable crops; what they were Charlie could not have said. Between the white posts ran a straight metalled road, covered in muddy tyre tracks that stretched into the infinite gloom. Some distance away was a low range of red-brick farm buildings, and as he approached, Charlie noticed that the skyline was also relieved by several fibreglass tanks, and long breeze-block buildings with corrugated roofs.

He pulled up in the cobbled yard next to a green twin-cab Toyota pick-up, rather like the one he used to drive during his Yoruza days. The farmhouse beside it was quite extensive, but of no architectural merit: its most prominent feature was a large satellite dish. As he got out of his van, a man opened the nearest door and looked out to see who had arrived. This man wore a short black leather jacket, and had dark skin, black hair and a moustache: he might have been Turkish, or possibly Iraqi. He certainly did not look like a farmer, or a vintner.

He stared at Charlie and then, turning his head, shouted: 'Hansi!'

Then he disappeared back inside. A moment later a very tall man emerged through the doorway, bowing his head so as not to strike it on the lintel. He wore a checked shirt and jeans. He had ruddy cheeks and blue eyes in a round face adorned by gingery mutton-chop whiskers, and topped with receding wiry hair. When he saw Charlie, who was picking his way across the muddy courtyard, he opened his arms wide and said: 'Mr Summers! Welcome to Chateau Kloof!'

They shook hands and went inside. The door opened straight on to a large kitchen. At a long table sat the first man, reading a newspaper; a slatternly-looking woman with straggly blonde hair who was nursing a baby with a runny nose; and a small boy who played continuously with a hand-held electronic game.

Charlie had a picture in his mind of what Chateau Kloof should look like: an expanse of turrets and leaded roofs; stone walls mirrored in the glassy waters of a moat with swans gliding by; a drawbridge leading to a vaulted tunnel and an inner courtyard where he might have been greeted by his host in a quilted silk smoking jacket. He had expected at least some display of wealth and elegance; certainly nothing like the scene before him.

Over a cup of coffee they discussed business. Charlie had many questions, and the answers he received seemed either incomplete, or unsatisfactory. No, they did not grow the grapes here: there was another farm, in the south, where the grapes were grown and harvested. The wine was produced here, though, and Charlie would see how it was done. The technology was the very latest; more advanced than even the best vineyards in California. They had their own special, secret method of maturing the wine. Would Charlie please sign the non-disclosure document, and hand over the euros?

Charlie did sign and, with some misgivings, handed over the cash he had brought in his briefcase. He might not have done so, but when he asked to see the wine first, Mynheer Kloof and the other man in the black leather jacket had suddenly looked so unfriendly, and the atmosphere had become so chill, that Charlie remembered he was alone miles from anywhere, and that he might as well fall in with their wishes.

After that, everyone began to smile again and Charlie was taken on a tour. He gazed, uncomprehendingly, at a stainless-steel vat full of a purple liquid in one of the low buildings he had observed on his arrival. He witnessed a row of barrels in which many thousands of litres of Chateau Kloof were said to be maturing. There was an odour, everywhere, that re-minded Charlie of school dinners. The explanation for this familiar smell became clear when Hans van der Kloof said, 'And now, Charlie, I tell you our great secret, what gives our wine its special flavour and bouquet. Some growers mature their wine in oak barrels to give it a special taste. This is very old fashioned nowadays, I think. We are different. At Chateau Kloof we grow many fields of beetroots, and pickle them to preserve them. We use the same vats to mature our wine. That is the secret of our special flavour and colour.

Now you see how much I trust you: this is private information, known only to ourselves.'

After this revelation, they returned to the kitchen. Charlie was handed a few packs of marketing literature. It was the first thing he had seen on his visit of which he could thoroughly approve: glossy photographs of sunlit hillsides covered in rows of vines; a long pedigree of the Kloof family, not unlike Charlie's own family tree, proving the descent of the Kloof bloodline from the Emperor Charlemagne, who had caused the first vineyard to be planted; reproductions of several gold medals said to have been awarded at various wine festivals; and some lyrical description of the wine and the winemaking processes which omitted any mention of beetroot.

The dark-haired man in the leather jacket helped Charlie load the van with the cases of wine. These too were well presented and adorned with ornate labels in blue and gold inks. Charlie's spirits rose for a moment. Perhaps this really could work, after all: at any rate, it all looked very convincing.

Once the van was loaded, Charlie went back into the house to bid farewell. On the kitchen table stood an open bottle of rich red wine.

'Now you must taste the wine,' said Mynheer Kloof. He poured out three glasses and handed one to each of them, then proposed a toast.

'To the success of our first English distributor,' he said. '*Proost!*'

'Down the hatch,' replied Charlie.

'What did you think of the wine?' I asked Charlie, later, when he reached this point in the story.

'I don't know much about wine,' he replied. 'I'd be the first to admit that a pint of beer is more in my line. This stuff had quite a powerful taste. I don't think I would have wanted a refill. I thought it might go well enough with a strong curry, or something of that sort.'

Toasts exchanged, and after many more expressions of mutual esteem and invitations for Charlie to come again soon, he left. He was thankful that he had been able to leave at all. The whole set-up had filled him with uneasiness from the first moment.

'They were all smiles most of the time,' he told me, 'but if I'd tried to short-change them I think I might have ended up in a field, pushing up beetroots.'

Buying the wine turned out to be the easy part. Charlie took a different ferry back to England, arriving this time in Hull. From there he drove to York and used his credit card to rent a room in a hotel outside the city centre. He chose York because he had not been to York before: it was one of a diminishing list of towns or cities where he was, as yet, unknown. He knew York to be a prosperous sort of place where no doubt plenty of people drank wine. He managed to insert an advertisement in the local paper the day after his arrival, and to have some leaflets run up advertising a wine tasting. Then he spent several hours distributing the English-language brochures Mynheer Kloof had given him, in the leafier and more genteel suburbs where he felt wine drinkers might live. No one could say Charlie did not put his back into it: he was quite done in after two days and had to lie in his hotel room watching television for most of the next day until he recovered.

The evening of the wine tasting arrived. It was to take place in a function room provided by the hotel, who also undertook to announce the event on a welcome board in the foyer. Charlie had some business cards printed which bore the legend:

Charles Edward Gilbert Summers Esq.,
Master of Wine

The cards gave a mobile number, but no address.

Charlie set out a few rows of the marketing literature on one table. On another was a row of bottles of Chateau Kloof, which he had opened; in between these were small plastic pails for spitting out the wine, as Mynheer Kloof had instructed him, together with some plates of water biscuits, and little saucers laden with lumps of Cheddar and a few pickled gherkins. Then Charlie put on his grey suit, now slightly wrinkled, and his shiny black shoes, and waited for the customers to pour in.

Trade was slow. A couple of men in suits wandered in early on. Charlie had seen them at the hotel bar on the previous evening and presumed they must be visiting businessmen. One of them said, 'Mind if I try some of that vino?'

'That's what we're here for,' Charlie replied. The man poured himself a generous measure, and drank about half the glass. Then he screwed up his face.

'Where do you get that stuff, mate? What is it?'

Charlie offered them a Chateau Kloof brochure and gave them the marketing spiel, but they were already leaving. After this unpromising start the evening did not improve. A couple of elderly ladies appeared in the doorway giggling and clutching at each other nervously. When Charlie welcomed them, they admitted to having been lured to the hotel by Charlie's leaflet campaign. They helped themselves to small measures of wine, sniffed it and sipped, and then left again without saying anything. Another man in an old overcoat fastened with baler twine came in, a woollen cap on his head and several days' growth of beard on his chin. He nodded pleasantly to Charlie, poured himself a full glass of wine, and drank it in a single gulp.

'Cheers, mate,' the connoisseur said, giving Charlie a wink.

Then he helped himself to a refill. After he had drunk two or three more glasses Charlie asked him to leave. There was no rancour; the man thanked Charlie and said he'd send in an order for a few cases just as soon as he had an address for Charlie to send them to. And that was it. No other visitors came. Charlie's first (and last) wine-tasting event was over.

The following day Charlie packed up his rented van. He filled it with diesel at a nearby garage, and when he went to pay, he found that the card reader rejected his credit card. So that game was over: he had to pay for the fuel from his diminishing reserves of cash. There would be no more wine tastings. In any case, the evening in York had not encouraged him. Not knowing where to go, or what to do, he instinctively turned for the town that had once been his home. He drove north to Middlesbrough.

It occurred to him that his life, as it had been conducted for the last two decades or more, was coming to an end. The sense of inevitable failure that had filled him as he drove out to Holland now returned stronger than ever. The feeling was so profound that, as he drove, his vision blurred with tears. He did not know why he was weeping, or what would make him stop: he knew only that he had a vanload of undrinkable, unsaleable wine to get rid of; after that, the future stretched in front of him as barren as a polar desert. Charlie was returning to the place where he was born: but no friends, no family, no warm fireside awaited him.

Sixteen

The morning after my disturbing phone conversation with Nick, I went to the local newsagents and bought an armful of papers. I thought I should have a good look at the job advertisements. I had spent most of the previous day trying to decide what to do with myself and coming up with no answers at all. I thought perhaps I had better stay in London for a while and at least try to get another job. Once I gave up and went back North, I knew I would never return to the capital. On the other hand it was unsettling to consider that somewhere out there might be a group that felt its collective chances of entering Paradise would be greatly enhanced if they did something unpleasant to me. Ridiculous as it seemed that anyone would bother after all this time, I couldn't quite dismiss the idea. My professional experience told me that the chances of any jihadi wasting his time and energy coming after me were very slight: nevertheless, I felt jumpy.

I spread the newspapers out on the kitchen table and began to turn the pages of the *Daily Mail*. A picture on page three caught my eye. It was a photograph, an old army mugshot: the head and shoulders of me, inset against the background of a rocky valley that could have been anywhere. The clue was in the headline: 'The Butcher of Gholam Khot'.

It continued:

In November 2000 Major Hector 'Eck' Chetwode-Talbot guided a strike force of American gunships in an action that led to the deaths of eight innocent farmers in eastern Afghanistan.

Major Chetwode-Talbot was leading a team dedicated to rooting out al-Qaeda operatives and punishing their Taleban allies for giving them safe harbour. At that time no state of war existed between the United Kingdom and Afghanistan and no British troops had any legal right to operate in that country, let alone call in air strikes against its civilian population.

Military sources, who have asked not to be named, have provided the *Mail* with evidence of this incident, including a copy of a report by Major Chetwode-Talbot made on his return to base in Oman.

Major Chetwode-Talbot is currently employed as a salesman for a firm of stockbrokers in the City.

The *Mail* would like the Ministry of Defence to answer the following questions:

WHY were British troops allowed to enter another sovereign state illegally when no state of war existed?

WHY was a group of innocent Afghan farmers targeted for destruction by American planes?

WHY has Major Chetwode-Talbot never had to face an official inquiry or court martial?

I clutched the paper in my hands and stared at it. I felt dazed and sick; for a moment I thought that I might even throw up.

I rang Nick and got his voicemail. It was noon before he rang me back.

'Yes, I saw it,' he said. 'The same story is in all the other nationals and made it on to Sky News and BBC breakfast TV this morning. I was worried this might happen. Someone's leaked these details to the press. I'm afraid things are going to be difficult for you for a while. It looks like a piece of carefully orchestrated spin. The Internet sites flash up messages about your forthcoming punishment and the papers are fed the story of Gholam Khot to stoke the fires.'

'So what do I do now?' I asked him.

'Get over it,' he said. 'The story in the papers will be denied by someone in the MoD or, at any rate, defused. It's not in anyone's interest for this to run too far. The big question is: who put it there and why now after all this time? The events happened six or seven years ago. Some of our press may push the boundaries at times but they don't, so far as I know, willingly allow themselves to be used as propaganda tools by al-Qaeda or anyone else of that sort.'

I struggled to get my thoughts and feelings under control. The newspaper story was bad; very bad. But in a year's time, would anyone care? Did anyone really care now? I was one of the good guys and the dead Pashtun might – whatever the papers said – have been on the other side. All I had to do was stay tight lipped whenever the press rang me for a quote or comment, as they surely would.

'Do you think someone will come after me?' I said.

'I think you've seriously annoyed a few people, including Aseeb. He was trying to find a way to bring money into the UK and we were trying to see how he would do it. You joined up the dots for us. Aseeb is a key figure in the Taleban drugs trade, shipping drugs west, and cash and munitions east. Behind most religious or political insurgencies you'll find a very sound business network for selling Class A drugs. This lot are no different. Laundering money through Bilbo was just one of several operations Aseeb was involved in. Unfortunately we can't get to him at present. We don't know where he is. He's not in Dubai.'

'Bilbo started this,' I said. 'What are you going to do about him?'

'He's skipped,' Nick replied.

'What do you mean, skipped?'

'We went to his house in Kensington Gate first thing this morning. His butler was there, no one else. "Mr and Mrs Mountwilliam have gone on holiday, sir. Can't say where, sir. No, sir, I don't know when they will be back." He was a big help.'

Bilbo and Vanessa Mountwilliam had driven to Ascot very early that morning and taken their two daughters out of school. The school had been told some story about a family bereavement. Then the whole Mountwilliam clan had driven to Heathrow, and had left the country while I was still making breakfast. They had a flight booked to Paris. After that, their destination was unclear. So far, Nick had not traced anyone by the name of Mountwilliam registered on any outbound flights from Charles de Gaulle airport that day.

'It may take us a while to find out where they've gone,' said Nick. 'They could have had a car waiting at the airport. They could have booked a flight under another name – unlikely but possible.'

'Doesn't the office know where he is?' I asked.

'I'm glad you asked about the office,' said Nick. 'We went there too, around seven thirty this morning. It was still locked up.'

'That surprises me,' I said. 'There's usually someone in by that time.'

'We had a warrant,' said Nick. 'So we waited in our cars to

see what would happen. After a while your former colleagues started to turn up, found the door locked, and stood about in the street, talking into their mobiles. Later, someone with a key arrived – Mr McNisbet, he was called. We produced our ID and warrant and all trooped inside.'

Nick paused.

'What do you think we found?' he asked.

'How should I know?'

'Nothing,' said Nick. 'We found absolutely nothing. None of the computers worked. None of the servers worked. Someone had been in and cleaned all the files from the hard drives. The back-ups had been taken from the office safe. We know that other back-ups were kept in a safe at Bilbo's house in Kensington Gate. Your IT guy gave them to Bilbo every night. We've sent someone to look for them but I don't suppose he'll find anything. It seems like quite a thorough job. There would have been some interesting names on the client list, I'm sure, but we'll have to see if our specialists can retrieve anything. Whoever did the clean-up was very professional. Too professional – it could almost have been one of our lot.'

'It can't have been Bilbo,' I said. 'He barely knew how to switch on a computer.'

'Maybe not,' agreed Nick, 'but Bilbo arranged to have it done.'

The implications of what Nick had just told me sank in.

'Wait a minute,' I said. 'All the servers are down? All the memory gone?'

'That's what it looks like,' agreed Nick.

'Then how will the firm keep going?' I asked. 'All the trades will have been recorded there; all the client histories;

everything. The hard-copy records are always hours, if not days, out of date. What a mess!'

Suddenly, not being employed by Mountwilliam Partners seemed a very sensible decision; even if it had been Bilbo's, not mine. All the same, I felt for Doug and the other people I worked for.

'Don't worry too much,' said Nick. 'Mountwilliam Partners is insolvent anyway. It received margin calls last week. The banks and brokers wanted their money back. Didn't you know? By last night, it was on a deadline from its main funding bank. The Financial Services Agency rang and told us this morning. Obviously they knew of our interest, or, at least, one of the senior staff did. We know that Bilbo told Alan McNisbet late the previous night, but we gather that even he was only told there was a bit of pressure from your prime broker. He took some of the calls that afternoon, so Bilbo had to tell him something, I suppose. If Bilbo hadn't closed down Mountwilliam Partners' operations in his own special way, someone else would have done it for him.'

I was silent for a moment, trying to work out the implications of what I'd just heard.

'But they will owe hundreds of millions, maybe billions,' I said. 'If they have to unwind all their positions at once they will lose a fortune.'

'Yes,' agreed Nick. 'The banks will put in an administrator to sort it out. That will take a while, since your ex-boss has done his best to destroy all the records. Then the administrators will take their cut. Insolvency practitioners don't work for nothing. There won't be anything left for the punters, I'm afraid. I'd be surprised if there was enough left to pay the milk bill.'

I listened to this in horror. Henry Newark and the dozens

of other friends and acquaintances I had introduced to Mountwilliam Partners would lose every penny they had invested, and all because I had talked them into putting their money into the firm. Good old Eck, he may be thick, but he's straight: if he says it is all right, you can take his word for it.

Except that Mountwilliam Partners had lost all the money.

'What do I do now?' I asked Nick.

'One way or another, it seems like quite a good time for you to leave town.'

I knew he was right. If I stayed here God knows who might come calling on me: journalists from the national press; TV cameras doorstepping me; perhaps even more troublesome visitors. There was no longer any reason to stay in London, and plenty of reasons to leave it.

'Where will you go?' asked Nick, after a moment's silence in which I tried to think about what would be best.

'I'll go back home.'

'Oh yes, I forgot – you've got a farmhouse somewhere near Darlington, haven't you. That sounds like a good idea.' Then he added, 'Pity you ever got involved with that lot, Eck. It wasn't really you, was it?'

'It was the money,' I said sadly. 'The money was too good to turn down.'

Nick was right. I had never been cut out for the job I did at Mountwilliam Partners. I had never understood the products I sold, nor did I understand how we appeared to make so much money. As it turned out, the money had probably never really been there: every trade was rolled over to fund the next one, everything was always in the future. We had disregarded the most basic equation in investment: high reward means high risk. As for me, my stock-in-trade had been my friend-ship with people like Henry; the clients had trusted me because they assumed I knew what I was doing, and that the funds were as safe as I had told them. They weren't safe. The punters had listened while I talked about straddles, and box trades, and swaptions, and short selling, and long selling. They liked the sound of all those mysterious terms: it was more exciting than the things other stockbrokers talked about, and seemed to be much more profitable.

But I hadn't a clue. I barely understood the terms myself. I had read about three textbooks and studied other people's lecture notes and crammed what fragments of knowledge I could into my head in order to pass a couple of exams. After that, I just did what Bilbo said; if he told me the sky was pink, then for me pink was the only colour that the sky had ever been.

You couldn't argue with the results: that's what Bilbo had told me, and that was the message I repeated. If the market was the house, then Mountwilliam Partners always beat the house.

I had been a fool; had I also been a knave? I looked into my heart, and when I did so, I wished I hadn't. How honest had I really been? Hadn't some corner of me known, or at least suspected, that this world of exponential returns was, in the end, an illusion? Hadn't it been the case that I was simply not prepared to be the man who stood up and said: hold on, how does this work again? How come we're so much cleverer than the rest of the world?

I had never questioned the wealth that flowed around me and through me over those last few years. Now I had probably bankrupted Henry Newark, one of my oldest and closest friends, by selling him a story about a fund which – it turned out – bought sub-prime debt in the Midwest of the United

States. How on earth could I have done that? How could I ever look Henry in the eye again – or any of the others?

What, in the end, was the difference between me and someone selling Japanese dog food or revolting Dutch wine? There wasn't one, except no one really went bust buying things from Charlie Summers. I remembered what I had said to Nick.

It was the money: the money had been too good to turn down.

Seventeen

And so I went home, back to Pike's Garth Hall. I packed a suitcase with a few clothes; the rest of my possessions – the furniture and pictures I had inherited – were all at Pikes Garth. Then I drove north.

When I arrived and climbed out of my car, I thought as I stood and surveyed the wide dark skies, and the moorland and pasture of Upper Teesdale, that perhaps being here might wash away all my troubles. As I looked up the valley, glimmers of late afternoon sunshine broke through the clouds, lighting up corners of fields here and there so that the grass looked as fresh as if it were spring. Sam and Mary Pierce's cottage was a hundred yards farther down the hill, and there were one or two neighbouring farms not far beyond.

There was a peaceful, almost empty feeling to the valley. I fell in love with it again every time I saw it after coming back from London. I wondered, for a moment, how soon it might be before the outside world intruded. I didn't really believe anyone would take notice of those websites. They were just part of a long game being played out to win over the hearts and minds of disaffected young Muslims the world over, and no doubt their creators would already be busy with the next propaganda campaign. But even if I was physically distant here, I could still be reached by phone or post. I dreaded answering the phone.

The collapse of Mountwilliam Partners barely made it to the front pages of the business news. The main television channels didn't bother to cover it: the story was too technical, not easily compressed into a sound bite capable of being understood by a vast audience of viewers munching their morning cornflakes or sipping their glass of wine in the evening. Besides, there was enough in the news to worry about already: a bank run; obesity; the correct way to throw out your rubbish; whether antidepressants made you more or less depressed; was the heavy rainfall of recent weeks a tipping point in climate change; was buy-to-let still a good idea? There was always enough to agonise over from a safe distance: were the prisons too full, and should we let offenders out early? Did too much coffee give you Alzheimer's, or prevent it? Why couldn't we remember which of these views was the latest theory?

The viewers and readers munched their cornflakes or drank their wine, and shook their collective heads in disbelief at the general state of things. Around them, at first almost unnoticed, parts of the financial world began to fracture. There were warnings of more bank runs and bank closures in England, France and the United States. Other creakings and groanings from the engine room alarmed the more discerning financial commentators, but the world as a whole did not concern itself too much with the news that one hedge fund had collapsed.

A number of people, however, had particular reasons for noticing that Mountwilliam Partners had disappeared off the map.

The first couple of times that Henry Newark called me on my mobile, I couldn't bring myself to answer it. I saw his caller ID appear on the screen and couldn't face speaking to him. I simply did not know what I could say to Henry that would be of the slightest use. On the third occasion that he rang, I was sitting at a low wooden table outside my house, looking beyond the stone dyke that formed the boundary of the garden, to a small patchwork of pastures, beyond which the heather-clad hills were beginning to emerge from the morning mist. It was going to be a glorious summer's day. Today and every other day, I had absolutely nothing to do except to sit here, and drink coffee. The mobile was lying on the table next to my coffee cup and it started ringing at me. So I answered it. I couldn't put this off for ever.

'Eck?' asked Henry. 'Is that you?'

'Henry,' I said, with false cheerfulness. 'How are you?'

'How do you think I am?' asked Henry. 'I've been trying to get hold of you for days. Your office appears to have closed. You can't be at your flat because I must have tried that number a dozen times. You don't answer the phone at Pikes Garth. Are you on holiday?'

'No, I'm not on holiday,' I said. 'I'm unemployed.'

'So what's the story?' asked Henry. 'I can't get any sense out of anyone I talk to in London. There's a stupid rumour going around that Mountwilliam Partners has closed its doors . . . What do you mean, you're unemployed? Are you joking? I'm not really in the mood for jokes. I'm worried sick, Eck, and I was hoping you could put my mind at rest.'

I tried to arrange my thoughts. What could I tell Henry that would ease his mind? The shape of the hills was sharper now as the atmosphere heated up and cleared. Soon, one would have the impression of being able to see for ever, across the green and unspoiled world of the Pennine dales.

'Mountwilliam Partners has gone bust,' I said at last. 'I

don't know any of the details, but it appears that some of its trades went badly. There's been a lot of negative talk about the company in the market over the last few weeks. Then the company tried to refinance itself, and couldn't get the funding.'

I had been home for just a few days, but already life in London was becoming a distant memory and the world of Mountwilliam Partners seemed increasingly remote. Somewhere, out in the wider world, Bilbo was no doubt sunning himself on a beach, and waiting for it all to calm down. I, too, was a fugitive. Old Sam Pierce had cut the rough grass patch that passed for a lawn in honour of my return to Pikes Garth; otherwise my arrival here appeared to have gone unnoticed.

'So what does that mean?' asked Henry, breaking my reverie. 'My money's still safe, isn't it? I mean you said that the Styx fund invested in bank debt and was safe as houses, didn't you?'

'I'm afraid that may not be the case, now,' I said. 'I don't know what's happening any more than you do.'

'What do you mean, you don't know what's happening!' Henry was almost screaming into the phone.

'Calm down, please, Henry,' I said, 'and I'll do my best to explain. I've been sacked. I haven't been in the office since last Thursday. My guess is that an administrator will have been appointed by now and he will have been closing out all the company's trades as quickly as possible. You might find your units in the Styx fund have lost value as they were designed to make money over five years. If the administrator sells them now they could be worth very little. I couldn't be more sorry, but it's out of my hands.'

'I don't understand,' said Henry. 'You're saying that the

investment isn't as safe as houses now. Have I got that right? You're saying the opposite of what you and Bilbo told me a few weeks ago when I put the money in?'

'I don't know, Henry,' I answered. I felt myself getting hot, as if the whole of my body were covered in a single, enormous blush. Beads of sweat trickled down my back. 'The world has changed in the last few weeks. It's likely you have lost money, that's all I'm saying. If I knew anything for sure, I really would have told you before now.'

There was another silence, while Henry thought about his next question. Then he asked, 'Suppose, just for the sake of argument, the value of my investment has fallen? Let's say it has fallen to zero.'

'Well, that's rather a worst-case scenario, Henry,' I began to say, but he interrupted me.

'Mountwilliam Partners going bust *is* rather a worst-case scenario, wouldn't you agree? I'd like to know what could be worse than that?'

'OK,' I agreed weakly. 'Let's suppose.'

'And Mountwilliam Partners arranged for me to borrow two million pounds against the value of the Stanton Hall estate so that I could buy units in their fund. Now that the fund is worthless – in my worst-case scenario, Eck, before you say anything – are they entitled to ask me to repay the loan, when they've lost it all?'

This was the hardest part. I had to make Henry understand what I knew.

'It won't be Mountwilliam Partners who asks for the loan to be repaid. They sold the debt on straight away. The debt will be with a third party specialising in equity release. They are the people who will be asking for the money.'

'They've sold my debt on to someone I don't know?'

shouted Henry. I held the phone away from my ear for a moment.

'Yes, I'm afraid that's standard practice,' I told him. 'It's in the contract you signed. I remember pointing it out to you.'

'Oh, in the small print, was it? I must say, Eck, you do sound quite the City boy now, don't you?'

The sneer in the voice hurt me more than anything he had said, yet I knew in some part I deserved it. Then he asked, more quietly: 'So someone I've never heard of might turn up one of these days and ask me to pay back two million pounds I haven't got. Is that right?'

'It could happen, Henry,' I told him. 'I really don't know what the position is at the moment. It might not be as bad as that. But, yes, it is possible. That's the truth.'

For a while there was silence at the other end of the line, and I might have thought Henry had hung up, except that the screen on the phone showed that we were still connected.

'So your advice, your *honest* advice, would be to prepare for the worst? See what I can sell that might raise two million pounds in a hurry? Offhand I don't know what that would be. The woodlands might raise some cash. I could sell them off, or fell them. We have some cottages we could sell. That would help, but the rent from those keeps Stanton Hall going.'

His voice trailed off; then came back again louder.

'What the hell am I going to tell Sarah? We were all right as we were. What in God's name have you got me into, Eck? How could you drag me into a mess like this?'

He hung up before I could reply. For a long while I sat at the wooden table, wondering whether I should return the call and, if I did, what I would say.

There was nothing I could say. Every word Henry had

uttered was true. He had lost his money; I was in no doubt about that. He would have to sell up some – or perhaps all – of an estate that had been handed down in his family for nearly two hundred years. It was all, in the end, about greed: I had baited the hook and he had risen to take it. I hadn't meant to ruin my oldest friend, but that's what I seemed to have done. That was how I had earned my living. And the call from Henry might be only the beginning. How many other phone calls like that might come?

I stood up, and took the empty cup and saucer inside and stacked them beside the sink. Then, as I had done for the past few days, I wandered around the house, trying to find odd jobs to do. Nothing needed doing. My mind would not focus. I still had a creepy feeling of being under threat. I hoped the feeling would go away soon. In the daylight I rarely thought twice about it, but when night fell, I remembered what a lonely place I now lived in. None of my neighbours except for the Pierces knew I was permanently back at home. I hadn't rung any of them, and none of them had rung me.

The previous night I had gone to the gun cabinet, unlocked it and taken out one of my shotguns. I had loaded it and slept with it by the bed, where my trailing fingers could find it in the dark. I lay awake for a long time, listening to the creaks and sighings of an old house cooling down after a warm day, feeling embarrassed by my own nervousness.

Now, as I moved restlessly about the house, I was thinking of the words Henry had used: '. . . your advice, your *honest* advice'.

My advice had been well intended: I had not set out to deceive Henry. I was paid to take money from people like him and give it to our traders, in the sincere belief that one day they would return it to him in greater quantities than he could have dreamed of had he sent it anywhere else. Better yet, I had shown him how to put his capital to work: he had once told me that he was 'land rich, but cash poor'. Mountwilliam Partners had shown him how to extract value from his land and put it to work for him.

I believed that I had been honest. But what I, what we all, had forgotten about was the price of risk. We had behaved as though risk had been banished; but, like some awful monster crouching in the shadows beneath the stairs, it turned out to have been there all the time.

I cannot remember a worse twenty-four hours than the day and night I passed after Henry's phone call. Was that how everyone would now think of me: as a sharp salesman, who had drawn a fat salary while his investors – and his friends – lost their money? I had to assume that I too had lost my investments in Mountwilliam Partners; soon, no doubt, I would have to sell off my London flat to pay for the equity I had 'released' from it in order to buy more units in one or other of their funds. The same debt collectors who would soon call on Henry would also be calling on me.

It was time I moved on and started to think what to do next, how I would manage to pass the days and earn some sort of a living.

It was exactly a day after Henry's call that the phone rang again. I looked at the screen. I wasn't sure I wanted to speak to Henry if it was him, but I knew I would have to. It wasn't Henry; it was Harriet.

'Eck,' said a distant voice, and yet it was as if she were in the room beside me.

'Harriet,' I said. 'I was going to ring you.'

'I've just seen last week's newspapers. I never get round

to reading them until the following week. I saw the articles about you in Afghanistan,' said Harriet. 'How could they say such awful things about you? You were only doing your duty.'

'Someone thought it would make a good story,' I replied.

'Well, someone ought to be taken out and shot,' Harriet pronounced fiercely. 'You must feel awful. What do people at work say? Are they being supportive?'

'That's the other thing,' I said. 'I'm not at work any longer.' I explained as briefly as I could about the demise of Mountwilliam Partners.

'So where are you?' asked Harriet. 'What are you doing?'

'Well, it's only just happened, so I'm not doing anything. I'm living at home, at Pikes Garth Hall, for the moment. Don't tell anyone that, Harriet, because I don't want people to come and bother me just now.'

There was a pause, and I had an irrational but strong conviction that Harriet was waiting for me to ask her to come and join me. There were a lot of reasons why I wasn't going to do that just yet. To start with, I wasn't sure how safe she would be in my company. I didn't want Harriet to come here and walk into a team of investigative journalists, or perhaps something worse. And even if I was overreacting to recent events, I wasn't going to be very good company for a while. I longed to see her, but I couldn't bring myself to do anything about it at that moment.

Harriet spoke again: 'Are you still there, Eck?'

'Yes.'

'You should have rung me before now.'

'Life's been a bit muddled,' I said. 'There's been a lot of other stuff going on that I can't explain over the phone.'

'Well, unmuddle yourself, then,' said Harriet. 'I'll call

tomorrow and you can tell me the rest of it. Look after yourself, dear Eck.'

She put the phone down before I could reply.

When the mobile rang the following morning I was all set to explain everything to Harriet. Now wasn't the time for us to be together; there were problems; it was related to what had happened in Afghanistan. I rehearsed various versions of this speech but none of them made any sense, even to me. When I looked at the phone, the screen simply said 'Unknown Number'. For a moment I hesitated. It could be anyone: it could be Bilbo; it could be a car salesman from Audi wanting to pitch a new model; or it could be Osama Bin Laden. I decided I had to answer the call however much I didn't want to.

'Hello?' I said cautiously.

'I say, old boy, is that you?' asked a familiar, but for the moment unrecognisable, voice.

'Who's that?'

'It's Charlie, don't you recognise my voice? Charlie Summers speaking here. You gave me your mobile number, remember?'

'Charlie,' I said. My voice must have sounded rather flat; I couldn't quite bring myself to be any more enthusiastic.

'Am I calling at a bad time, old chap? Are you in a meeting?'

'No, Charlie, I'm not in a meeting.' I thought he might possibly be somewhere in London, wanting to cadge a few pounds from me, so I added: 'I'm in my house in Teesdale.'

'Teesdale! Well, that *is* a nice surprise! I'm just down the valley from you, in Middlesbrough.'

'What on earth are you doing there?' I asked, dismay

creeping into my voice. Then I remembered that Charlie had once told me he had family in Middlesbrough. 'Are you staying with your family?'

'All passed on,' said Charlie. 'I've got an auntie in Stockton, but we're not on speaking terms. No, I'm calling you from the Sally Pally in Trimdon Road.'

'The Sally Pally?'

'Salvation Army Centre, old boy. I'm a bit low on funds at present and the council has very obligingly given me B&B accommodation for a few nights. I drop in here because it's somewhere to go. They give you coffee. They're jolly kind. Quite a lot of praying goes on, though, and it's Ladies' Fellowship Night tonight, Eck. I'm not sure I can face it.'

When Charlie had begun the conversation he had adopted the tone of martial bonhomie he sometimes used in my company, as if we were both temporary members of the same officers' mess; but now his voice cracked as he told me about 'Ladies' Fellowship Night' and I thought I could hear him crying.

'Are you all right, Charlie?' I asked.

'Just got a bit of a cold,' he said, clearing his throat noisily. 'Anyway, I won't bother you any further, Eck. I just thought I'd say hello and have a bit of a chinwag. Don't want to disturb you if you're busy. Hope things are going well. Hope you get together with that dishy-looking girl in the photograph. I'll say goodbye now.'

He hung up. I expelled the breath I didn't know I had been holding in a sigh of relief. Thank God for that. The last person I wanted to see was Charlie.

I walked about the house some more, congratulating myself on my escape from Charlie Summers and his importuning ways. I didn't think he would ring back. He had sounded very down; almost desperate. That was the last sort of person I needed for company.

What had he said? He was broke? He must be at a low ebb indeed if he was staying in council accommodation for the homeless, and spending his days in the local Salvation Army drop-in centre. It sounded as if Charlie really had, at last, reached rock bottom. The wine business, unsurprisingly, mustn't have worked any better for him than the dog food business.

I sat down at the kitchen table and found myself drumming my fingers on the tabletop. Thinking about Charlie made me uncomfortable, for some reason. He was nothing to me, and I had a great many more important things to think about, including deciding what to do with my own life. With an effort, I banished him from my mind.

Half an hour later I was in the Audi, and on the road to Middlesbrough.

Charlie looked thinner and his face more lined than when I had last seen him. He was wearing a very crumpled grey suit and a grubby, open-necked shirt. He suddenly seemed years older. At first he couldn't believe it when I walked into the hostel. He was sitting at a table by himself, nursing a mug which turned out to be empty.

'Eck,' he said. 'My God, Eck! What on earth are you doing here? You're not down and out yourself, are you?'

'I've come to offer you a bed for a couple of nights, Charlie,' I told him. 'Just a couple of nights, that's all.'

His face, an old man's a moment before, split from side to side in a beam of pure joy.

'I say, old boy, that's awfully good of you. Are you sure?'

'Don't ask,' I said. 'Do you want to come, or not?'

'I don't have any other engagements at present, Eck. I don't mind telling you my diary is pretty empty.'

'Then we might as well go.'

'My things,' said Charlie. 'I'm stopping a couple of streets from here, and all my belongings are there: my pyjamas and my toothbrush. Would it be a bother to collect them?'

We collected Charlie's scant belongings, which were still in the same battered canvas holdall, and then drove back up the valley to Pikes Garth. In the car Charlie kept looking at me sideways. I thought he was going to thank me again, in which case I would have to tell him to shut up. He surprised me by saying, 'Are you all right, Eck? You look as if you've had a bit of a rough time yourself.'

'I'm fine,' I told him.

'I saw that story about you in the papers, you know,' said Charlie shyly. 'I just want you to know that I wish we had more soldiers like you in our Special Forces.'

'Thank you, Charlie,' I said. 'It's something I'm trying to forget about. And I'm not in the army, any more.'

Charlie winked at me and said, 'I quite understand, old boy.'

We drove on in silence until we came to the winding lane that led between dry-stone walls to Pikes Garth.

'My goodness!' said Charlie. 'What a heavenly spot you live in, Eck. I can't think how you can bear to spend any time in London with a home like this to come back to.'

'Don't be using the address for any credit card applications, this time,' I warned him as we parked outside the house. Charlie looked embarrassed. 'Sorry about that,' he muttered. 'I hoped you wouldn't be troubled by anyone, as you said you were going to sell the place.'

We went inside. I showed Charlie a spare bedroom, and the linen cupboard, and told him to make his own bed. While he was doing that I looked for my mobile, as I had forgotten to take it with me when I left the house. It was on the kitchen table. To my annoyance I saw that it was showing a missed call from Harriet. I rang back, but there was no reply.

Charlie came back in.

'All shipshape,' he said cheerfully. 'Now, how can I be of use? Why don't you let me cook lunch, Eck? I once had a job in the kitchens on a cruise ship. There isn't a lot I don't know about cooking.'

It turned out later, as we sat sharing a bottle of beer and eating corned beef hash, that Charlie's job had been more in the washing-up line; but, as he said, 'you can learn a lot watching top chefs in action', and the corned beef hash was surprisingly good.

After lunch Charlie excused himself and said he needed a rest.

'I haven't slept a lot recently,' he explained apologetically. 'I'm at a bit of a turning point in my career, and I've had quite a lot on my mind. Two hours of Egyptian PT will put me right, I'm sure it will.'

It was early evening before he re-emerged in the kitchen, awakened no doubt by the smell of roast chicken. I had dug the bird out of the freezer after lunch in order to provide some dinner for the two of us.

We sat and drank whisky together before dinner. He told me what he had been doing in the time since we had last met: about his trip to Holland, and Chateau Kloof, and the disastrous wine-tasting evening in York. But he was quieter than he had been in Cirencester, when I had found it difficult to get him to stop talking. Now Charlie's manner could almost be described as thoughtful.

'I've got to get my life straightened out, Eck,' he said. 'I'm sure your turning up at the Sally Pally was providence. I couldn't think in there. People were always coming up and asking me if I wanted to share my worries with them. They meant to be kind, of course. I expect they thought I was going to top myself.'

'I hope you're not,' I said.

'Life's very strange, isn't it,' Charlie mused later, over roast chicken, chips and peas. 'I mean, we come from different walks of life, but you and Henry have both been very good to me. I now see the mistake I've made: I tried to take too many short cuts through life. You look around you and you see other chaps with big cars and smart houses with two garages and a jacuzzi, and you think: Why not me? I've tried to climb the stairway to success two steps at a time and it hasn't worked. In fact, to be frank, it's been a total bloody disaster. You and Henry have got it about right, I reckon. You work hard, lead regular lives, keep your head on your shoulders, and your shoulders to the wheel. My problem is I've always believed that with the right scheme, it would be possible to get rich quick. But looking things squarely in the face, I couldn't really be any poorer than I am now.'

'Have some more wine,' I said. I didn't feel very comfortable being singled out as a role model.

'I will, thank you, old boy. It's slipping down a treat. I'm afraid the Chateau Kloof stuff I sent you was a bit rough on the palate. Perhaps it was too young. I don't know whether you noticed? As I was saying earlier, I need to get straight. I need to think things over. It's time to prove to myself that I can do something worthwhile before it's too late. Don't worry, old boy, I won't overstay my welcome . . . you've done a good deed, bringing me here, and I'll make sure you don't regret it.'

Eighteen

When I awoke the next morning, the sun streaming in through curtains I had forgotten to close the night before, I saw a light blinking on my mobile indicating I had a text message. I sat up and picked up the mobile from the bedside table. The text said: '*Coming to stay with you meet me Newcastle Airport Wednesday 15:35 flt from Nice xxx Harriet.*'

The message was dated earlier that morning. I looked at my watch. It was ten o'clock: I couldn't believe I had slept for so long. I still felt slightly muzzy from the extra whisky or two that seemed to be a feature of evenings with Charlie Summers, but it wasn't just the drink, I admitted to myself. I had been short on sleep for a while and somehow Charlie's presence, the arrival in my house of someone so much worse off than I was, had allowed me a dreamless sleep.

It was too late to phone Harriet to tell her not to come. She would be on her way to the airport in Nice by now. Besides, I knew that I badly wanted to see her. I got up, showered, shaved and dressed and then, feeling lighter of heart than I had for a while, went and looked in Charlie's bedroom. He was still enjoying his night's rest, lying flat on his back and snoring gently. I decided it would be cruel to wake him with the news that he had to leave; I was quite sure that if Harriet was coming to stay, I did not want Charlie around for much longer. Good deeds can easily go too far.

I went into the kitchen and made myself some coffee, then took it outside to the wooden table. The dew had dried on the seats, so I sat down and contemplated the view, wondering what I would do when Harriet arrived. I looked at my watch and realised there was not that much time – I would have to be at the airport in a few hours. Meanwhile, the house needed to be smartened up; food and drink had to be purchased; clean linen and towels organised.

I wrote a note for Charlie and left it on the kitchen table.

'*Dear Charlie – my cousin Harriet has just been in touch to say she is coming to stay tonight. I'm afraid that means I'm going to have to ask you to move on . . .*' – here I paused and decided it would be too harsh to throw him out today, so wrote – 'tomorrow. I will be out until about five or six. Eck.'

Then I went to the car, climbed in and drove down to the Pierces' cottage at the bottom of the lane. Sam Pierce was in the garden clipping a yew hedge. I stopped and wished him good morning.

'Another lovely day, Mr Eck,' he said, putting down his shears as if he was ready for a good long chat.

'Isn't it?'

'Still, we deserve it after the cold spring we've had,' said Sam, offering me the opportunity to comment on the weather so far.

'Is Mrs Pierce around this morning?' I said. 'Only I'd be very grateful if she could come to the house and give it a tidy up and change the linen – I have an unexpected guest coming tonight. And I've another staying in one of the spare bedrooms, a Mr Summers.'

'She's gone to the village for some milk,' said Sam, 'but I'll tell her when she gets back.'

'I must dash,' I said. 'I'll see you later.'

I drove to Newcastle and spent a couple of hours shopping. There was almost no food in the house and very little left to drink, after the previous night, so I crammed the back of the car with carrier bags full of supplies, and hoped that Harriet didn't have too much luggage with her.

Then I drove to the airport, arriving at least an hour too early. For a while I sat in the car, then got out and went to the arrivals area, where I drank a cup of coffee, looking up at the board about every ten seconds. At last it showed that Harriet's flight was landing. My heart began to hammer and I felt a painful sense of anticipation. I tried telling myself that it was only my cousin Harriet, whom I had known for years, but it made no difference. How will I greet her, I wondered: a peck on the cheek? Should I make it clear to her that I was taking nothing for granted? While I was debating these questions she came through the arrivals gate wheeling a suitcase behind her. As soon as she saw me, she flew straight into my arms.

On the drive back I said, 'I have an unexpected guest at home.'

'I thought I was the unexpected guest.'

'You are, and the nicest possible surprise. But I've another: Charlie Summers.'

Harriet was delighted.

'I'm so looking forward to meeting him.'

'Make the most of it. I've told him he's got to go tomorrow morning.'

'That sounds hard, Eck.'

'People like Charlie always need deadlines,' I told her.

Then Harriet said, 'Are you glad I've come?'

'You know I am.'

'Only, when we spoke on the phone, I wasn't quite sure.

You said your life was in a muddle, and you couldn't explain it.'

'Ah, yes, I did say that,' I agreed. 'I'm very glad you're here, but some things have happened recently that . . . it's not easy to explain while I'm driving. Can I tell you about it when we get to the house? In fact, it might have to wait until I've got rid of Charlie Summers.'

Harriet frowned, but asked no more questions. And as things turned out, the matter explained itself in a way I could never have imagined.

When we turned into the lane that led up to Pikes Garth Hall, we found a police Land Rover parked across the road, its blue light flashing. I felt a sudden knot tighten in my stomach. I hoped to God Charlie hadn't topped himself after all. It wasn't possible to drive around the Land Rover, so I pulled my own car on to the grass verge, and Harriet and I got out and walked towards the house.

'What's happening?' asked Harriet.

'I haven't the slightest idea.'

Two more police cars were parked outside the house. A uniformed policeman was standing at the foot of the steps that led from the garden into the lane, talking to Sam and Mary Pierce. Mary was very pale; Sam red faced and flustered. Another officer and a man in plain clothes, presumably a detective, came out of the house.

'Are you Mr Chetwode-Talbot?' asked the detective when he saw us.

'This is Mr Eck,' cried Sam, before I could speak. 'Oh, Mr Eck, the most dreadful thing has happened.'

As far as I could piece the events together, what had happened had taken place a couple of hours after I had left the house. The event that I had dismissed as so improbable that it was not worth thinking about had, in the end, occurred. The websites had stirred up the desire for action among the jihadists of the valleys of North Lancashire. Perhaps a message had come to them from Aseeb. After all, who knew what friends a man like that had? Perhaps this abduction had been carefully planned, or perhaps it was a spur-of-the-moment initiative by a local group acting on their own. This last possibility seemed the least likely: as subsequent events showed, a certain amount of organisation had gone into the kidnapping.

Mary Pierce had been straightening Charlie's bedroom upstairs. Charlie himself had risen from his slumbers and was enjoying a mug of coffee in the kitchen. Whether he had read my note telling him to go, I cannot say. I hope he did not see it. Mary Pierce heard the noise of a van coming up the lane. Of course, she took no notice: it might have been the postman, or a special delivery.

Charlie must have risen from the table when he heard the van, and gone outside to see whether it was something that required his attention. No doubt he had wanted to be helpful. The van – Mary couldn't see more than the roof from where she stood – had parked at the foot of the steps, and two men were getting out of the cab. Then two more men got out of the rear of the van. Charlie knew trouble when he saw it. He must have realised in that instant that something was very wrong indeed. Mary Pierce rushed downstairs and hid in the hallway, from where she could see the open door and Charlie standing with his back to her.

She heard the sound of raised voices outside, and one in particular, speaking in an accent that was more Lancashire than Pashtun: 'Are you the lad that killed our brothers at Gholam Khot?'

Her description wasn't much use to the police: tracksuit bottoms and trainers, leather jackets, woollen hats pulled down over the men's dark faces. She saw that one, perhaps more than one of them, had a gun. She was paralysed by fear: it wasn't only the sight of the guns but something more than that – the posture and voices of the men communicated a sense of absolute menace.

She heard Charlie say in reply, 'I am Major Chetwode-Talbot, yes.'

He stood at the top of the steps, facing them. I can picture him standing there, a slight smile playing on his lips. I believe that I know exactly what was going through his mind: he was Gordon of Khartoum – he was Charlton Heston playing the part of Gordon – standing on the steps of his palace by the Nile, unafraid and unarmed, confronting the blood-maddened hordes of the Mahdi, and staring boldly down into their faces.

'What do you want?' asked Charlie.

Mary Pierce saw one of the men raise his gun and point it at him. She said she nearly fainted. Charlie did not flinch.

'You are going to pay for your crimes,' the man hissed, pointing the gun.

'Have you come from Afghanistan?' asked Charlie.

'Nay, lad, we're from Oldham. But where *you're* going is another matter.'

The other man said: 'Come on, let's not fuck about here all day. Get him in the van.'

Charlie did not move. There was no struggle. The men came up the steps and grabbed him by the arms, then frog-marched him down to the van and pushed him into the back. By now Mary Pierce was frantic. She said that Charlie made no attempt to deny their mistaken identification, and went quietly with his captors. When she heard the sound of the van starting up, she ran to the door and saw an old blue Ford Transit that then disappeared down the lane. The only concrete clue Mary was able to give the police was the first half of the number plate.

'He did look a lot like you, Mr Eck,' she told me much later when she finally felt able to talk about it. 'Only a bit older, and more tired.'

I believe that Charlie, who had lived by his wits for most of his life, appreciated the situation as soon as the four men got out of the van. Despite everything I had told him to the contrary, he had always insisted on believing that I still worked for my country in secret. He must have thought very quickly, much more quickly and coolly than I would have done in those circumstances. He may have seen one of the men looking at a photograph of me and realised as soon as they spoke that they presumed that he – poor, lost, battered Charlie Summers – was Eck Chetwode-Talbot, hero of countless secret actions against the forces of evil. It was simply too good an opportunity to resist.

I also believe that, in the few microseconds available to him for any form of rational thought or judgement, he came to a decision. All his life he had tried to live by deception, by confidence trickery of a minor sort, and all his life he had seen it go wrong and ended up having to cut and run. He no longer had the strength or the will to go on. That much was already clear to him – and he had made it clear to me, as we talked the evening before. Perhaps he simply surrendered to the fate that awaited him, because in the end it was a solution to the unbearable question of what to do with the rest of his life.

I have played the scene of Charlie's abduction over and over in my head times without number and have come to another conclusion about Charlie, and the life that he led.

In the ranks of the world's debtors, Charlie stood very low. He had never really done serious harm to anyone but himself. In the balance sheet of his own life, however, it was otherwise. For him, each deception – whether practised on me, or Henry, or Sylvia Bently, or the dozens of other people he had tried and failed to manipulate in the course of his varied and hopeless life – was a creditor unpaid, a debt as painful as a wound. This final deception, in the last few seconds of freedom and choice that he ever had, was, in his eyes, an opportunity for redemption: a moment when all his debts might be cancelled by a single act. I am imagining all this, putting thoughts into his head, and yet I feel as sure about it all as if I had been there beside Charlie. In my mind Charlie gave up his life for mine, so that I could go on living happily ever after, with the 'dishy girl in the photograph'.

Of course, there was a great deal of fuss that day. More and more policemen arrived and stood about, doing nothing except talking to each other. Nick Davies called me on my mobile to find out whether I was all right, and I explained what had happened.

He laughed when he heard. 'You killed the wrong guys, they kidnapped the wrong man – I'd call it a draw. I think you might be lucky. I doubt they'll try again once they find out their error: too embarrassing.'

'I'm luckier than Charlie, anyway,' I said tersely.

'Who?'

'Charlie Summers, the man they took. He was a sort of friend of mine, Nick. I hope you're looking for him.'

'Yes, of course, the police will do their best. Don't worry; we're looking for the people who did this as hard as we can.'

I spoke to Nick a couple of weeks later, and he told me that they had searched through a few hundred miles of CCTV tapes and found a blue Transit van whose number plate matched the partial description Mary Pierce had given them. It was parked near the docks at Teesport. The theory that emerged in the end was that Charlie had been put on board a vessel moored at the grain terminal. The ship had sailed later that day, bound for Basra with a cargo of wheat. The particular vessel they suspected was Panamanian flagged and the ultimate ownership was traced to Dubai, but nothing was ever proved one way or the other. What was meant to happen to me, or Charlie, after arrival in Basra, was never made clear: onwards to Iran, or Pakistan, or Afghanistan?

'It could be that they planned to ship you out to that part of the world for some sort of video trial,' said Nick. 'It would have been a tremendous propaganda coup for the Taleban, of course, and would have guaranteed a huge number of hits on their websites. They screwed up, of course.'

Nick promised to keep in touch but somehow I didn't expect to hear from him. I was no longer of any use to him. Yet I couldn't help hoping that one day Charlie would simply pop up at my door with some other new scheme.

The local press picked up the story, but their version was so garbled and incoherent that the nationals didn't run it. There was some other story that day: rumours of a snap general election filled the front pages, and as no one was quite sure what had happened to Charlie Summers, or who he was, or where he had been taken, it was never followed up.

Poor Harriet had endured a baptism of fire on her arrival

at Pikes Garth Hall. I told her, 'That was what I was worried about; that was why I didn't want you to come.'

'Well, I'm here now,' she replied.

She has stayed.

Mountwilliam Partners was finally wound up owing hundreds of millions of pounds to various banks, not to mention losing all the money it had invested for its hapless private clients. Henry's call was not the only one I received, and after a while I let Harriet answer the phone. She did so very briskly, and few callers rang back more than twice. But the whole affair was a five-minute wonder and I had been only a minor player.

For a long time after, I was reluctant to go about in society. I felt like a pariah, but after a while Harriet made me face up to the world.

'It wasn't you who lost the money,' she said. 'Everyone knows that you were acting in good faith.'

I wasn't so sure that acting in good faith had been enough. But if one or two of my friends whom I put in to Mountwilliam Partners still treats me rather coolly these days, I find I can live with that. No one has a perfect record: not me, not them.

I haven't seen Henry and Sarah Newark since the collapse of the fund. My annual pheasant-shooting invitation has disappeared, along with the pheasants and, Henry told me over the phone, the woods they used to live in.

'I managed to keep the bailiffs from the door in the end,' he told me when he rang one day, a few months later. 'We clear-felled the woods and sold the mature timber – luckily for us, timber prices have been on the up lately.'

I thought of the ancient stands of oak and the tall

beechwoods that had adorned the Stanton Hall estate, the bluebell-filled glades that were no more. Henry sensed my thoughts and said, 'I should have cut them down before now, but it would have spoiled the shooting. That doesn't matter; I can't afford to shoot any more. The woods were a cash crop, and I needed cash. I've had to sell my guns, too. And we sold most of our cottages.'

'How has Sarah taken it all?' I asked.

'Oh, she's been an absolute brick,' said Henry. 'She likes a drama. She's playing the part of the wronged and heroic wife to perfection. No, I'm being unfair: she *is* the wronged and heroic wife.'

I winced. I could imagine how Sarah would be handling the situation all too well.

'The children have had to come out of private education, of course, and go to a state school,' said Henry. 'Personally, I think they're happier than they were at boarding school. They have so many more local friends now. Sarah's been very good about that, but she's rather worried the children will end up speaking with an accent. And we're a bed and breakfast now.'

'A bed and breakfast?' I asked.

'We advertise for American visitors who want to get the inside track on life in a mini-stately home in Gloucestershire. I have to sit and have a whisky with them before dinner, and bullshit on about my ancestors while Sarah cooks dinner. We don't have a cook or a housekeeper any more. Sarah says she doesn't mind, but I know she gets tired. The trouble is that she has very high standards.'

'I remember,' I said.

'Anyway, keep in touch,' said Henry. 'I hear that you've cornered the lovely Harriet at last. Well done. Give her my love. I'd ask you to bring her to stay, but this B&B business keeps us both rather busy at the moment, and we don't often have a spare bedroom.'

'I'm glad it's going well, at any rate,' I said. Henry and Sarah pouring drinks and cooking for passing tourists was hard to imagine. Thousands of other people did it, however; why not them?

'And Eck,' said Henry, just before he rang off. 'No hard feelings. I mean, about all that Mountwilliam Partners stuff. It takes two to do a deal like that and I was greedy. I saw other people, who I didn't think deserved it, driving around in bigger cars and spending their money like water. It was envy. I couldn't bear to think that I was poorer than all these people who suddenly appeared from nowhere. I wanted part of the action. I wanted to put my capital to work too. Those times are over now, aren't they?'

'For a while, anyway,' I agreed.

That was typical of Henry – being generous in spirit, always concerned not to hurt the feelings of anyone he met. I knew, however, that things between us could never be the same.

I heard from someone – I think it must have been Doug Williams – that Bilbo is now living in Dubai. He is said to have bought a house and some beach frontage on one of those new islands they have reclaimed from the sea. SOCA is trying to seize his assets in this country but Nick Davies told me the last time we spoke that it is very complicated.

'The house in Kensington Gate is still worth millions, even after the property crash,' he said, 'but the ownership is a bit confusing. It appears to belong to a trust registered in the Cayman Islands. There are all sorts of jurisdictional arguments. And we think Bilbo owes Mountwilliam Partners several millions of pounds in bonuses he paid himself just before the collapse. We'll catch up with him in the end.'

I doubt that.

The investigation into what happened to Charlie Summers dragged on for a while longer. The DI in charge of the case told me that they weren't sure who Charlie Summers actually was. Based on the information I had given them, they had checked at the Salvation Army Centre in Middlesbrough.

'The trouble is,' said the DI, 'the social security number he used to get accommodation in Middlesbrough belongs to someone called Billy Skeggs. "Charlie Summers" seems to have been an alias.'

To me this information appeared to be irrelevant.

'Never mind what he is or isn't called,' I said. 'Charlie Summers will do now. Do you know any more about what has happened to him?'

But the DI didn't know and Charlie's fate continued to play on my mind.

It was quite by chance, talking to a man from my old regiment at a dinner party at Catterick one night almost a year later, that I heard a story that might shed some light on the matter. We were talking about life in Basra, where he had been stationed until very recently, and he recalled some of the strange things that happened out there, the type of story that was never covered by the press.

My informant said that for a while they had been hearing that a European was being held hostage somewhere on the outskirts of the city. That was nothing special: there were usually two or three contractors being held to ransom at any one time. But in the case of this European there had been no demands for prisoner exchange or money, and no one appeared to be looking for him. So it wasn't even certain that this particular kidnap victim existed.

'Then we picked up a group in an unrelated raid,' my new friend told me. 'We knew they had dirty hands, and were supposed to have killed a Swiss oilfield engineer. So we took them in and – assisted by the Iraqis – we interrogated them. They told us something rather odd.'

It turned out they'd bought a captive from another group who had sold him on the grounds that he was a British officer, and was worth a fortune in ransom money. The new group – the one that had bought him from the original kidnappers – tried to ransom him, but no one was interested. Eventually, they discovered they'd been had: the man was no more a British officer than they were. The local spooks – our spooks, I mean – couldn't work out who the man for sale actually was or why anyone would want to ransom him. They had the Foreign Office breathing down their necks about half a dozen more important cases and the British press had never picked up on the story, so no one was under pressure to do anything about the situation.

'In the end,' my friend said, 'his captors just took him out and shot him.'

'They shot him?' I said in disbelief. I don't know why I was so surprised, though. If this unknown captive had been Charlie, as I was beginning to think it was, it would have been much of a piece with the rest of his luck.

'Why did they shoot him?' I asked.

'It was cheaper and safer than releasing him, I suppose. They said they actually liked the guy. He made them laugh. But what does a bullet cost? And if they'd simply handed him back, the guy might have given away something about the identity of his captors, or their location. Plus they'd have looked silly releasing someone they paid good money for in the first place. Shooting him was the simplest way out.'

There was a silence. I could not speak. The grief I felt was sudden, and overwhelming. I told myself this was only a story, long on suppositions and very short on facts. Even if the story were true, how could anyone be sure that the prisoner was Charlie?

'They'd kept him for six months in some tenement on the outskirts of As Zubayr,' continued my friend. 'Half the time he would have been bound and hooded. It can't have been fun, but the people we interrogated said that the guy was as good as gold: never complained. They gave him a radio to listen to and he sang along to some of the music. They liked hearing him sing.'

'That's good, then,' I managed to say.

'Here's the thing that made the story stick in my mind,' said my friend. 'It's probably just one of those urban legends, but apparently when they took this guy out to shoot him, he began to sing. They said that they all thought it was very beautiful, and that he had a very good voice. They waited until he had finished before they shot him.'

I knew, then.

I knew for sure who it had been. And I knew for sure what he had sung. They had walked Charlie out from his miserable cell, perhaps down into the dry bed of a nearby wadi for greater discretion. Charlie would have known what was coming; he must have expected it, and probably longed for it. The last few months can't have been comfortable for him. I can't imagine what it must have been like to have your head bagged inside a hood with two air holes for most of the time, while the temperature outside soared past forty degrees: not knowing where you were, or who your captors were, listening to their voices when they raised them, wondering whether they were arguing among themselves about what to do with you. He must, by then, have been sick at heart, and probably was physically ill too.

Still, he had the heart to sing:

'*Panis angelicus*
Fit panis hominum
Dat panis coelicus
Fuguris terminum
O res mirabilis!
Manducat Dominum
Pauper, servus et humilis.'

I remembered the words. I could hear them in my mind as clearly as if Charlie were in front of me at that very moment. I could picture him singing them in a green Provençal dusk, the swifts and bats swooping in the airy gulf behind him. I could recall the feeling of enchantment the song had produced in me.

Charlie Summers had found peace.

Epilogue

Harriet stayed. She made a few trips back to France that autumn and winter to wind up her affairs and arrange for her small stock of worldly goods to be packed up and shipped over to England. By the following spring, Harriet and I had both found jobs not too far from Pikes Garth Hall. Harriet worked part time as a consultant to a firm of land agents in Ripon. I ended up as secretary of a charitable trust. Neither of us earned much money, but between us it was enough. I remembered the contempt with which Bilbo had forecast such an outcome for me, and was glad things had turned out as they had. At least there was no moral hazard in this job.

Life had to be conducted on fairly frugal lines. The money we made from the sale of Aunt Dorothy's house in Cirencester was saved up for our future life together, although Harriet for a long time remained reluctant to discuss the future.

I sold my flat in London just before the property market really crashed, and was able to pay off my mortgage and my loans I had used to invest in Mountwilliam Partners. There wasn't any change. I sold the Audi, and since then have had little call for any of the dozen or more suits I used to own. I wear the tweed one for Sunday lunch parties, if I wear a suit at all, and the pinstriped one for funerals and regimental reunions. The rest are hanging in a spare bedroom, and the moths are welcome to them.

One evening Harriet was watching the latest series about celebrities dancing or ice skating or some such; the kind of programme she watches with a great deal more enthusiasm than I do. It was a warm spring evening, so I went outside and lit a rare cigarette, and thought about how the music that the rest of us had been dancing to for the last few decades really had stopped, at least for the time being. For a long while its compelling, seductive rhythms, its jazzy tones, captivated all of us and we went out and spent. We spent, and we worked harder and harder to earn what we had spent, and when that wasn't enough, we went out and borrowed some more.

Now, at least for the moment, the players had mislaid their scores.

In the silence, it was just possible to imagine that there might be other music being played somewhere else. If I listened hard enough, I thought I might hear it.

Harriet's television show came to an end and she joined me on the terrace. She began to talk about our plans for redecorating the house. We couldn't afford to get someone in: we would have to do it ourselves, and in a very modest way. Money was always going to be tight with us, but it didn't matter any more. We had what we needed.

Out in the dark, an owl screeched. Harriet gripped my hand for a moment and said, 'I love it here.'

'So you're going to stay for a while longer?' I asked her.

'I don't know,' she replied, but she was smiling.

THE END